SECRET WITNESS

SECRET WITNESS

Madison C. Brightwell

SECRET WITNESS

This is a work of fiction. All of the characters, names, incidents,
organizations, and dialogue in this novel are either the products
of the author's imagination or are used fictitiously.

iUniverse books may be ordered through booksellers or by contacting:

iUniverse
1663 Liberty Drive
Bloomington, IN 47403
www.iuniverse.com
1-800-Authors (1-800-288-4677)

ISBN: 978-1-4917-5117-6 (sc)
ISBN: 978-1-4917-5118-3 (e)

Library of Congress Control Number: 2014918971

Printed in the United States of America.

iUniverse rev. date: 10/29/2014

For my grandfather
Donovan William Rymer
A gentle, good man

CHAPTER ONE

THE COUPLE WAS dancing altogether too close. Too close, as far as Maddie was concerned. His cheek was pressed against the top of the girl's head, his brawny arms holding the small of her back as if waiting for the opportunity to move lower down, his eyes dreamily closed and a soft silly smile on his lips, ostensibly heedless of everything surrounding them.

But Alan was aware that Maddie was there, watching him and his dancing partner. She had seen his eyes flicker open and glance in her direction briefly. So he was galling her on purpose. Perhaps he got some perverse pleasure from hurting her by doing the exact opposite of what he'd promised. Maddie detested him at that moment, for humiliating her in front of her friends. This was *her* party, wasn't it? In honor of *her* birthday. And she had chosen Alan to escort her. Yet here he was, flaunting the rules she had tried to establish in their relationship, throwing her previous jealousy in her face. She could feel her body glowing hot with fury. She glared at the couple slowly gyrating on the dance floor, as if her rage could bore a hole through their bodies and make them notice her, or at least make Alan open his eyes. But he and the girl just

1

kept dancing, their bodies moving in time to the smooth rhythm of the music.

She heard a tinkling laugh at her left ear and turned to see Sharon, her understudy, clutching a glass of red wine. "Spilt a bit on meself. Idiot." She giggled again and a few more drops of red liquid sprayed on to her white satin blouse. Her eyes were glazed and she made a half-hearted attempt to wipe off the stain with her fingers, still giggling at some private joke, her unsteady hand shaking the glass so that more wine slopped out and on to the carpet.

"Watch it!" warned Maddie, taking the glass from her and putting it on a nearby coffee table. Three spots of red had already stained the once-pristine beige carpet. Maddie knelt down to inspect the damage, which was difficult to see in the gloom. Her crossness over Alan's treatment of her welled up in her throat and out of her mouth. "You are a cretin, Sharon," she snapped. "Bella told us to be careful. This is a brand new carpet. Her dad'll have a fit when he sees this."

Sharon belched loudly and covered her mouth with her hand. Maddie's admonitions had only increased her amusement: "Shall I get a...hic...cloth..." She was giggling so much she'd bent almost double.

"No, I'll do it" Maddie flung back at her. "You just stand there. And try not to do any more damage." She waded through the dancing bodies to the kitchen, elbowing backs and arms in her irritation, and encountered Paul hovering over the garlic bread. She considered briefly that he was one of those types who always ended up on his own in the kitchen. He wasn't an unattractive guy. Just a bit boring, perhaps.

He raised his head and his face lit up when he saw Maddie. "Hi. Have you come for a top up? Have a bit of this bread - it's hot stuff. Bella's really gone to town on the garlic."

"No thanks. I need some salt." Maddie didn't have time to pay him much attention, but headed straight for the cupboard where she knew the condiments were kept.

"Whassat for?" he enquired amiably, watching her red dress slide over her slim figure, as she reached up and ran her fingers over tins and packets.

Having located the jar, she pulled it down and waved it in passing at Paul. "There's been a little accident" she replied with a smile, heading for the door.

"Whoops - not the red wine on the..."

"Yep. On the carpet. Sharon's a bit drunk."

"What a surprise" said Paul with irony.

Maddie shrugged her shoulders. "Well, she's only young." She moved out of the kitchen and Paul called out after her, "Superwoman to the rescue!" Despite the irony of the words, Maddie's ego was boosted by the obviously genuine admiration in his voice and she felt more well-disposed towards Sharon - she could be a stupid girl sometimes but she was harmless overall.

Maddie returned to the scene of the crime, to find Sharon carefully propping herself up against the wall with a sour face, her giggling fit having subsided. Maddie bent down to cover the stains with salt, and a pair of dancing feet virtually knocked the jar out of her hand. She put down the jar and shook her hand to remove the sting of impact, then looked up to see who the culprit was. It was Alan, now doing an enthusiastic if clumsy jive with the same girl he'd had in his arms a few minutes before. Maddie felt her anger well up again, and her cheeks flushed. He'd sworn he wouldn't do this. He'd agreed that it was Maddie's special day and he'd promised he wouldn't flirt with other women or act as if he was at the party on his own. She was still smarting from the fact that he hadn't given her a birthday present, just a rather cheap card with a soppy message over which he'd scrawled some crude joke. And now he'd broken his promise to her as fast as he could, waiting only till she'd disappeared to the kitchen to top up *his* drink, before grabbing another woman and giving her the attention he ought to be giving his girlfriend.

Sharon was mumbling something to her, fixing her with a vacuous gaze, and Maddie had to lean in close to hear what was said against the thudding beat of rock 'n' roll music. "What d'you say?"

"I said, I thought he was your feller, Alan."

Maddie was stung by the remark, maybe more so because it wasn't intended maliciously but was merely the casual comment of someone too drunk to be tactful. As Maddie contemplated how to reply, the music finished and the dancers paused for breath. In the interlude, a hand tapped her shoulder and she turned to see Alan leering at her. "Hello beautiful. Wanna dance?"

"No, I bloody well don't." Maddie blustered, wishing she could have managed a better retort, a real putdown like sophisticated women make in films. She inwardly commanded her face not to betray her, but it rebelled and sent an angry red flush stealing from her temples to cross her cheeks.

Alan raised his eyebrows and turned down the corners of his mouth: "What's up with you?"

"Oh, don't give me that innocent expression - you know bloody well what's the matter!" Maddie thought she caught a giggle from Sharon behind her, and her back arched. She silently prayed not to have another slanging match with Alan and give the cast more ammunition to hold against her. She knew that already her relationship with Alan was the subject of gossip, being notorious for its tempestuousness.

Alan merely smirked and shrugged his shoulders: "What you getting so upset about? My little dance with Gilly? You was in the loo anyway, so what am I supposed to do, sit on my own in the corner till you come back?"

His actions sounded so innocuous, he made her look like a fool now to be complaining. She gave a sharp breath out, her hands on her hips, while she stood her ground and decided how to reply. "It wasn't just a *little dance*, and I came back from the toilet ages ago. Anyway, you promised you wouldn't." She hated the sound of her whiny voice, like a nagging wife or a stupid clingy girlfriend who was over possessive. She had intended to be cool with Alan, whatever he did, but yet again her emotions had got the upper hand. She hated the way he always stayed calm, he always made her feel that she was in the wrong even when she knew she was right.

"What's the harm?"

She was ready with her retaliation this time: "You came with me."

"I'll dance with you now, darling. I asked you, didn't I?"

She turned away from him, sulking. "I don't want to now, thanks..."

"Look - I wouldn't care if you danced with another bloke."

"No, you bloody well wouldn't" she muttered under her breath but loud enough to be audible to Alan and the small group of people clustered around them who were attending to the argument.

Alan laughed at her discomfiture. "So, it doesn't bother me, all right. Sorry, but I'm not the jealous type."

"And I suppose I am?" She was glaring at him. She knew the answer to her question - he'd told her many times - but she couldn't help asking again.

He tutted loudly and reached into his pocket for his cigarettes. "Give it a rest, will you." He turned away from her, with a look of disgust, scanning the room briefly for his former dancing partner who'd now wandered off. "I've had enough of this," he grunted. "You women are all the same."

He prepared to saunter away, shoving a cigarette into his mouth with tar-stained fingers, till Maddie brought him back with her voice: "Oh, and you'd know, of course. You know all about *women!*" she flung at him, spitting out the last word, "You've slept with most of them."

Alan turned to her with a face like thunder. She knew it was dangerous to continue, but she couldn't control herself now. The momentum of her anger had propelled her on to a familiar collision course. "You're not very choosy, are you? You've probably slept with most of the girls in Bristol." She gulped and waited tensely for his reaction, aware that the room had suddenly gone quiet and she was the center of attention. It was like being on stage or in some badly written soap opera, with the cliché words flowing out of her before she could stop them. "What's your problem, Alan? Have you got to prove yourself or something? I bet you don't really like women at all. I bet you're really gay."

Before she fully realized what a hit she'd scored with her final comment, Alan had stridden across the floor and punched her in the solar plexus, knocking her backwards. There was a gasp from the onlookers as Maddie collapsed against the people standing behind her, who grappled with her back and shoulders, cushioning her ungainly fall to the ground. Maddie sprang up immediately, her eyes ablaze. Before anyone could stop her, she ran at Alan and pummeled his retreating back with her fists, screaming "You bastard!"

At that moment, Maddie felt strong hands gripping her arms as Bella appeared at her side and dragged her away from Alan's unresponsive shoulders. "Come on now, come on now. Calm down. It's all right."

The watching crowd had begun to whisper and mumble and Alan slipped through the press of people and disappeared like a thief in the night. Bella meanwhile steered Maddie - now sobbing and wetting the edge of her friend's dress at the shoulder - into a chair at the side of the room. "Sit down for a minute, love. Don't worry. You have a good cry. Here, take my hanky." Maddie's sobs started to subside, as Bella knelt by her chair and squeezed her shoulders.

The cassette tape - a compilation album of music from the 50's - had now stopped and so had the party. For the moment, everyone was too stunned to know what to do. "Hey, everybody" Bella announced in a loud voice from her kneeling position, in an effort to inject some fizz into the now flat atmosphere: "Is this a party or a funeral wake? Don't stop having fun. Haven't you ever seen a lover's tiff before?" Embarrassed smiles and muffled remarks followed this last comment. "Terry, put on a CD, will you" Bella commanded her long-suffering lover, who had entered the living room with her and now stood by the door anxiously wiping his hands on his jeans. Terry obeyed, loping over to the CD player and selecting a disc of the liveliest music he could find, and gradually the guests began to herd together in clumps and dance or talk again in muted voices.

Bella watched till she considered the party atmosphere regained, her hand still on Maddie's shoulder, then she focused her attention back on her friend: "Feeling better, flower?" She gently smoothed away some damp strands of hair from Maddie's forehead. Maddie nodded dumbly. "I don't want to say I told you so, but..."

"You told me so," Maddie admitted with a wry grin and a sniffle.

"I'll tell him to piss off, shall I? He's probably gone into the kitchen for another drink."

"No need. I bet he'll leave anyway. He doesn't like scenes."

"That was quite a scene." Bella looked at Maddie to gauge if she was still feeling vulnerable, then she started to laugh.

After a few seconds Maddie joined in, as she suddenly appreciated the funny side of the situation. "Did I go red in the face?"

"Did you ever! You were like a bloody hellcat on wheels. I've never seen anything like it." Bella threw her head back and her large body shook with laughter. "It's a shame we didn't have any casting directors here, they'd have given you a part as the injured wife in a soap opera any time."

"Oh God, was I really that bad?" Maddie asked, her eyes wide and her hand over her open mouth in mock horror at the mental image of herself in full spate.

"I wouldn't want to get on the wrong side of you, that's for sure."

"Oh come on, I'm not a bitch. Am I?" Maddie's forehead abruptly creased in anxiety. "Was I wrong to be angry?"

Bella threw her arm around her friend's slim shoulders and squeezed them tightly. "Kiddo, you're not a bitch at all. D'you think I'd be your best mate if you were? Anybody'd be angry to be treated like that; the guy's a complete arsehole - as I've pointed out before, not that you took any notice. I think you were a saint to put up with him as long as you did. I'd sure as hell give Terry a bollocking if he danced with someone else on my birthday."

"He wouldn't though, would he" muttered Maddie enviously.

"Well, it's your own daft fault," replied Bella, not unkindly. "What d'you see in jerks like Alan? I could see he was a rat the minute I clapped eyes on him. You know, those sort of blokes, they've got an aura around them, it might as well be tattooed on their forehead - *Stay away from me, I'm trouble.*"

"I dunno. I don't know why I do anything. P'rhaps I'm a masochist" Maddie responded quietly, shrugging her shoulders and looking down.

Bella gave her friend an affectionate kiss on the cheek. "You're a twit, that's what you are. There's lots of nice men about."

"Where?" asked Maddie, making a dismal face. "I never seem to find any."

"You're not looking in the right places, my love. C'mon - let's not sit here moping. D'you wanna come and get a drink? We might find a nice man in the kitchen."

———⁓⁓∿⊙⊱⊙⊰⊙∿⁓⁓———

An hour or so later, Maddie found herself dancing with a young man. The music had a heavy rock beat and she was enjoying throwing her body from side to side, abandoning herself to the intoxication of the rhythm and concentrating on the movement to help empty her mind of thoughts. She'd instructed herself to forget all about Alan and their earlier confrontation, repeating the mantra that a rat like him wasn't worth bothering about, as Bella had asserted. But his rejection of her still rankled deep inside, and it took an effort to throw off the negative emotions of guilt and self-blame that were threatening to destroy her pleasure and confidence even now.

To console herself and boost her ego, she had agreed to dance with this young man, who had winked at her as she sat disconsolately nursing a drink by herself at the edge of the room, and with a gesture offered to be her partner. His black hair was closely cropped and his compact boyish body was clothed in slashed blue jeans and a black t-shirt advertising *Iron Maiden*. He also sported a pair of dark sunglasses, which gave him an image of cool maturity belied by his young voice and childish giggle. His dancing was fluid and confident and less inhibited than Maddie had previously encountered with other young men. But although she felt a certain attraction to him, Maddie wasn't in the mood to flirt with strangers - her fracas with Alan had stripped her of any desire for male company beyond the brief respite of the moment. Every time the young man swayed towards her, Maddie envisioned Alan's face and the dark leer of his expression as he'd dismissed her hurt feelings so callously. She cared so little about the boy she was dancing with that she hadn't even bothered to ask his name or tell him hers, knowing they'd have found it impossible to hear anything over the roar of the music anyway.

Terry had chosen a compilation CD where the tracks flowed seamlessly from one to another, and now the rhythm of the music slowed to something less frenetic and more sensuous. Maddie felt sweat glowing on her cheeks and she pushed back her damp hair from her forehead, as the boy came close and wrapped his body around hers. The stench of smoke and stale sweat from his neck was close to her nostrils and she squirmed and tried to wriggle free of his strong grip, but her arms were pinioned beneath his. Her heart started to race in anger at his assumption that he could do as he liked with her, but she quelled her rage and submitted to his embrace, too weary to protest. She couldn't bear another scene, to relive the humiliation of people watching her and judging her a fool. So she closed her eyes and tried to empty her mind, to enjoy the music of a song she liked and lose her awareness of external events.

When he pushed his greasy face next to hers and the plastic of his incongruous dark glasses dug into her temples as he started trying to kiss her, sliding his tongue insistently between her teeth, she knew she'd let things go too far. Abruptly, she brought her arms up to his chest and pushed him away, saying she needed to visit the toilet in a hurry. It was the ideal opportunity to get rid of him and she seized it eagerly, wishing she'd never embarked on the dance with him. What had started out as a childish attempt to get back at Alan - futile anyway since he'd left the party directly after their argument - had gone distinctly sour, and now all she wanted was to be among friends.

Maddie staggered through the press of dancers and into the dimly-lit front room, where she was smitten by the pungent aroma of marijuana. Here the actors from the cast of *Puttin' on the Ritz* had their enclave, away from the music and activity of the adjoining room, where no sounds were heard but the drone of familiar voices reciting jokes and anecdotes. Jonathan - who played the juvenile lead in the show - was entertaining a group of admirers with his Laurence Olivier impressions and a few members of the chorus sat in the adjacent corner passing round a joint. The atmosphere of the room felt safe and comfortable to Maddie, who immediately squatted on the floor beside her onstage partner and patted his knee with fraternal familiarity.

"Hi there" gushed Jonathan when he noticed her beside him: "If it isn't Lady Macbeth herself! Where've you been hiding? You know, this girl's more dramatic off stage than on." Everybody laughed, including Maddie. "Sorry to steal your limelight, Jonnie. I know you're the one who's supposed to have the tantrums round here."

All at once, Maddie felt serene and suffused in an atmosphere of warm friendship, and the evening's previous events receded into unimportance. The frown lifted from her forehead, she smiled and felt her previous anxiety evaporate like sweat from the pores of her skin. It was good to be back in the bosom of her little theatrical family. Her comrades surrounded her on the carpet like an impermeable barrier, and when she later glimpsed the young man she had danced with standing in the doorway looking at her, she confidently ignored him. She knew that now she was unassailable. With their mutual laughter and affection, her group had formed a close coterie, which excluded any outsiders.

It must have been some time later - Maddie wasn't sure exactly when, as her head was woolly with the effects of alcohol, enjoyment and tiredness - that Peter, the musical director, extracted Bella's old acoustic guitar from its resting place behind a dusty cabinet and began plucking the nylon strings. As the familiar tunes of jazz standards floated on the air, the group sang along in a straggly chorus. Maddie's voice rang out above the others in a confident soprano, the effects of the beloved music and words magically clearing the fuzziness from her brain, and her friends clapped her and encouraged her to do a solo. It was while she was giving her rendition of *Cry me a River* - her voice soaring in a plaintive wail on the words which seemed to have a particular relevance for her that night, "Now you say you're lonely, you cry the long night through, well you can cry me a river, cry me a river, I cried a river over you..." - that Maddie became briefly aware of the young man's face amongst the crowd watching her. After that, he vanished from the room and from her mind.

———————

At 5 a.m. when dawn broke and a weak sunlight started to filter through the velvet curtains of the front room, only a few stragglers remained at the party. The music had long since ceased, a sleeping man was snoring on the sofa in the living room and a small knot of people lingered on the carpet in the front room conversing in tired sentences strewn with pauses. Maddie was propped against the draining board in the kitchen slowly supping a mug of coffee that Bella had prepared. She marveled at Bella's undiminished energy and smiled as her friend made comments and jokes in a loud voice only slightly hoarse with tiredness and overuse.

Bella picked up an empty bottle of vodka and tossed it into the swing bin, where it clanked against the others. "I can't understand why people drink that stuff. It tastes of nothing and leaves you with a filthy headache the next morning."

"Do you want me to help you clear up?" Maddie offered in a bleary voice.

Bella chuckled: "I can tell you really want to, flower. No - no need. Terry and me'll do it in the morning, won't we Tel?"

"It *is* the morning," remarked Terry benignly.

"Oh yeah" said Bella with a glance at the clock on the wall. "Well, sod it. I can't be bothered now. Anyway, I object to doing dishes until the dirt's encrusted on them. I'm not a bloody housewife, am I?"

"You're certainly not," agreed Terry, getting up and squeezing Bella in a bear hug. "But I love you anyway."

Maddie suppressed an envious stare and put her empty mug on the draining board with a sigh, then straightened up. "I'd better be going, I suppose."

"Don't go home, flower. We've got a spare room. It's clean, you know, no one's thrown up in there yet."

Maddie laughed. "You hope! No, I should go home. I know what'll happen if I stay here, you'll never stop gabbing and I won't get to bed at all. And I'm wrecked, I need my beauty sleep."

"What a wimp" Bella commented to Terry, who was still gripping her round the waist and nuzzling her shoulder. "Hey, get off." Terry sat down again at the kitchen table and rubbed his forehead with his knuckles. Maddie thought he was probably longing for his bed himself, but was staying the course for Bella's sake. "There won't be any buses yet, you know," said Bella. "They don't start till seven on a Sunday."

"That's O.K. I'll walk."

"Walk? You're kidding! You can't walk all that way at this time of the morning. Terry'll take you in the car, won't you love" volunteered Bella, turning to her boyfriend.

Terry opened his mouth to protest but Maddie got in first: "In his state? Don't be cruel - I don't think he could keep his eyes open long enough."

Terry grinned sheepishly and nodded. "I would you know, only...I've had a bit to drink."

"I'll call you a taxi, then" persisted Bella.

"No. Really. I'd rather walk. I fancy some fresh air."

"You sure?"

"Yes, I'm sure."

"All that way, on your own. What if you get attacked by a mad axe murderer?"

"In broad daylight? Don't be ridiculous. I'll be fine."

"Don't be such a Mother Hen, Bella. Maddie can take care of herself," said Terry, with only a touch of irritation.

Accordingly, a few minutes later, Maddie hugged her friends goodbye, promised to meet them for a picnic that afternoon if the weather stayed fine, and set off for home. She was a little chilly in her red party frock and summer sandals, but a few seconds of brisk walking soon warmed her body. Despite having been awake all night, she was surprised at how fit and clearheaded she felt as soon as her steps settled into a regular rhythm and propelled her forward by their momentum. The exercise invigorated her and livened her spirits, making her glad she had chosen to walk.

She stopped for a moment and adjusted the strap of her canvas bag - an old one she'd bought in Greece a couple of years back - as it was biting into her shoulder, being crammed full and therefore heavier than usual. Besides the usual rubbish accumulated there - like her skin cream, vitamins, a book on Buddhism, purse and house keys - was Bella's birthday present, hastily unwrapped and rewrapped during the interval, a large ceramic aromatherapy burner.

She noticed no one else in the street as she walked, and she enjoyed strolling through the sleeping town and being the only person awake at that hour, as if she was the only person alive and the whole world had been created just for her. The dawn chorus was just reaching its peak, the birds seeming to compete with each other to produce the most noise, and the summer morning air smelt fresh and clean as if it had just been washed.

Maddie had been walking for about half an hour when the Clifton Suspension Bridge came into view ahead of her. She was no longer walking quickly but ambling along the road, enjoying the solitude and with no particular rush to get home. It was about then that Maddie first became aware of sharp and determined footsteps behind her. She was initially surprised, having thought herself alone on the street, but not unduly worried. At first, she quickened her pace slightly, thinking to outstrip the person behind her. But the footsteps quickened also and kept up with her. At this point she started to feel a little nervous and wondered if she was being deliberately followed.

The footsteps continued. Maddie debated with herself whether to turn around and accost her unknown follower. Would her pursuer take that as encouragement? She decided to keep walking, faster and faster, without actually running. She'd read in a book somewhere that women walking on their own should walk confidently and not show fear, so as not to look like a victim to a potential attacker. So she strode purposefully towards the bridge, hoping that whoever was behind her would eventually give up.

But her pursuer didn't give up. The footsteps reverberated against the pavement, sounding closer and closer, and Maddie felt her heart thumping in her chest with fear. Perhaps it had been foolish of her to choose to walk home, such a long distance on her own. But what danger could befall her in broad daylight? She tried to console herself that she was just being paranoid: the person behind her was simply eager to get home.

"Hang on a minute." The voice sounded vaguely familiar to Maddie. It was a male tone with a strong urban accent.

Halting, she whirled round to face the stranger and was astonished to recognize the young man she'd danced with at the party. He had a grin on his face that was halfway between cheeky and cunning. In the daylight, he seemed younger than she'd remembered him, and his body now didn't seem so much compact as slight. He swayed slightly as he stood, the early morning breeze ruffling his short black hair.

"What are you doing here? Why are you following me?" Now that she knew who her pursuer was, Maddie was no longer afraid, just irritated at the unwelcome intrusion.

"Not following you" he replied, his grin looking more inane and childish with this denial.

"Look..." Maddie began to explain, then realized she didn't know what to say to him. "Just go away. Go home... or wherever." She was suddenly weary, as if the events of the past few hours had caught up with her all at once. Seeing that he made no response, she turned to walk away.

"Can't go home" he called after her retreating back.

She gave a heavy sigh and turned again. "Why not?"

"Home's in Cardiff." He giggled.

This time she made no reply but glared at him with disdain and made to leave.

"Hang on. Come here." The voice behind her was demanding now and Maddie was reminded of the insistence of the young man's kiss at the party. There was something strange and unsettling about him. He was too intense. She didn't know what he wanted of her. And she felt a little stab of fear at the thought that he was maybe less harmless than he looked.

He walked briskly up to her till he was at her left side, and grabbed her arm in a proprietorial gesture. "Can I walk you home, miss?" he said in a singsong tone.

"No you can't. Get off!" She'd had enough of his games. Maddie pulled her arm out of his grasp and carried on walking, making an effort to ignore him.

"Don't be so unfriendly" he whined, attempting to take her arm again. This time, Maddie confronted him.

"Look, don't walk with me, I don't want you to. OK?"

"Why not?"

"I just want to walk on my own, all right? Just...just... leave me alone."

"All right" he responded, hanging his head sheepishly.

Maddie walked on, nearing the bridge, thinking she'd got rid of him. But the voice resumed its soliloquy behind her and the footsteps continued in her wake.

"Come on darling, give us a kiss, you're a good kisser, give us another kiss then, come on sexy, show us your tits, I wanna see your tits, you got big ones..." Between every phrase he giggled, as if playing a part he'd seen in a movie and slightly embarrassed at the things he was saying.

Maddie could contain herself no longer. She turned and shouted back at him. "Go away! Piss off, you little creep!"

But he seemed to take this as encouragement. Maddie marched ahead and he continued his verbal assault, laughing all the while.

Maddie was just about to break into a run when she felt his arms around her waist. The shock of it made her gasp, and she couldn't react quickly enough as he spun her around, pushed her back against the low stone wall at the beginning of the bridge and started to fumble with her skirt, trying to pull it up.

She couldn't believe this was happening, something so sordid and ugly. She felt shocked, like an animal that has just fallen headlong into a trap. Her hands fought the youth's desperately and she swung her head from side to side in an effort to avoid his leering face with its ugly smell of booze and smoke and stale sweat.

"Get off me!" she screamed in choking gasps, "Let me go, you bastard, let me go!"

But his hands seemed to be all over her. His deceptively slight frame contained a wiry strength, the full force of which was pinning her down. She could hear his desperate breathing in her ear. She scanned the horizon frantically for help, but there was no one there, no one to hear her call for assistance. She shouted anyway, as loud as she could, but the weight of his body was nearly suffocating her. He pinioned her against the cold stone, while with his hands he pulled down her knickers and fumbled with the zip of his flies.

Maddie could feel nothing but panic and the pain of his belt buckle digging into her stomach. She felt she was in some kind of nightmare. She craned her head round and saw the swirling water of the river many feet below. The seagulls seemed to be screaming for her, "No, no, no!"

———～〜◦◦◦✚◦✚◦◦◦～〜———

About a mile away, Gabriel Thatcher had just walked into the small cylindrical building where he worked every Sunday. Puffing slightly with the exertion, he ascended a steep flight of stone steps to a circular room at the top of the building, which housed nothing more than a large white chunk of stone in the center. Pushing open the creaky wooden door, a slow smile of contentment crept over Gabriel's face as he entered the room. He never tired of the sensation it gave him to close the door behind him and see how the light from above hit the stone and threw an image across its surface. It was like being held inside the body of a camera, looking out at the world from the inside. Withdrawing a cloth from his pocket, he wiped the surface of the stone slab to clean it. Then he grasped a wooden handle at the side of the slab and the image projected from above changed as he turned. As if looking from an airplane flying low over the scene, the image swept over the green grass of the park outside the building, over the river to the other side and back over the Clifton Suspension Bridge.

Suddenly, Gabriel saw something that caught his attention and he stopped and peered at the stone. Two moving figures could be seen at a distance, one wearing scarlet and one black, the strong colors contrasting sharply with the pale morning light. On to the slab was projected an image - clear and focused and as perfect in every detail as if he was standing outside and close by looking at it - of a scene currently being enacted on the bridge between a woman and a man who appeared to be attacking her.

Gabriel had witnessed many things during his years as curator of the Camera Obscura building - couples furtively lovemaking in the bushes, men taking the opportunity to urinate, even a purse snatcher once running off with his booty and hotly pursued by his victim - but never something like this. His mouth went dry and his heart started to pound at the realization that he was observing a real-life drama. If this had been something on the television he would have switched to another channel, but here was a scene he couldn't turn off. And some voyeuristic instinct kept his eyes riveted on the slab.

He stood still for several seconds, an unwilling onlooker at the two figures struggling on the bridge. The couple was alone, dwarfed by the iron edifice rising above them and the expanse of air below, where the river - now at its height - churned and gurgled and seemed to echo their distress. The girl's head twisted wildly and her arms flailed against her assailant's back but the man's body held hers firm beneath him. Inside the room it was eerily quiet, and Gabriel saw the scene unfolding mutely before him as if in a silent film.

On a sudden impulse, he turned and fled from the room, dropping his white cloth on the floor in his haste, and descended the narrow stairs as quickly as he could.

⎯⎯⎯ ⫸⫷⫸⫷ ⎯⎯⎯

It was then that Maddie saw the knife. She caught the glint of it as a ray of sun struck the shiny surface. Her mouth opened in horror and she tried to scream, but as in a nightmare, the sound lay gagged in her throat. The youth was poised above her, holding the knife's razor sharp edge to her neck: "Don't you scream. Don't you dare bloody scream, or I'll cut you wide open." His voice was low and intimidating. The words had such an unreal ring, they reminded Maddie of phrases uttered in thriller movies, and she suddenly had an insane urge to giggle. Instead, her terror made her breathe in and out in quick gasps, almost as if she were sobbing. Her wide, unblinking eyes were trained on her attacker. She saw that all the boyishness had gone now from his face. He lowered above her like a fully-grown man, determined and invincible.

Her panic had paralyzed her. She couldn't move, either to scream or escape, her eyes mutely pleading with the youth to just let her go. All she could do at that moment was pray that he wouldn't touch her face with the knife, that he wouldn't scar her face.

Suddenly, some sound or movement in the street distracted the youth and he turned his head away from Maddie, relaxing his grip momentarily. Her body apart from the right arm was pinned down and incapable of escape. Her heavy bag had slipped down that arm during the struggle and come to rest in the crook of her elbow. Seizing her chance, she summoned up all her reserves of strength. She straightened her arm, letting the strap of the bag slide to her hand, then gripped it as firmly as she could and swung the bag with all her might at her attacker's head. The bag whipped round his neck, catching him on the side of the cheek, and he stalled for a moment startled by the impact, and released the pressure on her body.

Maddie swung the bag again with all her might, throwing the weight of her newly liberated body behind the blow. This time the weapon hit home, smacking the youth full on the back of the skull with an audible crack. The force of the collision knocked him sideways and sent him reeling away from her, his arms up in an instinctive gesture to protect his head and his mouth emitting a yowl of pain. Without his hands to steady him and with the momentum of his reaction carrying him backwards, he tumbled against the low stone wall. His spine arched over the wall, his legs were catapulted from the ground and he keeled over in a backwards somersault, mouth still open in astonishment, arms flailing in a futile attempt to save himself, as his body plummeted in a slow and graceful arc and a few seconds later hit the river's full waters with a splash which drowned his screams, as he sank into their cloudy depths many feet below.

Maddie stood rigid with shock, unable to comprehend what had happened with such terrible suddenness. Unable even to turn and see the dead weight of the youth's body as it plunged into the icy water. She just stood, staring stupidly at her shoulder bag, which had sprayed some of its contents out into the street while travelling through the air and now hung limply in her shaking hand.

A grating sound made her look up, and now Maddie saw what it was that had startled her attacker and made him relax his grip on her for that crucial moment: a tall, elderly man with white hair was standing a few yards away watching her. He had a gentle, handsome face and a dignified demeanor. He and Maddie regarded each other for a few seconds, both too shocked to speak. Then, as the man held out one hand and approached her, opening his mouth to say something, Maddie turned and fled without looking back.

Gabriel had run down to the bridge from the Camera Obscura building as fast as he possibly could. But the distance was a good quarter of a mile, he was an old man and not strong, and by the time he'd arrived within view of the scene he was gasping for breath and had to halt for a few seconds to recover. When he straightened up and looked again, he saw the knife flashing in the sun, as the youth pressed it to the girl's throat. The sight filled him with horror and his heart thumped painfully in his chest. Calling out, "Hey!", he lurched towards the couple. But just at that moment, as the boy noticed him and turned his head towards the sound, Gabriel saw the blur of an object whizzing through the air and suddenly the young man was thrown off balance and precipitated into the river.

The body descended, almost beautifully, in the slow motion of a dreamscape. And yet, the whole event had happened so quickly that Gabriel could hardly take it in.

Now he saw the girl's face, numb with shock, and her look of blank despair as she saw him and grasped that someone else had witnessed the incident. He searched his mind desperately, wanting to call out to her, something helpful and encouraging, but before he could find the right words, the girl ran away.

He'd arrived too late. He berated himself, as he remained on the now empty bridge. Why did he always come too late to do any good? Why were his good intentions always so ineffectual?

Gabriel shambled crestfallen away.

CHAPTER TWO

THERE WAS ONE sachet of instant coffee remaining on the saucer by the electric kettle, and Maddie ripped it open and emptied the granules into her cup with trembling fingers. Her hot bath had soothed her a little, but her brain was still buzzing with feverish ruminations. Her arms felt raw and burning after the way she'd scrubbed at her skin, as if she thought by doing so she could wipe out the past. Her long soak in the blisteringly hot water had necessarily been curtailed, in case Mrs. Evans - her incorrigibly nosy landlady - had noticed the amount of time she was spending in the bathroom and ventured upstairs to knock on the door, precipitating a conversation leading to awkward questions about the night before.

Maddie wore the pink cotton nightdress she'd donned immediately on entering her bedroom a few hours before, but the sheets on the bed remained uncrumpled. Abandoning her attempts to sleep, Maddie had sat in an armchair reading a book as a distraction from her memories, until the morning was sufficiently advanced to warrant her leaving her room. She hadn't gone down to breakfast at ten o'clock, as was her usual habit on Sunday morning, intending to use a severe hangover as her explanation to

Mrs. Evans. The mere thought of food - ordinarily one of her greatest pleasures in life - this morning made her feel like retching.

She sat on the edge of the bed drinking her coffee, and tried to collect her thoughts as they whirled confusedly about her head. Even now, she was afraid to close her eyes for longer than a blink in case the images, which were waiting behind her lids, sprang out and forced themselves upon her wary consciousness. Her head felt as if somebody was playing a drum inside it and her body felt heavy and slow like she'd been drugged. She was unused to these sensations and they frightened her. Her body had suddenly become unpredictable and unfamiliar.

She sat in silence, without any music from the radio or cassette player, seeming to stare vacantly into space, terrified that any noise would alert Mrs. Evans and induce her to come upstairs and start an unwelcome discourse. At the moment, Maddie didn't feel capable of conversing in a natural way with anyone, much less her inquisitive and gossipy landlady. She knew she would have to face the world soon and adopt a mask of normality, but she intended to stall that moment for as long as she could. She wished she could hide herself away from prying eyes and burrow into the earth, like an animal in its lair.

She rose and went to the window, gently parted the flowered curtains and gazed out, feeling some trepidation about viewing the street. But it looked perfectly normal and ordinary, as it did every day. A large apple tree stood in the front garden, covered in blossom only just beginning to fade; a couple of children argued over a football in the yard across the road; cars meandered down the street weaving between their parked counterparts. For some reason, she had been anticipating an expectant menace in the air, from a world already apprised of what she had done and waiting to pounce on her. Of course, she recognized, that was only paranoia. But although she tried to reassure herself that she was still the girl she'd always been, still a part of things, still a valued member of her team, all at once she was overcome with a feeling of alienation, as if she had been cast out from society, an outsider who could never fit in. It was like being in a play where everybody else but she knew the plot. Or like one of the nightmares she had frequently, where she stood backstage due to make her entrance any minute but unable to remember any of her lines. She shook her head and tried to pull herself together, tried to clear a logical pathway through the fog in her brain, but her constantly shifting emotions disorientated her too much to think at all.

Maddie dressed quickly in jeans, t-shirt and jumper, then shook the contents of her handbag out onto the bed. Her eyes flickering briefly over the familiar objects, she noticed two things: first, that her birthday present, the ceramic aromatherapy burner, was broken into three pieces. Maddie knew when it must have happened. The events of that terrible morning replayed themselves in her mind and she saw herself swinging her handbag through the air and the noise that it had made as it struck. She shivered and shook her head again, trying vainly to dislodge the memory.

She forced herself to return to practicalities. Should she try to repair the burner with superglue? No, there was no point - she decided, weighing the pieces in her hands. There was no hope of making the joins invisible. Better to buy another identical one and say nothing. She was acquainted with the shop where Bella must have purchased it.

Secondly, there was something missing, something essential to her welfare. Maddie had a stand by for use in emergencies, but that wasn't what concerned her most. The item must have been jettisoned from her bag when the other things were chucked out into the street, and she hadn't stayed long enough to check. It was the only object from her handbag lost in that moment that could definitely be traced back to her. She would have to go back to the scene and attempt to retrieve it, maybe tonight, under cover of darkness.

She huddled inside her jumper, shivering, only partly with cold. She wished that life were like a computer screen, where memories like words could be erased at the touch of a button. She felt so lost and confused. The same thoughts circled around and around in her head without ever being resolved, and the same questions to which she couldn't find the answers. *What should I do now? Give myself up? But who would believe my story? Should I run away? But that would mean giving up my job - and anyway, wouldn't that seem more suspicious? Should I stay and pretend that nothing's happened? Would I be able to keep up the pretense? Will anybody find out? What about the old man? Did he see me clearly enough to recognize me? Did he know that I was being attacked? Will he come looking for me? Should I go looking for him? What should I do?*

She longed suddenly for Bella. Bella was her best friend. And she was such a sensible girl; she would know what to do in any situation. But Maddie knew that there were some burdens even best friends couldn't be expected to carry. She had to deal with this alone. There was no one she could tell.

————✦————

Gabriel kept a bottle of whisky in the bottom of the sideboard in his living room, behind the cut-glass decanter that had been a retirement present from his work at the *Bristol Evening News*, and several bottles of more innocuous substances, such as Ribena and Stone's Green Ginger wine, to which he turned more frequently.

The sunlight was just starting to slide through his pale green curtains and make a dappled pattern on the living room wall. Outside, it was a still and silent Sunday morning, enlivened only by the sound of next door's cockerel, which always crowed later than it should. Gabriel reached into his cupboard and felt around the dusty surfaces for the whisky bottle at the back. He grasped it with shaking fingers and tipped some of the amber liquid into a tumbler balanced on his knee. He felt guilty and ashamed of his actions: if anyone had walked in at that moment he would probably have blushed and denied that he was helping himself to an alcoholic drink in the morning. It was an unusual act for him, but he needed Dutch courage to do what he was intending. In fact, the whisky felt so good and strong and warm when he drank it that he poured out another portion and consumed it quickly before guilt could stop him. Then he replaced the bottle.

Thus fortified, he collected his brown suit jacket from the coat stand in the hall, checked that he had the slip of paper with the address in his pocket, and departed from the house. It was a glorious summer morning - fresh and clear with the scent of flowers in the air - and as he walked he didn't think about what he was going to do but just enjoyed the feel of the breeze on his skin and the confident sound of his own footsteps tapping out their solo rhythm on the pavement.

He was a sturdy walker despite his age, and it didn't take him more than half an hour to arrive at the police station in Heston Road. As he neared the grey brick building, he could feel his heart beating faster and his stomach churning with nervous tension. But he was determined; he couldn't turn back now.

He approached the front door and saw through the glass that a man in uniform was seated at the reception desk, his head down over some form that he was filling in. Gabriel's confidence was evaporating with every moment. He had half wished the police station would be closed on Sundays, so he could tell himself that at least he had made the effort. He realized now, though, what a vain hope that had been. Of course policemen worked every day of the week, crime wasn't a nine to five business.

He rapped softly on the glass and attracted the attention of the officer, who indicated with a nod that he should enter. Once inside the building and standing in front of the young man - who regarded him with a briskly questioning stare - Gabriel realized the finality of his situation for the first time. He was actually here, in a police station, where he'd come to report a crime. Now he would be expected to make a statement, which somebody would write down, and later possibly he would be asked to repeat everything he'd said to another officer. In a few weeks, or however long it took, he would be expected to appear in Court and say the whole lot again, this time to a roomful of people (all of them sniggering when they heard his voice). And if he deviated from his original statement he would be questioned with suspicion, as if he were the culprit. Gabriel had watched all the police dramas on the television and he knew how things operated in the world of the Law.

And yet he had made the effort to come. He had told himself it was the right thing to do, and he wanted to do the right thing. He wanted to prove - if only to himself - that he was not the spineless fool Helen had thought him, not the "observer of life" his mother had called him, always unwilling to get involved with other people, on the sidelines, watching events.

Gabriel took in a gulp of air and steeled himself: "I w...w...want to r...r...report a..." Gabriel's stammer was exacerbated by his nerves and he could hardly get his lips to move at all, the consonants sticking on his tongue like sentinels guarding the escape of his thoughts. And the final word of his sentence was lost in a welter of confusion and indecision - *what had he come to report anyway? A crime? A rape? A murder? Who was he trying to help, by telling what he'd seen?* To Gabriel's immense relief, the young policeman was suddenly called away from his desk by one of his colleagues in the next room. He apologized briefly to Gabriel for keeping him waiting and said he'd be back in a moment.

Gabriel - left alone to ponder the consequences of his actions - stared at the bulletin board on the wall. It was covered with notices of various types - some personal messages on postcards or slips of paper, and some printed leaflets advertising services. One large notice in the center of the board had a bold headline that shouted to be read, underneath which was a photocopied magazine article:

RAPE CRISIS CENTRE
OFFERS TRAINING FOR W.P.C.s
IN COUNSELING TECHNIQUES FOR
FEMALE VICTIMS OF RAPE

"WHO'S ON TRIAL HERE? How can we expect the female victims of rape to come forward, when only 5% of rape cases that come to trial end in a conviction? For a woman who's just been through a harrowing experience, the added trauma of a police investigation, Court appearances plus possible harassment by the media during which her entire sexual history will be dissected (as if relevant to the issue) would be sufficient to deter most women, who could be forgiven for preferring to let the matter disappear quietly into obscurity. The added ignominy - and potential danger - of having her assailant acquitted, only exacerbates her feelings of helplessness and frustration. It's time for a change of attitude in the police force. Let's see some money put into proper training for police officers - male and female - who are attempting to deal with the problem, so that at least they can understand what female victims of rape go through."

Gabriel was a believer in Fate. Was it Fate that had led his eye to fall on that particular article at that precise moment? He believed it was. To him - in his ambivalent state of mind - it was a sign that he should never have come. Why was he here, preparing to tell the police about a man he'd seen falling into the river? What did he hope to achieve, by telling them he'd seen a girl struggling with him before he fell? They might find the girl and charge her with murder. They might think it was irrelevant that she was being attacked at the time. Did he really want to be responsible for that? What the hell did he know about the situation anyway? He'd only seen it from a distance and then briefly from a few yards away. He wasn't even sure himself exactly what had happened, the events had moved so swiftly.

If he did nothing, maybe the body wouldn't be found for a while, until the water had done its best to destroy the man's identity, giving the girl a chance to escape. Gabriel heard the sound of voices from the next room. Somebody said, "See you later, Bill. I've got a chap in the front." The young policeman was coming back. Gabriel turned and left the building, and hurried back down the street towards home.

CHAPTER THREE

"COME ON MADDIE my love, have another egg sandwich. This'll put hairs on your chest." Bella thrust a packet wrapped in foil under Maddie's nose. Her large red hands smelt slightly of the onions she'd been chopping earlier that day.

"No thanks, really. I'm not very hungry."

"That makes a change" Bella replied, laughing, and threw the rejected sandwich back into the plastic container. "Oh well, more for us then."

Maddie averted her face from the other two and stared at a nearby oak tree, feigning interest in the actions of a blackbird in one of the high branches. She could feel her nose growing hot and a pricking at the corners of her eyes that warned of the onset of tears. With a concentrated effort, she willed herself not to cry. She was desperate not to cry in front of her friends and be forced to endure their questions and their pity, neither of which she could answer. Only her hands betrayed her inner distress, as she plucked a blade of grass to pieces with quivering fingers.

She drove the black introspection from her mind and tried to dwell on the present. A few days ago she could have taken sensuous pleasure in the warmth of the air and the seductive country aromas, the sight of the lush grass speckled with white daisies, the wind moving softly through the trees and the birds warbling their carefree melodies. She wanted to be joyful and at peace. She would have been happy if it weren't for her memories, knocking on the doors of her consciousness and crashing in like unwanted guests at a party.

Terry's soft, high voice seemed to reach her from a great distance: "I said you're quiet today, Maddie. Anything wrong?"

Maddie awoke from her daytime reverie with a start and gave a sheepish smile. "I was just... enjoying the sunshine."

"She's still pissed from last night," suggested Bella, with a wink at her boyfriend. "Can I really not tempt anyone with some more eats?" she said, indicating the pile of foil-wrapped parcels, packets of nuts and crisps, apples and oranges lying in the picnic hamper. "Come on folks. If you don't have 'em now, I'll give you it all for supper with your milk."

Maddie turned to her friend and puffed out her cheeks, holding her stomach. "Sorry Bel, I'm stuffed. Why did you make so much?"

"She always makes enough for an army", Terry replied, grabbing Bella's arm affectionately and looping it through his. "She forgets that you dancers have to keep in shape."

Bella stuck her tongue out at him and gave him a playful punch on the shoulder: "I have to keep in shape too, you know."

"It wouldn't make any difference how little you ate", continued Terry unabashed, "you'll always be an Amazon." He kissed her on the tip of her broad nose.

"Thanks, titch." Bella rummaged around in the Tupperware container, selected a doorstopper of a tuna salad sandwich, removed the foil wrapping and took a huge bite.

Maddie watched the couple with a hint of envy, then resumed chewing a blade of grass. "It doesn't make any difference how *much* I eat, I never put on weight" she interposed.

"Poor old you" teased Bella. "I wish I had your problem. But hang on, you do worry about your weight sometimes, because you wouldn't try my chocolate cheesecake the other day, d'you remember? Even though I told you it was made with low fat ingredients."

"Such as cream, soft cheese, chocolate and biscuits--" smirked Terry.

"I wasn't worrying about my weight" explained Maddie.

"Yeah, yeah. Pull the other one."

"No, didn't I tell you? I can't eat chocolate and that. Not ordinary chocolate, anyway. I'm diabetic."

"You're what?" asked Bella, her mouth dropping open in amazement.

"I'm diabetic. You know. I can't eat anything sweet or my blood sugar level goes haywire."

"Wow! I never realized. You're a dark horse. D'you have to have a special diet and things?" Bella mumbled through her sandwich.

"Not really special. I just have to watch my sugar intake. That includes alcohol, unfortunately."

"God, and I thought you were just stronger willed than the rest of us."

"No, I'm not strong willed at all."

Terry was regarding Maddie with fascination. "Does that mean you have to, er..." he began, with a gesture as if injecting himself with a huge needle.

Maddie laughed in spite of herself at the crudeness of his mime. "Yes, I have to er..." and did a mime of her own. "It's quite easy."

"Where do you do it?" Bella asked with a grimace.

"People always ask that. Well, you don't always do it in the same place. You can inject anywhere; in your legs, in your arms, in your bottom. I usually do it in my bottom, 'cos my arms are a bit skinny."

Bella whistled ironically: "Whew - how sexy!"

"How often?" asked Terry, with genuine interest. He was training to be a nurse, and people's physical problems were a source of continual glamour to him.

"Four times a day, before meals."

"Four times!" Bella's eyes widened. Maddie had to laugh at her reaction.

"It's really not a problem."

"Will you have to do it today?" asked Terry.

"Yes, I injected before I came out. I've got one of those portable pen things. You just bung it in, it gives you the right amount of insulin and it doesn't even hurt. Look, I'll show you." Maddie started rummaging in her bag. "I've got it somewhere in here... in the side pocket I think. It's great having such a portable thing to carry around. Actually, this is my back up pen. I haven't used it in a while but I keep it for emergencies. My normal pen got lost..."

Maddie was gratified that her betraying face was partly hidden in the large confines of her bag, because

39

suddenly her heart started beating very fast and she could feel her cheeks flushing cherry red. She prayed that the others would fail to grasp the significance of what she had just spilled out, would not ask questions exposing her motives to inspection. She silently commanded her hands to stop shaking, as she located the pen and handed it to Bella to look at. Maddie was grateful that Bella and Terry were so intrigued by the pen and busy examining it that they took no more notice of her for a few seconds.

"Complicated stuff--"

"It's a really neat device. See how you can program the little dials to give you just the right amount of insulin..."

Maddie couldn't keep her face averted from her friends by pretending a fascination for the nearest tree forever. Yet she was conscious that her heightened emotions were currently very near the surface. It had always been her misfortune to betray her slightest emotions by blushing a sentinel red.

Terry turned the pen over in his hands, then passed it back to Maddie, asking: "Have you always been diabetic?"

"No, they only found out about me eighteen months ago. I sprained my ankle doing a difficult dance step and had to go to casualty. They did a routine blood test and that was when they discovered..."

"You mean you didn't know before that? Or is it just something that sort of...comes on?" asked Bella between mouthfuls of another sandwich.

"I dunno, really. I don't know if I'd had it for a while or if something I did aggravated the condition. The doctors didn't say. Just told me I had to be careful from now on."

"It's hereditary, isn't it?" asked Terry with interest.

"Yes...I think so."

"The doctors should have known to examine you for it earlier, since you're at a greater risk than most people." Terry sat forward and his face took on an earnest expression, as if he were practicing his counseling skills.

Maddie looked down at the ground and hesitated for a moment. Sensing her unease, Terry added: "Oh, I'm sorry. Didn't mean to pry or anything."

"Are either of your parents diabetic?" quizzed Bella, who had been too engrossed in delving between the sandwiches for a tomato quarter to notice Maddie's discomfort.

"Don't be such a nosy parker" admonished Terry, nudging Bella gently in the ribs. "She's not obliged to give you her life history, you know."

"It's O.K. I don't mind. Erm...I'm not sure about my parents. My mother...I think...I believe she was diabetic as well. I don't know about my father."

"I'm awfully sorry," said Terry. "I didn't realize your mother was dead."

Maddie was silent, her expression undecipherable.

"But your mum rang during rehearsals, didn't she?" blurted Bella, not registering the look on Terry's face. "I spoke to her on the stage door telephone and gave her your digs number. I'm sure she said she was your mum."

"That's my adoptive mum. I don't know my real mother. Or my father."

"What do you mean, adoptive?" asked Bella, too fascinated to be tactful. Terry sat in tense and embarrassed dumbness.

"I'm adopted. I don't know my real parents" Maddie announced, hating the familiar look of mingled pity and dismay on her friends' faces: "I mean I don't know who they are. My mum...my adoptive mum I mean...she wouldn't tell me. She said I'd only be upset." The others were too stunned to respond, so Maddie carried on, with a weak smile that attempted to lighten the atmosphere. "I only found out about the hereditary diabetes thing by accident, because my mum had to let the doctor at the hospital know and he told me. And that was the first I knew about it."

"That must have been... quite a shock" Bella whispered, her earlier bonhomie crushed and with genuine compassion in her eyes. "Not just about the diabetes, I mean. Finding out that you'd been adopted."

"Yes, it was" Maddie agreed flatly, wishing she could change the subject.

"Was that really the first you knew about it?"

"Yes."

"But aren't there adoption agencies or something?" Terry interposed. "I mean, even if your adoptive parents don't want to tell you, there are other ways you can find out who your natural parents were...are..."

"That's right" Bella agreed, raising one forefinger enthusiastically, as if convinced that between them she and Terry could solve all Maddie's problems: "I saw a program on the telly about this woman who'd been abandoned on the moors when she was a baby. She's in her fifties now but she hasn't given up trying to trace her natural mother. She went to all these different organizations and experts and stuff. I don't think she did find out anything in the end. But it would be different for you. You're so much younger. And they keep records all over the place. I'm sure you have a right to know who your parents are, your real parents, I mean."

Maddie shook her head sorrowfully. "I know, I know, you *do* have a right, I do have the right. Believe me, I've already explored all the possibilities."

For a few moments the three friends sat in a silence charged with unanswered questions, listening distractedly to the birdsong, which continued unabashed around them. Bella gazed at her sandwiches and Terry at his feet, both seemingly stumped for a response.

Maddie appeared to reach an inner decision. She inhaled deeply in preparation for divulging a story no one else had heard: "When I first found out about being adopted, it was such a shock, I couldn't do anything at all for a few weeks, you know? It was as much as I could do to come to terms with it, to sort of adjust to the knowledge that I wasn't who I'd always thought I was...I didn't talk about it to friends or anything, guess I felt sort of ashamed, like it was my fault or something. I don't know. At first I pleaded and pleaded with mum to tell me the truth but she wouldn't. I said to her, how could it upset me more to know the truth than to be kept in ignorance? But she didn't take any notice, she wouldn't budge an inch. God - she can be stubborn when she wants! Sometimes I'd plague myself, you know, imagining there was some terrible secret that nobody dared tell me, that my mother was a prostitute and my father was a..."

Maddie had been on the brink of saying *murderer*, but the word stuck in her throat. It was such an unpleasant reflection of her current circumstances...

"...had done something terrible. Anyway, I was also working at the time and that took my mind off things. But when I finished that tour and I got back to London, I went to the local library and looked at some books on adoption. I just think I wanted to find out more about the whole subject, you know?"

Bella nodded sympathetically, her brown eyes now fixed on her friend.

"I thought I'd go to the Citizens Advice Bureau and I rang them loads of times and they were always engaged or closed and when I found out where my local office was and the opening times I popped round there and I picked up a few leaflets but I didn't speak to any of the helpers. They all looked so busy and unsympathetic. For some weird reason I still felt like I wanted to be anonymous and discreet about things and if I had to have an interview with somebody...oh well, I gave up on that. But at least I found out that if you're over eighteen and adopted you have a right to know who your natural parents are. I was so glad I'd discovered something that actually said in black and white that I had some rights, that I was a person who deserved to know about my background."

"You were probably right not to bother any more with the Citizen's Advice people. They're pretty useless in my experience," grumbled Terry.

"Anyway, go on. What happened next?" encouraged Bella.

"So I rang my mum right away and crowed about it. I said if she wouldn't tell me, there were other ways I could find out and I wasn't afraid to try them."

Bella smiled and punched the air with her fist: "Atta girl!"

"I threatened to go to the National Registry Office - it's in central London somewhere - and look up my original birth entry in the records. Or I could write to...I can't remember their name...there's a national organization and you can fill out a form and they'll send you a copy of your birth entry and it's got to have the names of your parents on it. I actually wrote a letter to them asking for the form and they sent the form to me. I've still got it back home. I've even filled it in...most of it...but it made me nervous because they said I had to have counseling, from some official counselor, before they'd tell me the information or something and I didn't like the sound of that."

"Anyway, I told mum I'd done that. I'd written to the agency and I'd got the form and I'd filled it in and I was about to send it off. I suppose I wanted to hurt her with it, make her feel bad, I don't know. Anyway, I upset her just as much as I wanted to. More. She begged and begged me not to take it further. She actually cried on the telephone, she's never ever done that before. I don't remember her crying in front of me, ever, she's not that sort of person. But she was really upset. She went on and on about how this natural parents thing was like a curse, and if I knew the truth I'd regret having the knowledge."

"Oh really - what a thing to say! How can the truth be a curse?" Bella opined, with a look at Terry.

"She obviously just feels threatened. I've heard of this sort of reaction before. She wants you to accept them as your parents. After all, they're the ones who brought you up--" Terry rejoined.

"It shouldn't stop you looking, though" remarked Bella.

"In the end, my mum said that..." Maddie hesitated and blinked fiercely, gulping back her emotion. "She swore to me that...both of my natural parents are dead now and I'd never be able to meet them. Knowing who they were would make no difference at all, if I couldn't meet them and talk to them you see. So when she said that, I sort of gave up. I thought maybe she was right. Knowing who my real parents were would just make me feel worse. If there was something terrible about them, perhaps it's better that I don't know. At least this way, I can imagine...pretend to myself that they were special or famous or something."

Maddie gave a short laugh and shrugged her shoulders. "So I put the whole thing behind me. Forgot about it altogether, and got on with my life. And I'm over it now. I never even think about it," she asserted in a bright voice that failed to convince.

With an impulsive gesture, Bella put her arms around her friend and pulled her near, hugging her forcefully. "What a story! I'm so sorry, love. Never mind. You've got me and Tel now. Don't you forget that."

Maddie's emotions were a mixture of shame and gratitude, as she allowed her head to rest on Bella's large and comforting shoulder. And now, nestling in the warmth of her friend's arm, she allowed a few hot tears to fall. It *had* been a shock, she recalled, finding out that her parents were not her parents and she was not who she'd thought she was. It had pulled the ground out from under her feet, and destroyed all her solid notions of the world and her secure place within it, at a stroke.

But she'd also been relieved to finally have certain things explained to her. Why her father (or Jim, the man she had thought of as her father) had always been so distant with her and so seemingly uninterested in her progress. Why she had felt so unmoved by his death. And why she and her "mother" had never got on. Maddie had always felt separate and different from the two people who'd called themselves her parents. She didn't even look remotely like either of them. So it had almost been a blessing to find out that she didn't after all belong to them, the knowledge vindicating, as it did, her feelings of separateness.

At the same time this knowledge proved an uneasy burden for Maddie - who had never really given up wondering about her origins - to bear. Mrs. Wetherby's reticence on the subject verified in Maddie's mind that her adoptive mother had no comprehension of her feelings - since if she'd possessed an inkling of her "daughter's" suffering she'd have put her out of her misery by revealing the truth - and this had only exacerbated the strained relations between them.

Maddie couldn't put her dilemma into words or express its significance to her. But there was something so terribly inconclusive about not knowing where, or who, she came from. Sometimes she felt like a ghost or a refugee who belonged nowhere. Maddie shivered and tried to stop wallowing in self pity, as Bella's arm held her tighter. Not knowing was the worst torture, much more terrible than anything her invention could conjure. Perhaps - when she returned to London - she would steel herself for the counseling and send off the form.

Maddie wept slow and silent tears. She cried for herself, and for her real parents, whatever they had done and whoever they had been.

———— ⚬⚬⚬ ————

Gabriel Thatcher took down the old leather-bound photograph album with gilt edges from the bookshelf that was lined with similar albums, all conscientiously numbered in sequence and marked with a title on the spine to indicate what pictures they contained: "Fishing Trip 1982", or "Christmas with Rex and family 1979". This one simply said "India and Nepal". The calfskin leather, which had once been a mustard brown color, had darkened round the edges from many years of fingering.

Gabriel sat in his favorite armchair by the empty grate, underneath the light of the standard lamp with the tasseled shade. He sipped every now and then from a glass of sherry on the small wooden table by his side. His cat, Liquorice, lay curled up in front of the hearth, as if still judging it the warmest place, even in summer with the fire unlit. She was an old cat with coarse black fur that had gone rough in patches and one eye clouded with cataracts. It had been years since she'd caught a mouse or chased a bird: these days she preferred to spend her days asleep or staring out of the window at passers by. Another owner might have had her put down, but the cat had been Gabriel's constant companion for the last sixteen years of his life, and she occupied that part of his heart that may otherwise have been filled by a loving wife.

Gabriel turned over the first page of the album and around his lips a faint smile hovered, as the pictures brought the memories flooding back. He didn't need to read the little sentences written beside each photograph explaining where and what it depicted. He knew them all by heart:

"Summer 1968 - Helen and Gabriel set off on a mystical journey into the unknown."

[A young couple are standing, their arms entwined around each other, faces beaming. She is younger than he, in her early twenties perhaps, and very pretty, with long straight dark hair under her bandana. She is wearing a long Indian skirt, leather sandals and a sheepskin jacket, and in her right hand is a bunch of flowers. He is the young Gabriel, not instantly recognizable with his long hair and beard, loon pants, brightly colored shirt and strings of beads. In front of them on the ground is a bulging canvas suitcase and behind them a 747 Boeing aircraft with passengers in various stages of disembarking.]

"Oh wow, Gabe, isn't this fab!" enthused Helen, after she had taken back their Kodak brownie camera from the small Nepalese boy and given him what Gabriel considered to be a disproportionate amount of money.

"It's very n...nice," he agreed. He wasn't as relaxed as her: he'd already started worrying about where they were going to find a hotel to sleep at the height of season, arriving at Kathmandu airport in the sweltering heat of mid-afternoon, but she had pooh poohed his suggestion that they book in advance.

"It's so hot! Man, I could get into this; I mean I could live like this. It's the real McCoy, isn't it? God, let me get

this thing off" she said, throwing off her sheepskin jacket and letting it fall to the ground, then opening her arms wide and lifting her face to the sun in an abandoned, ecstatic gesture. "This is how people should live, I mean really be! Away from the concrete jungle, where things are real!" She started running down the tarmac with a whoop of joy, while the few other straggling passengers stared after her in amazement. Gabriel smiled rather sheepishly at them, picked up their bag and her jacket, and lumbered after her to the arrivals check-in. He didn't take off his suede fringed jacket, even though the uncomfortable heat was already making rivulets of sweat run down his chest, because he thought wearing it was the most sensible way of carrying the weight.

It only took half an hour for the couple to check in, as they didn't have to wait for their suitcase on the conveyor belt, having elected to travel light. To Gabriel's surprise and relief, they were met in front of the airport - while trying to hail a cab - by three men offering them cheap accommodation. Well, perhaps assailed might be a better word, by the men, who vied with each other to offer the best bargain bed in Kathmandu. Then there were several small children in rags who materialized from nowhere and pulled at Gabriel's trousers asking for coins. He tried to ignore them - which was difficult because Helen meanwhile was doling out what seemed like most of the coins they had just received in exchange for sterling at the airport - picked on the least threatening of the three potential landlords (an older man with a wide smile and quick nimble hands that grabbed their bags) and agreed to his offer. The three of them piled into the so-called taxi and sped at heart-racing pace through the shabby streets till they arrived at a small, rather rundown but bustling establishment in Freak Street, which the driver referred to as "the cleanest hotel in Nepal", with Helen enthusing all the way.

Despite its external appearance, the inside of the hotel wasn't bad, and their room was clean and a very reasonable price. They didn't have an ensuite bathroom but there was a shower down the hall, which Gabriel availed himself of immediately, while Helen chatted to the proprietor's wife about what there was to do in the area. By the time Gabriel arrived downstairs in the lobby, freshly washed and changed into cooler more comfortable clothes, Helen had already learned the location of the best local markets and eating places, and had made friends with the proprietress and her three children. She proudly demonstrated to Gabriel the all-purpose Nepalese greeting, Namaste - along with appropriate praying gesture, fingertips together - as they set off on their first evening stroll through the dusty streets.

Gabriel couldn't restrain himself from castigating her for giving money to every beggar that they passed - of which there were many - but she reminded him that to these people, Westerners were unbelievably rich. "It's only money, anyway. Material things aren't important, you know." Gabriel couldn't help loving her for her generosity of spirit, and he rebuked himself inwardly for the miserliness that kept him worrying about the small amount of traveller's checks they had with them and wondering whether they could last the three months in the Far East they had planned. He didn't really believe it was possible to live on as little as everybody said, even in a country as obviously poor as this.

The sight of the poverty around him at once appalled and fascinated him - the leper with no legs on the edge of the street, the emaciated dogs scrabbling in the dirt for food - and with a photographer's instinct, he wished he'd brought his camera out with him so that he could record all the myriad, conflicting images. Helen disapproved of his "little black box" as she called it. She said that his memory was the best camera there was.

When they got to Thamel - with its colorful sights and sounds - his wish became even more fervent. This was surely the real Nepal he'd been expecting to see after looking at the guidebooks. Even Helen was impressed with the variety and quality of goods on display, though she usually scorned such plebeian activities as shopping. Gabriel felt a sudden urge to buy something for her, something really special. Partly to give her something and express his feelings for her, which were so often bottled up in his own shyness, and partly as a memento, a reminder of their first holiday together, to record and retain for posterity this moment.

They came to a stall where a small brown-skinned lady in a beautiful Tibetan costume knelt on a mat, selling shawls, which she said she'd made herself (she spoke no English, but she managed to indicate this with a variety of hand gestures and a plethora of smiles). Before Helen could argue, she had been draped by the smiling saleswoman in a brilliantly colored silk shawl, whose rich blues and greens and golds suited her coloring perfectly.

"I th...think you should have it. I think it s...suits you."

"Oh, I don't know."

"Yes. Yes, I'll take it." Gabriel - in an uncharacteristically forthright gesture - paid the woman the price she'd asked (who, having expected to be haggled down, beamed even more in amazed gratitude) before Helen could gainsay him. She looked so beautiful in the shawl.

A slow smile spread over Helen's face, and then she threw her arms round Gabriel's neck exclaiming, "Oh, I'm so happy Gabe. This really is going to be the perfect holiday!"

Gabriel glowed. To him her words were worth a thousand shawls.

CHAPTER FOUR

IT WAS HALF past ten on Sunday evening when Maddie departed the *Bunch of Grapes* pub, and set out in a heavy downpour to walk the two miles or thereabouts back to her digs. Bella had offered to drive her home - if Maddie wanted to wait another half hour or so while she and Terry downed another drink - but Maddie declined, saying she'd be certain to pick up a bus. What she really wanted, rain or no rain, was to walk across the Clifton Suspension Bridge to the spot where she'd been that morning and attempt to retrieve the pen she'd been brooding about ever since she'd noticed its absence. Accordingly now - as she strode along quickly and decisively, with head bent against the piercing drops and feet splashing through puddles caused by broken paving stones - she fervently hoped that the pen would still be there and she'd be able to find it.

When she reached the bridge she was relieved to see that there were no other people behind her in the street, although the occasional car did swish by and a solitary figure was retreating into the darkness ahead of her. She came to the low stone wall, which marked the beginning of the bridge proper and recalled exactly the spot where the young man had pressed her back against its hard, cold surface. She had a sudden, almost painful memory of that moment as she relived the physical sensation of being trapped under his weight, choking on her useless screams. Dragging it from her mind with an effort, she forced herself to concentrate on the matter in hand.

Maddie scoured the ground in the immediate vicinity with her eyes, but it was hard to pick out a small object in the dark. She dropped to her knees and began looking more intently, feeling over the surface with her hands as well. If she hadn't been so desperate to find the pen, the sensation of cold muddy stone and the potential embarrassment of being discovered by a passing stranger would have made her give up the search quite quickly. But as it was, she spent over an hour - most of it on her hands, the knees of her trousers becoming sodden with rainwater - searching up and down the pavement near the spot where she had swung her handbag. When she didn't find anything there, she tried the pavement on the other side of the street, then walked down the Zigzag Path all the way to the river, in case the pen had fallen further than she'd thought. Having failed in all these places, she even tried searching in the middle of the road, having to run back to the pavement to dodge a passing car every now and then. But all her efforts were in vain.

Two hours later, freezing cold and worn out, she finally decided to give up. She concluded that the pen must have fallen into the river. She knew she hadn't lost it before the assault, because she remembered injecting herself at the theatre before the party and putting the pen away in her bag. Once at the party, the bag had remained securely fastened all evening. For safety, she'd left it on the bed in

Bella's bedroom upstairs, only retrieving it when she went home. And, unless someone had deliberately stolen the pen from the bag during that time (which seemed highly unlikely) it must still have been in the bag when Maddie started walking home.

She would have felt a lot safer if she'd actually found the pen. But there didn't seem any chance of that. At least - she reasoned to herself by way of reassurance - once it had vanished and been swallowed up in the depths of the water, it was highly unlikely that the pen would be discovered by anyone. That being so, there was no physical evidence to place her at the scene of the crime.

Of course, that didn't solve the problem of the old man who had witnessed some or all of the event. Maddie had no idea what to do about him. She wished now that she hadn't just turned and run away when she'd seen him there. Perhaps he would have been sympathetic, if she'd explained. Perhaps he would have been an ally rather than a foe or a potential accuser. But she'd been too shocked to reflect on that then. It had happened so quickly that now she couldn't even recall the expression on his face, in order to judge what his reaction had been.

He'd seen her face. She felt sure that he would recognize her if he saw her again. But would he give her away? That was the question she couldn't answer. If he'd gone straight to the police - as he could have done - they would already be on her trail. And it wouldn't take too long to find her. She was in a popular show at the Bristol Old Vic theatre. As the female juvenile lead, her face shone out from all the posters, appeared in all the advertisements in the local papers. She was hardly the most invisible of people!

But the police hadn't come looking for her yet. If the old man didn't tell, who else would? No one else had seen.

At half past midnight it was still raining and she dragged herself home, longing for her bed. She determined not to lose sleep over her worries: what use was worrying further, she asked herself? She'd made a thorough search for the pen, and for the moment, that was all she could do.

CHAPTER FIVE

EVERY SUNDAY, GABRIEL visited the *Beggars Alms,* which was the largest pub in the village of Lower Popple just outside Bristol. He liked it because there was no jukebox or fruit machine and the clientele were mostly local folk, few of them under thirty years old. It was always clean and quiet and well ordered, and the landlord - showing unusual artistic flair - had a penchant for designing elaborate pictures in colored chalks, on a blackboard proclaiming the daily lunch menu. The inn had been built in the 17th century and still retained its Tudor beams and whitewashed walls. The large floor area had been subdivided into various sections with carved wooden semi-partitions between each block of six or eight seats. It was in one of these blocks that Gabriel sat, nursing his pint of cider, and listening to his nephew Ian telling about a recent mishap with one of his sheep dogs.

"And then the silly bugger started chasing me instead and I said, go back, go back, I'm not a blasted sheep..." There was a ripple of laughter from the group.

The little knot of people gathered around Gabriel were all related to him in blood or law, and knew him well enough not to expect much of a verbal contribution to the conversation. He was the sort of person who carried on a perpetual dialogue with himself that rarely travelled through his lips to the ears of others. Nevertheless, he was loved and accepted by all.

"I hear Kate's moved back to the village," said Rex aside to Gabriel, as the other conversation continued. Rex was Gabriel's elder brother, Ian's father and the owner of Willow Farm, which Ian and his wife now helped to manage.

"Is that so?"

"I believe her old man died recently."

"Really? She could have stayed in Scotland, surely. I thought she had some children."

"Yes, but they've left home. Anyway, she wanted to come back, be near her family and all that. I must say, I never did understand her moving up North in the first place. Too damn cold up there, if you ask me."

"Well, how would you know? You've never even left the West Country" Brenda interrupted, with an indulgent smile at her husband. She was a homely dumpling of a woman who reminded Gabriel of his late mother.

"You don't have to visit a place to know what it's like, do you" Rex argued. "I don't see the sense in all this traveling about people do nowadays. What's wrong with staying at home, when you come from the best part of the country? If a thing ain't broke, don't fix it." Rex enjoyed quoting sayings or homilies that appealed to him, usually knocking the table with his fist as he did so to stress the importance of his pronouncement.

Gabriel murmured and nodded his head in agreement. He was glad he'd never left Bristol, never abandoned his roots like so many people did. Gabriel liked the well-known, the tried and tested. He didn't need the so-called thrill of foreign travel. Of course, he had been to the Far East - all those years ago - but that had been at Helen's instigation. And the trip had hardly turned out well for him.

Gabriel took his camera from the window ledge - where it was perched rather precariously - and handled it lovingly, enjoying the feel of the smooth cold metal. Machines fascinated him; the intricacy of their levers and mechanisms seemed a thing of mystery and exquisiteness, far more dazzling than any human beauty. His camera was always with him, like a talisman or a faithful friend. It was his joy to take photographs of the family, Ian's children, the village or the farm. Never mind that the scenes seemed to change little. To him, the pleasure of a fresh angle, new colors, a fractional alteration in the quality of the sunlight, were always enough to justify another picture. There was invariably something new to interest him: a flower just beginning to blossom in Spring; freshly fallen snow hanging pristine white on the trees in winter; little Lucy on her bicycle or Wendy standing by the back door stretching up to show that she had grown even taller since last Sunday. The family tolerated Gabriel's single passion with good humor, though they rarely asked to see the fruits of his work.

At about a quarter to two, Ian remarked that lunch would be ready by now, and the five family members trooped out of the pub into the afternoon sunshine, blinking a little as their eyes adjusted to the light. Ian, Sue and Brenda piled into the car and the two elderly brothers meandered up the hill to the farm. The village was especially pretty at this time of year, and Gabriel stopped a couple of times to photograph the lilac in bloom.

"Been a mild summer so far" remarked Rex, as he waited for Gabriel to put the camera back in its case. "How are your tomatoes doing?"

"Splendid crop this year" replied Gabriel, "I think I'll have quite a few."

It was a curious fact that Gabriel's stammer - so noticeable to strangers - almost entirely disappeared when he talked alone with Rex. Perhaps Rex was the only person with whom he felt completely at ease. At any rate, when he was with Rex, he blossomed into an almost normally articulate person, free of his usual shyness.

Many years ago, when they had both been children, an incident had occurred which was consciously forgotten but not erased, like the white patch of skin where an old scar has healed.

In those days, Rex and Gabriel went to the village school along with about fifty other local children of all ages. It was during the English class one afternoon, that a certain little girl called Mary - who was blessed with a mop of flaming red hair and thus often singled out for pranks - leapt up from her desk with a scream of horror, as a small, four-legged creature scuttled away across the floor. Some "obnoxious boy" - as Mrs. Carruthers the English mistress referred to him - had placed a live rat in Mary's desk in order to frighten her, and this boy must be brought to justice. Having roared for the culprit to come forward of his own accord, Mrs. Carruthers roved about the classroom fixing her steely eyes on first one cowed child and then another, but the pupils were silent and no one admitted to the crime.

Finally Mrs. Carruthers singled out Rex - who seemed the most likely candidate, as he was seated next to Mary. Furthermore, he was a cocky lad, and the teacher fancied she had heard him imitating her shrill voice behind her back and was therefore glad of a chance to bring him down a peg or two. She admonished Rex for his disgraceful behavior - brandishing her long, steel ruler as she did so - and ordered him to go to the headmaster's office at once. Gabriel - and indeed the whole class - knew what going to the headmaster's office would mean. The cane, applied liberally and painfully to the victim's rump or hands, so that it would be difficult for several days thereafter to sit down or pick up a pen to write one's homework.

Gabriel couldn't bear the thought of his beloved elder brother being punished for a crime he hadn't committed. Mrs. Carruthers had ignored Rex's claims to innocence and continued commanding him out of the room. In fact, Rex was half out of his chair reluctantly to do his teacher's bidding, when Gabriel leapt up in his brother's defense and burst forth with a torrent of explanations: "It wasn't Rex, it wasn't Rex at all, I know because I saw! Before you came in, Miss, I saw Larry put that rat in Mary's desk. It was Larry, not Rex!"

At least, that was what he meant to say. Those were the words that formed in his brain and struggled to trip off his tongue. But all the rest of the people in the room heard was a series of exploding consonants: "Wa...wa...wa...wasn't...I no...no...no...know...b...b...b...b.." as the words fell over one another and died unspoken on Gabriel's lips.

Needless to say, children being proverbially cruel, the whole class erupted with mirth at the sight of Gabriel's incapacity and in the end he was forced to sit down again, his defense unfinished.

Fortunately, Rex didn't have to go to the headmaster after all. Although Mrs. Carruthers hadn't understood a word of Gabriel's tirade, the sight of the little boy with his angelic blonde curls defending his elder brother would have touched the stoniest of hearts, and she elected to forgo punishing anybody.

The fact that he had saved his brother from punishment was no solace to Gabriel. The humiliation of that experience, the laughing faces of his classmates and the sound of his own voice as it failed so dismally to communicate, remained with him forever. From that moment on, he had sworn he would never stand up and speak in public again.

———————

It was Monday afternoon before Maddie was able to get to the Diabetic Clinic at Bristol General Hospital. Having called up her own specialist in London, he had recommended a local doctor who would be able to help her, and she'd made an appointment as soon as she could. Sitting in the waiting room and reading a copy of *Cosmopolitan* she didn't feel too nervous at the prospect of meeting this new doctor, as she'd rehearsed and prepared her story.

She didn't have to wait long before the doctor - a young Scot with ginger hair and freckles and an approachable manner - poked his head round the door of his consulting room and called her in. They exchanged the usual few minutes of pleasantries and chitchat before Maddie came to the point.

"I'm afraid I've lost my BD pen," she announced.

"Lost it? Oh dear. That was a bit careless wasn't it?" he replied with a good-humored grin, as though he suspected her of being frequently scatterbrained.

"I went on a picnic on Sunday - in the woods near the Downs. I got my pen out of my bag to inject myself before we had lunch and I must have left it on the grass somewhere, because it wasn't in my bag when I got home."

"All right, well these things happen don't they. I'll get the nurse to give you another. Just don't make a habit of this, will you? The NHS can't afford it."

He smiled at her and proceeded to ask her about her blood sugar monitoring and she showed him her patient's diary, which she kept dutifully. Maddie was relieved at the doctor's tolerant attitude, and the fact that she hadn't blushed while lying.

An hour later, she was out of the clinic and on her way to the local leisure center for a swim and a sauna. She wanted to try and relax and get in the right frame of mind for the show that evening. It would be her first performance since the "accident" (which was how she described the event in her head) and the first time she'd seen the others in the cast apart from Bella. She'd hardly slept since the Friday night and her nerves were taut and frayed. She was worried that the others would see how on edge she was and notice that something was wrong. Particularly Jonathan, with whom she had the great majority of her scenes on stage, and who was notorious for his close scrutiny of people and his lack of tact in pointing out any observations. She didn't know if she'd be able to concentrate sufficiently to remember her lines, and her anxiety about the show only added to her feelings of panic and loss of control. She had to somehow regain her composure.

As she sat in the sauna soaking in the burning heat, she willed her body to loosen and her mind to throw off the images that were haunting it. There were two other girls in the sauna, teenagers who gossiped excitedly about their love life and who seemed to fill the enclosed space with their strident voices. Maddie could feel irritation setting her nerves on edge, but the more she tried to block out their company the more the girls intruded on her thoughts. The egg timer on the wall was half full when she finally gave up and stomped out of the small room with a glare, which was lost on her associates. She took a refreshing cold shower and washed her hair, enjoying the feel of her strong fingers massaging her scalp as she imagined some attentive lover's hands in place of her own.

As she stepped out of the shower cubicle and fumbled for her towel with eyes half-closed and stinging with soap, the door to the ladies' changing area opened and a bearded face appeared. A young man carrying a nylon hold-all stepped into the room, caught sight of the naked Maddie and immediately lifted his hand to his mouth: "Oh! I'm terribly sorry. My mistake..."

A surge of anger welled up inside Maddie. Without thinking, she threw her plastic bottle of shampoo at the young man's retreating back, shouting: "Get out of here! What do you think you're doing!" The young man beat a hurried retreat and Maddie felt immediately ashamed of her outburst. She really had to relax!

CHAPTER SIX

MADDIE AND BELLA, as juvenile lead and main character actress, were allotted a tiny dressing room on the second floor of the grand old-fashioned theatre. It was a long scramble down narrow stairs to the stage so they had to leave their quick-change costumes in the wings, but they preferred the privacy of being only two to a room rather than competing with five chorus members in the main dressing room occupying the first floor. Their friends Peter and Nigel - musical director and pianist respectively - shared a dressing room down the corridor and often popped in for a coffee and a chat before the show while the females were in various stages of undress. Neither of the girls were accustomed to being modest about their bodies, and Peter and Nigel's obvious gay relationship made them no sexual threat.

Maddie threw open the small window which creaked with unoiled hinges, in an attempt to ventilate the room and expel the odors of stale cigarette smoke and wine. It was seven o'clock and Bella hadn't entered yet, although the performance was due to start at seven thirty prompt: frequently late to arrive at the theatre, she had twice been castigated by the Company Stage Manager for getting there after the "half". A couple of girls from the chorus who secretly coveted Bella's role, had one day in the Green Room openly censured her apparently flippant attitude to the show, calling her perpetual lateness all the more scandalous because she was the only member of the cast who actually resided permanently in Bristol. On overhearing these criticisms, Maddie had championed her friend, correctly pointing out that Bella never even missed one of her cues, never mind an entrance or a performance; she was always precise on her lines (more than could be said for everybody) and in Maddie's opinion Bella's tendency to lateness was a rather endearing part of her flamboyant and madcap personality.

The difference between the two friends could clearly be seen when comparing the adjoining halves of the dressing table they shared. Maddie kept her side scrupulously tidy, her sticks of make-up and bottles of cleanser and cotton wool in neat rows with a clear space in the middle. Bella's - by contrast - was always a jumbled mass, constantly in danger of spilling over the invisible line and encroaching on Maddie's side.

Maddie noticed the roses in an empty champagne bottle on the windowsill, both of which had been a first night present to Bella from Terry. The petals had faded from red to brown with age and the flowers were now less of an attractive feature than a reminder of past occasions. Maddie knew that if she didn't discard them nobody else would bother. With a sense of purpose, she grasped the stems and chucked the dead flowers in the already full wastepaper basket then washed out the evil-smelling green slime that had collected at the bottom of the bottle.

She threw the dregs of wine left in the bottom of two plastic cups down the sink and tipped out some lipstick-smeared cigarette ends from the glass ashtray.

Cleaning up was a habit she had acquired from her adoptive parents. It was her way of gaining control of feelings and therefore of events, and was something she was capable of doing almost obsessively when distressed. Maddie's emotions at that point had been pushed so far underground that she wasn't consciously aware of them, and to all outward appearances she was her normal capable self. The only evidence of her inner turmoil was the perpetual nausea that had gripped her ever since Bella's party, and the pain like a gnawing rat in her stomach that wouldn't cease.

Tonight she was more than usually irritated by the debris in the room, and she clicked her teeth while clearing up Bella's mess. She felt all pent up inside, like a coiled spring or a bomb primed to explode. She remembered a season she'd played at Worthing, when she and a friend had released their frustrations by racing down the shoreline screaming in the dead of night, their sounds wondrously engulfed by the roar of the waves. She wished she could do that now, but there was nowhere to run and no one to run with.

There was five minutes to go before Richard, the Assistant Stage Manager, called the half over the tannoy. Maddie regarded herself in the mirror, as she brushed her hair back into a tight ponytail. The act of brushing had a calming effect and she fantasized that a lover was caressing her tenderly. She contemplated her large honey-brown eyes and straight dark hair and wondered for the hundredth time who they belonged to. Of course, they belonged to *her*, but who before that? Who was responsible for the accident of her birth? If only she knew where and who she sprang from. She believed - with the irrational, childlike part of herself - that if she were acquainted with her real parents, they would offer support and help in her current plight. Over the past few months, these *real parents* had been built up in her mind and idealized into the perfect couple, all-wise, all-seeing, all-understanding and with a never-ending supply of love for her. She felt no more ability to turn to her adoptive mother in her present crisis than at other times in the past, a woman whom she didn't resemble in looks or temperament, a mother who had always seemed a stranger even when Maddie had been a child.

Bella burst in upon Maddie's reflections by swinging open the door with a force that sent it colliding against the wall with a heavy bang. She let out a long exhalation of breath to announce her presence. "Whew! Did I make it?"

The atmosphere in the room seemed immediately to brighten. Maddie turned and admonished teasingly: "You're bloody late. Richard's just about to call the half".

"Not my fault," pouted Bella. "Bloody bus - waited 35 minutes!"

"Aren't you in your car today?"

"No, had to do some shopping." Bella pulled a package out of a bulging plastic bag and slapped it on the dressing table in front of Maddie. "D'you like it? Got it for Terry." She unburdened herself of skintight leggings and velvet t-shirt which inadequately covered her sizable frame, flinging off high-heeled shoes and plumping down heavily into the chair beside her companion.

Maddie looked at the package, which was a heavy cotton shirt patterned in a bright orange and black check design and wrapped in cellophane. "Yeah, it's nice."

"Very Terry." said Bella, in her best Noel Coward voice. "Don't you think?"

"It'll suit him to a T" responded Maddie in the same vein.

"To a T-shirt" quipped Bella, chuckling at her own joke as she fumbled around the mess on her side of the dressing table searching for her eye make-up.

"Oh, ha ha. So, what are you buying him presents for anyway? Is it a special occasion?" asked Maddie.

"I'm just fed up with seeing him in *white*. Makes me think of hospitals."

"Makes sense."

"I know, but he doesn't have to bring his work home with him, does he? I feel like I'm permanently in an episode of *Casualty*. Apart from him droning on about all the infectious diseases I can catch and telling me grotesque anecdotes about his patients..."

Maddie giggled: "You probably bore him to death telling him about Lindsay corpsing in the coffin scene again or your latest improvisation when Sharon gets the cue wrong."

"Yeah, probably. Anyway, the present is for a special occasion. His birthday. Next Saturday. We'll be having a party again. If dad lets me. He was fairly miffed about the last one. Said someone spilt red wine on his beige carpet. Well, what does he expect." She spoke in jerky gasps, as she jabbed at her eyes with a mascara wand. "Hey, maybe you'll be able to stay over this time. There are advantages.

I make a mean omelet." She poked Maddie in the ribs with her elbow. Maddie gave a terse smile, and got up to collect her costume from the rail.

"Hey - I never asked...Have you made it up with your bloke? What's 'is name? Alan?" Bella often preceded her remarks with a loud *Hey*, which was like a sudden gunshot announcing the start of a race.

"Oh, him." Maddie reflected, surprised at herself, that the mention of Alan didn't start any butterflies in her stomach. In fact, she'd completely forgotten about him. Other matters had taken greater precedence in her thoughts. The realization felt strange to Maddie, remembering that only a few days earlier Alan had been the only thing on her mind: it had been his stubbornness, his betrayals, his insensitivity that had occupied her, and her anger at these had waged an incessant battle inside her head. "We've split up. Or, at least, I suppose we have. He hasn't called me, and I'm not too bothered to be quite honest. Could you do me up?" She slipped the dress over her head and presented her back to Bella, who began zipping with the expertness of habitude.

"You're better off, if you ask me" Bella replied without hesitation. "I never liked him. I said to Terry I always thought he was a bastard and you could do better. There's other fish in the sea."

"I know, but I never seem to find them," complained Maddie, wriggling to fit inside the tight bodice of her costume.

"They're out there, love, if you're looking properly," mumbled Bella, now back in front of the dressing table mirror, through a mouthful of hairpins.

Maddie had the vague notion she was being chided, as if by a sympathetic but disapproving mother. "What's that supposed to mean?"

Bella rampaged on, oblivious of the effect her words had on her friend: "Why d'you go for men like Alan? It's written all over his face that he's a woman-abuser. Any girl with an ounce of sense wouldn't touch him with a barge pole. I told you right away he gave me the creeps. But you wouldn't listen, oh no, you had to get involved with him."

"I made a mistake, O.K.? People do." Maddie was petulant and defensive now. She felt Bella had no right to chastise her for her bad luck with men. After all, Bella was well cared for, she had Terry, she had no idea what it was like to be on your own and vulnerable.

"It's not the first time, though, is it? You told me yourself." Bella saw the hurt look on Maddie's face and - maybe realizing her words had stung more than she intended - gave her pal a kindly pat on the waist. "I'm not being mean. I just don't like to see you putting yourself through this. Men aren't worth it, you know."

"I'm not going *through* anything," retorted Maddie. She even believed this herself. Nevertheless, she hadn't told Bella about the churning in her stomach and the sick feeling that was plaguing her. For a while, the two girls sat in silence, each preoccupied with her own make-up routine and her own thoughts. Maddie reflected that Bella was her best friend and the person she trusted most in the world. Bella may be blunt but she was honest, and she cared enough about Maddie to confront her with the truth. Maddie wasn't accustomed to people doing that, and although part of her resented the kindly meant intrusion, another part of her was gratified at somebody taking notice. Bella was almost like a mother figure, the mother Maddie had never had and always longed for. For all Bella's tactlessness, she had a perception, a wisdom almost. And a kind heart.

"I'm really not upset, you know" Maddie confided as she turned and looked at her friend. "I know I usually am. But this time... I don't know. There are too many other things to think about."

Bella beamed at Maddie, obviously relieved that the silence had been broken. "Yes, of course. The show and your part and everything. There's no time to worry about men, is there?"

Maddie was gratified that Bella had completely misunderstood the significance of her words. With a small hidden smile, she turned to the mirror and began applying her foundation.

"Hey -" barked Bella, "You tried your burner yet?"

Maddie gave an intake of breath as if going to reply, then clamped her mouth shut. Bella was struggling into her costume blouse at that point and so didn't notice Maddie's slight change of color. "Yeah, it's great." Maddie's training as an actress certainly came in handy when controlling a tremble in the voice.

Fortunately, also, her reply was overshadowed by a sharp rap on the door and a familiar cry from outside: "Are you decent?"

"No" shouted Bella in loud response.

"We'd better come in then." Peter entered, with Nigel hot on his heels. "You two got any coffee? I'm gasping."

Peter was a tall gaunt man in his forties, with a mop of frizzy grey hair that stuck out from his head and pale blue eyes that wore an ever-questioning expression. Nigel hovered behind him, silent and shy, a permanent smile on his boyishly handsome face, eager to please everybody. He was the same size as his friend, but gave the impression of being smaller and somehow lighter, as if he was trying to shrink and be as insubstantial as he felt.

"There's a bit. But no milk, sorry." said Bella. "Anyway, I'm late."

"Finish getting your slap on, girl" bossed Peter, with a quick glance of longing at the unused kettle. "Karen's on the second floor already."

"Shit!" Bella expostulated, "I've not even ironed my skirt yet!"

"I'll do it for you" said Maddie, carefully outlining her eyes, trying not to let her still shaking hand make the line on her top lid too thick.

"Really? Oh, you darling. I love you to bits." Bella gave Maddie a rather wet kiss on the cheek, smearing a little of her pancake foundation on to Maddie's face.

"It's O.K. I'm ready anyway." Maddie gave up on her eyes and made her way to the ironing board, which was stuck in a rather cramped position by the door.

"Hark at her - Goody Two Shoes," teased Peter.

"What's the house like?" asked Bella.

"How do I bloody know?"

"Oh come on, Pete. I know you always check the numbers with the front desk."

"Lots of bookings, but I don't give a hoot."

Bella raised her eyebrows in disbelief at this remark.

"His music critic didn't come again," explained Nigel in a soft voice.

"I mean, what is the point of me writing all this wonderful music for you girls to sing, if nobody hears it?" declaimed Peter, punctuating his remarks by throwing his hands in the air as if conducting an orchestra.

"The audience hear it", commented Maddie.

"Nobody *important*, I mean. Well, we can't stand here carping all day. Come on Nige, we'd better leave these girls to their toilets."

"Don't be rude" Bella chided, her laughter following the two men as they sidled out of the door.

"See you on the green" chirped Peter, and a brief laugh passed between the two men on their way down the corridor.

There was a buzz like the noise of a wasp, and Maddie picked up the intercom phone, which was on the wall near the ironing board. "Yes?"

"You got a visitor," hissed the voice of the stage doorman on the other end of the line.

"What - now? We're just about to go up." Maddie made a grimace at Bella.

"I told 'im that. Chap says he wants to see you."

"Who is he?"

"How should I know? Says he wants to see you."

The stage doorman was a grumpy retired train driver in his sixties called Jones (nobody seemed to know his first name) who delighted in taking out his irritation on the actors. Maddie knew she could by rights have insisted on knowing the name of her visitor, but she didn't feel in the mood for an argument. "All right. Send him up."

She put down the receiver. Bella looked at Maddie with a question in her face and Maddie shrugged. "Suppose two minutes won't do any harm."

"What the hell...?" began Bella, her lipstick poised in mid air.

"Don't ask me" replied Maddie, going back to the ironing board. "Some man wants to see me."

"Secret admirer? *News of the World*, is it? Want to interview you?"

Maddie gave a loud guffaw at this private joke. At the beginning of the run, when the two girls had been mere acquaintances, Bella had subjected Maddie to one of her notorious practical jokes, affecting the voice of a cockney journalist and ringing Maddie at her digs on the pretext of wanting an interview for her paper. Maddie - thrilled and flattered at the thought that her first leading role was receiving national press attention - had fallen hook line and sinker. And the story had been greeted with not inconsiderable amusement by the rest of the cast.

A few minutes later, the face of a young man appeared at the dressing room door. He seemed hesitant and unsure of himself. "Can I come in?" he stammered, remaining in the corridor.

"How can we help you?" Bella demanded in a booming voice, intending to amuse rather than frighten. Then she recognized the stranger. "Hey, I know you! You were at my party."

"That's right. I'm Ted." The young man had a strong Bristolian accent and the humble air of a peasant coming to visit his wealthy squire.

"Come in for a minute, if you like" offered Maddie, inviting Ted with a gesture into the tiny room. "I'm sorry, I don't remember you," she added sincerely.

"It's all right. Don't want to disturb you or nothing. You got to work." The young man seemed tentative and embarrassed, but still he stood there, shifting nervously from foot to foot, his eyes darting fleetingly from time to time at Maddie.

"Bags of time yet" said Bella, cheerily.

As if on cue, the voice on the tannoy system announced: "Ladies and gentlemen, this is your fifteen minute call."

Maddie continued with her ironing. "What was it you wanted to see us about?" she asked kindly. He seemed too vulnerable to be threatening and she felt quite sorry for him, standing there shuffling as if he couldn't muster the courage to voice the purpose of his errand.

"Your party on Saturday night - I went with a friend of mine. Darren Webster."

Bella looked blank but encouraging. "Oh yes? Do I know him?"

"I don't know. It's just...I haven't seen him since, since the party. And that was on Saturday. And now it's Monday. I was a bit worried, like."

Bella gave Maddie a wordless look that seemed to convey: *This boy's simple, isn't he? Why's he asking us?* "I'm sure your friend can take care of himself."

The boy had anxious eyes and they were trained on Maddie, hardly noticing Bella at all. Her words seemed to have little effect on him. "He was staying with me, see. In my house. And we went to the party. And he never come back."

Suddenly, Maddie had a horrible sinking sensation in the pit of her stomach. The nausea rose up almost into her gorge and she suppressed a desire to retch. Keeping her eyes down, she pretended to be concentrating hard on her ironing.

"I don't remember a... what's his name? Darren? What does he look like?" questioned Bella affably, as she dusted her face with powder.

"He's about my age - 23 that is - and he's short like me. But a bit sort of chunkier. And he has short hair, very short black hair." He was talking to Bella but looking all the time at Maddie.

"I'm sorry. I don't remember him at all. Do you, Maddie?"

"No." Maddie replied rather faintly, turning away to hang the newly ironed skirt on the costume rail behind her.

"It's just," Ted persisted, staring at Maddie, "I saw him dancing with you. Did he go home with you?"

"She's just said she doesn't remember him." Bella sounded irritated now. She was running late, and the novelty of the stranger's visit was wearing off.

Maddie didn't trust herself to speak and was eternally grateful to Bella for intervening. "Nobody went home with Maddie. I know, because she was at my house till 5 o'clock in the morning. Then she walked home on her own."

"That's right," said Maddie, emboldened by her friend's support, and she turned and faced the young man.

"But you did dance with him." Ted kept looking at her, shyly but insistently, like a timid dog that expects to be given a kick.

Maddie hated him at that moment. Hated his simple face with its earnest gaze. But she said calmly "I might have done. I danced with a few people. But I don't remember."

"She was drunk" laughed Bella, "We were all drunk. Probably your friend too. Maybe he just forgot to call you and tell you where he is."

"I told you. He's staying at my house."

"Is he not from Bristol, then?"

"He lives in Cardiff. He's my friend. He's on the dole, see. He wanted to stay with me for a bit, while he looks for work here."

"Have you tried the D.S.S.?"

"Er...no." The boy looked confused and out of his depth.

Bella had the air of a social worker dispensing advice: "I bet you they'll know where he is. He probably had to go back to Cardiff to sign on. Have you thought of that?"

"No. O.K." The young man hung his head. He looked sad and chastened now.

"I'm sorry," said Bella warmheartedly. "We'd help if we could. I'm sure he'll show up."

The five-minute announcement came over the tannoy. The young man cast a final desperate look at Maddie, but she kept her back to him. "Thanks anyway" he muttered and left the room.

"What a character!" said Bella with a wry face at Maddie, as she closed the door after him. "A real country yokel. He reminded me of a gardener we had once. Dad used to catch him picking his nose in the potting sheds. You all right, love?"

Maddie's face wore a peculiar expression: "I'm fine." Then suddenly: "Can I have a ciggie?"

Bella looked at her in amazement. "I didn't even know you smoked." Maddie didn't respond. "Of course, love. They're in my bag."

"I only have the odd one." Maddie found the pack and lit up gratefully. "I'm just a bit nervous tonight. Don't know why."

"You've no need to be nervous. We've been doing it for two weeks" soothed Bella. "Anyway, you know you're the star of the show."

The cigarette helped relax Maddie, enough to stop her heart pounding at least, and by the time Karen came up to fit their wigs she was feeling almost normal. With a Herculean effort, she managed to put Ted's visit and its implications out of her mind while she made her final last minute preparations. She thanked God that she had an early entrance in the first scene and there simply wasn't time for her to dwell on anything outside the show for the time being. It was a case of "doctor theatre" - as her friend Erik put it - coming to the rescue and taking her mind off her problems.

By the time the second act came around, Maddie was into her stride and had almost managed to jettison the whole episode from her mind. During the penultimate scene she had a habit of peeping through the curtains at the side of the stage, in order to judge the exact moment for her entrance just as the lights were dimming and the last dancer left the floor. She often scanned the audience at this point, to see from their expressions whether they were enjoying the show and were therefore in a responsive mood for her solo ballad at the close of the act, her only time alone on stage and the highlight of her performance. As her eyes ranged over the unknown faces - old and young, smiling and blank - she saw something which jolted her so much she sprang back momentarily from the curtain as if stung. It was a face she thought she recognized.

Drawn by curiosity and a need to know for sure, she pressed her right eye again to the gap between the curtains and scanned the audience for the countenance whose sight had shocked her. Surely, it was that old man. The man who had run up to the bridge on Sunday morning and caught sight of her before she ran. She thought she would recognize him anywhere, his tall gaunt frame and thick white hair. So, what was he doing here at the theatre? Had he somehow managed to follow her and find out where she worked? All sorts of terrifying thoughts flashed through her mind, as she sought desperately to find his face again, to verify what she'd glimpsed. But as she scoured the rows of people, the lights dimmed so that she could no longer see, and she realized that the music was slowing down ready for her cue and there was nothing for it but to go out on stage. She was trembling so much her legs could hardly carry her. But she forced herself to open the curtains and run on into her spotlight.

As the notes of the solo violin played the opening bars of her introduction, she stood with her head flung upwards as always, her heart beating so wildly in her narrow frame that she thought she might keel over. But she didn't. She took a deep breath and her voice floated out of her and over the heads of the appreciative audience. It was as if her voice wasn't joined to her at all, it was a gift from God that projected from her mouth whenever she wanted, with no effort from her. Her mind felt divorced from her body, giving her an unreal sense of not being wholly there. Her mind was racing ahead and seeing the future and frightened of what it saw.

And it was saying to her, over and over, *I must get out - I must get out - I <u>must</u> get out of here!*

CHAPTER SEVEN

B Y EIGHT O'CLOCK the next morning, Maddie was sitting in a compartment crowded with commuters on the Intercity train to London. During the two-hour journey, she leafed through her Filofax in a desperate search for a friend she could stay with temporarily, as her own bedsit in Notting Hill was being sub-let and wouldn't be vacant for another two weeks.

When she arrived at Paddington station, she descended unwillingly from the train. She wished she could have carried on traveling forever, enjoying the feeling of security and passivity and the freedom from having to make decisions. The train was like a great big steel womb, even its regular rhythm resembling a mother's heartbeat, and she didn't want to leave its warm embrace and step out into the harsh unloving world. Seeing a tramp seated on a bench, she thought for a moment how pleasant to have no responsibilities and be a person of No Fixed Abode. But she shook her head and chided herself inwardly - that was just a romantic notion, a dream of escape.

Now on the station platform, she had to take charge of her life. But she felt so alone and disorientated. Every decision facing her seemed impossibly difficult, even the tiniest ones such as whether to bother trying to find a bathroom for a freshen up or which friend to try first. People flung themselves past her and they all had a purpose, but she had none. With an effort she forced herself to stop feeling so negative and followed signs to the telephones. At least if she had a place to stay for a while, she concluded, life would start to improve.

She chose Sally from the list of names she'd scribbled. Sally had been a friend since drama school. Maddie felt confident that Sally would be sympathetic, whatever story she was told, and Maddie longed to hear her sweet and consoling voice on the other end of the line. But her ansaphone message left another number, which Maddie recognized as that of Sally's boyfriend in Stratford.

Next Chloe, a director friend whom she'd worked with once and knew less well, but who always had bright ideas in any emergency. Chloe announced in brisk tones on her ansaphone message that she was "unable to come to the phone right now". Maddie left a rather incoherent message anyway, just in case - "Hello Chloe, it's Maddie Cambay, from *The Unbroken Line*, remember me? I'm just in town for a couple of days and thought I'd look you up, I'll try again later, take care, bye now" - and then replaced the receiver miserably. Why had she even thought of Chloe? She was always busy anyway, the sort of person who's never there when you need them. She thought briefly of going back to her flat, where she would certainly be in the way. Or even of visiting her mother. God forbid! She pushed that idea out of her mind almost immediately and considered the other options.

The last person on Maddie's list was Erik, who she hadn't wanted to try but she was getting desperate. It wasn't that she actively disliked him; just that she wasn't sure how much of his rather chaotic company she could stand. But she had to go somewhere. She hadn't enough money with her for a hotel. At least Erik was always unemployed and was therefore likely to be in.

"Hello?" answered a sleepy voice after many rings.

Maddie compelled herself to sound cheerful: "Hi Erik, it's me, Mad."

"Hiya" He didn't sound surprised, but then he never did. Maybe he'd forgotten that she wasn't due to finish her stint in Bristol for another two weeks.

"Where are you, kid?"

"Paddington Station."

"Wow." Maddie laughed on hearing his predictable response. "Suppose you wanna come over."

"Can I?"

"Sure, that's cool. I'm not doin' anything special."

"Erik?"

"Yeah?"

"Could I crash for a few days? A couple of days?"

"Er...yeah, I guess so. What's up? Thought you had a flat."

"Yes I do, but I've got someone staying there at the moment while I'm in Bristol."

"Oh, right, Bristol yeah. O.K. kid. Come on over. We'll see what we can fix up."

"Thanks. See you later."

Maddie was relieved at having somewhere to go, although she wished it hadn't had to be Erik. But for the time being at least, she was determined not to look into the future and see its bleak face. Not just yet.

———∿∞◌❀◖❁◗❀◌∞∿———

Erik had assembled a put-you-up bed in the living room for Maddie to sleep on that night, and even a couple of grubby white cotton sheets he said had been his mum's and a tartan blanket full of moth holes. His tiny flat in Ladbroke Grove was permeated with the smell of a thousand cigarettes which never evaporated even when, as now, the window was thrown wide open to let in the fresh morning air.

After a breakfast of croissants and strong coffee - which Maddie bought from a nearby baker's out of gratitude for a roof over her head - Erik casually asked if the show in Bristol had closed early. Maddie was forced to admit that it hadn't. "Actually, I've just left. I've run away, sort of thing."

Erik looked at her with bemusement, as if he thought she'd been playing some spectacularly wild and crazy joke for her own pleasure. "Wow" he said, shaking his head so that his long greasy hair swung from side to side.

"No one knows I've gone. I just upped and left," she said almost proudly, pretending it was something she'd wanted to do all along. She knew this act of seeming rebellion would appeal to Erik.

"Pretty funky stuff" he replied with admiration. "But what's the story? Did the director piss you off or something?"

"No, nothing like that. Erik, can you keep a secret?"

"Sure, sure" he asserted, putting his head on one side and looking at her with curiosity.

Maddie knew that Erik was about as discreet as a tabloid headline. "I got into a bit of a fix with a fella. He started pursuing me."

"Far out!"

"He was making life difficult. I don't want him to find out where I am."

"But what about your play, man? I thought you told me it was a brilliant part. You mean you just gave that up?"

"Yes." Erik was looking at her with huge veneration now. Of course - Maddie realized suddenly - she had become his heroine, an actress who was so blasé about her career that she could walk out on the best part of her life at a moment's notice, on a whim, simply because some man was coming on too strong.

Erik declared that he would have done the same in her shoes. But it was one thing to affect indifference and another to act on it. In any case, Maddie privately doubted Erik's ability to land a plum role in the first place, having seen him perform only once in a worthy but dull fringe show. She recognized his little game and the way he professed to despise ambition because he couldn't aspire to it himself.

"You must have been good, though, kid. You know what, they showed a bit of your show on the telly last week, a sort of review on that late night arts program. And I couldn't see which one was you. Did you catch it?"

"I didn't see the program, but I know which bit they filmed. The big chorus number and part of my solo."

"Which one was you, then?"

"I sing *Anywhere my heart leads me*."

"What - that was you? The blonde one?"

"Yep. It's a wig."

"Wow, you look really different. I didn't recognize you under all that makeup, and with that cool wig. I'd never have known it was you."

All at once she felt a fool. Having to explain her actions to another person had made her realize the enormity and the foolishness of what she'd done. She was ambitious, hugely ambitious, and she had just forsaken the best part of her career because of a stupid moment of panic. And what Erik said about her being unrecognizable in costume made a lot of sense: would anyone think to connect the blonde girl in the show with the slim brunette who existed offstage? The photographs on the publicity board outside the theatre had been taken at the dress run when everyone was in full regalia. Fortunately for her, it was not a policy of the theatre to show standard head and shoulder publicity photographs of the actors appearing in musicals.

But what could she do now? She'd already taken the step. How could she go back now?

"So what are you gonna do?" asked Erik.

"I don't know," replied Maddie truthfully.

Later that morning, they sang songs and played with Erik's karaoke machine, which Maddie enjoyed. Losing herself in the music took her mind off her troubles and made her feel more relaxed. Erik rolled a couple of joints and tried to persuade Maddie to have some too but she refused. It wasn't only that her diabetes made her look after her health more assiduously than many people her age. The smell of marijuana made her feel sick. And she hated losing her self-control, which she thought was probably the very thing that endeared drugs to people like Erik.

In the afternoon, Erik wanted to watch a video he'd purchased cheap down the Portobello Road market, a horror movie from the 1930s so melodramatic it was laughable. Maddie would have much preferred to just collapse on the camp bed and sleep, to cure the exhaustion she was suffering over recent events: the night before, her mind had been so beset by anxieties that she had barely slept. But she was conscious that, in Erik's flat, it would be impolite to occupy all the space in his only living room sleeping when he wanted to socialize.

She wished she could reverse time and go back to Saturday morning, to her 25th birthday, which had started so well. She'd been happy and confident and everything had seemed right in her life. She'd loved her job in Bristol, the friends she'd made in the cast, even her little room in digs.

She knew she couldn't stay here, when everything about Erik's flat and his life depressed her. Even if he was happy for her to stay on - which she seriously doubted - she didn't think she would be capable of bearing it even for two days, never mind the two weeks before her sub-let ended.

Later that day, she tried a couple of other friends in her book, but one didn't reply and the other said sorry but she had relatives staying with her at the moment. Erik - as she had suspected - wasn't keen on her staying more than a couple of nights, though too bashful to say so directly.

"Maybe you should go back, huh? Tell this guy to piss off. I mean, you can't let him run you out of town can you, man? It's not fair."

"D'you think I can go back? How can I explain? They'll think I'm crazy."

"When's your next show? Not till tonight, right? Go back now and nobody'll even notice you've gone."

"I gave up my digs."

"Haven't you got any friends you could stay with?"

"Well...there's Bella I suppose."

"Cool. Bella. Get on the blower to Bella now and ask her. You can lie and say your landlady threw you out or something."

Maddie looked at him. What he said made a lot of sense. If only she'd seen it before. But she'd acted over-impulsively, as usual.

"I mean, like, you could stay here. I'd be cool with that but...it's kinda small and everything. You'd be better off going back."

Maddie realized that a conventional soul lurked beneath Erik's bohemian exterior. He didn't want her there. He liked his life to be orderly too, in his own chaotic way. She had no alternative but to go back. Face the music, if there was any.

When she considered it calmly, things weren't as threatening as she'd imagined in her panicky rush from Bristol. There was no physical evidence to connect her with Darren, even if Ted *had* seen her with him at the party. And she still wasn't certain whether the face she'd seen in the audience at the theatre was that of the old man who'd witnessed the attack. Perhaps, in her heightened emotional state after Ted's visit, she had simply over-reacted and assumed it was him. From that distance, she reassured herself, most old men looked pretty similar. With any luck, it would take weeks for the body to be discovered and she would probably have finished her run by then anyway.

She would be a fool to jack in her job now. The part in *Puttin' on the Ritz* was prestigious and had been hard won. She was playing one of the leads - her first leading musical role - and both the production and her performance had received rave reviews. What would it do to her burgeoning acting and singing career to walk out in the middle of a run? She'd probably never work again.

She had to go back.

CHAPTER EIGHT

JANE SINCLAIR WAS not very adept at rock climbing, but she had joined the outing organized by the Bristol Savers Building Society Climbing Group simply in order to spend one of her Sundays with Charlie Bast. Charlie was tall, blond and handsome in a conventional way, like one of the heroes pictured between the pages of *True Romances*, which Jane read avidly and clandestinely in her lunch breaks.

Jane had only worked at the office a few weeks and her lowly position as junior secretary to the Accounts Assistant gave her little opportunity to speak to Charlie, who was a bright young star in Finance. So she had been flattered and pleased to be asked to join the climbing group on one of its regular Sunday outings to assay the rock face, which overhangs the river near the Clifton Suspension Bridge.

To her disappointment, she'd hardly seen Charlie all day. His interest in rock climbing was genuine and she realized that the friendly smiles she had imagined as being especially for her were extended to all and sundry as part of his easygoing charm. After spending the morning on the so-called "easy slopes", the others were at this moment clambering up what seemed to Jane like a dauntingly sheer rock face, while she had elected to wait for them at the bottom. If she craned her head upwards, she could almost catch sight of an orange-colored jacket and the tip of the heavy climbing rope dangling many feet above. Their voices were dissipated in the warm afternoon air. Jane wished she had never come. The only thing to do now was make her way quietly home.

She sighed and looked around her. There were no other walkers on her side of the river - people didn't usually stroll this far up - although she could see someone on the other side nearer the bridge. She closed her eyes and lifted her chin, reveling in the feel of warm sun on her skin. It was a beautiful day and on impulse she decided not to go home immediately but to meander a little way downstream.

When she had walked for five minutes or so, she left the track and ambled down onto the grassy verge. Although she had heard that the river was filthy, the water with the sun sparkling on it looked cool and inviting and she felt an urge to dip her hands in it and wash off some of the rock dust that had embedded itself under her nails.

She sat on the edge of the bank, removed her shoes and socks and let her feet dangle in the deliciously cool and refreshing water. When she'd enjoyed that sensation for a few moments, she knelt down as far as she could go, cupped some water in her hands and splashed her face with it. She could see her own hands beneath the water - her two hands. Then, something appeared which filled her with horror.

There was a third hand in the water! A hand that was not her own.

She snatched her hands out of the river and sat motionless, too shocked to move.

The movement of the water that she had created had disturbed this third hand and now, as she watched, unable to avert her eyes, it slowly bobbed to the surface to reveal not just a hand but a whole arm, which was presumably attached to a body.

Jane stood up stiffly and backed away. A girl's screams filled the air, screams she didn't even recognize as hers until she felt two strong arms grasp her from behind and heard a male voice: "What's the matter? What on earth's the matter?"

Jane recovered sufficiently to cease her yelling and look up at her comforter, who had one arm around her protectively and was regarding her with warm brown eyes.

He gave a quick glance in the direction of the water and obviously registered what had upset her. "It's all right now. You'll be all right." She buried her head in his shoulder, trying to blot out the sight of what she had just witnessed. He didn't seem to mind but continued to hold her, soothing her with a soft caress on her back.

His voice was warm, too. Warm and concerned and friendly. He had wavy dark brown hair and tanned; muscular arms and a beautiful smile which came out in response to Jane's own.

Jane thought he was a lot better looking than Charlie Bast.

"But I only want to *know*, mother, can't you understand that? It's not that I'm going to do anything about it. What can I do, anyway?"

"Of course I understand. But as I've told you before--"

"No you don't, you don't understand. Why should you?"

"It's for your own good--"

"Oh, you always say that, but it's not *my* good you're concerned about. You just don't like to think that--"

"Of course it's *your* good I care about. Who else's would it be? You seem to forget that I brought you up. James and I. You've forgotten all those years--"

"Don't give me that guilt thing--"

"I was only saying that--"

"Look. I haven't forgotten anything. But it's not the same! Oh, why should I expect you to understand me? How can you? You're nothing to do with me."

"Now you're just being deliberately hurtful. I won't have you--"

"Well maybe I am, but it's the only way to get your attention, isn't it."

"I won't have you talking to me like that. After all we did for you. James and I treated you as our own."

"Why didn't you tell me? Why didn't you tell me before, then it wouldn't have been such a shock."

"We thought it was for the best. We wouldn't have done it otherwise. We genuinely believed it was better for you."

"And why not now? Now I know some of the truth, why not all of it?"

"What's the point? It wouldn't do any good, dear. You'd only upset yourself--"

"I don't see why it would be so upsetting to know who my parents are...or were... for God's sake. It's so bloody stupid!"

"And don't swear, dear. James and I thought it all out and discussed it before...before he died. We agreed. I promised *him*. If I tell you the names of your natural parents, it won't end there, will it? You'll want to know more and more about them. And you'd open up a whole can of worms. Believe me, things like this are best left alone. It's not as if you ever wanted for anything."

"Oh, this is useless."

"Do try to calm down, Madeleine. There's no need for these temper tantrums and they won't help you to get your own way. There are things you can't change. That you just have to accept."

"So that's where I'm different from you. I can't just accept things."

"You always were headstrong. We can't always have what we want in life. It's not like that, I'm afraid."

"Stop bloody moralizing."

"I'm not moralizing at all. But you're young. You don't realize--"

"I *do* realize. I realize everything. Now. I realize that I'm adopted and I don't know who my parents are."

"Don't shout, dear. It won't do any good."

Maddie played her trump card: "I could send off that form, you know. I've still got it. I have a right to know."

"Stop threatening to do that, Madeleine, please. Can't you see that it's *you* we've been trying to protect all these years?"

Maddie recognized the whining wheedling note in her adoptive mother's voice. It always had more effect on her than any amount of aggressive bluster.

"I'm not thinking of myself. Why should I object to your knowing the truth? It can't harm me. Believe me, I have only your best interests at heart."

Maddie sighed heavily. She had determined to be so strong, to demonstrate that she was an adult now, with rights which were perfectly reasonable. But she'd ended up reverting once again to childish bullying tactics. It wasn't even pursuit of the facts which drove her to wage this incessant battle of wills with her adoptive mother, as much as some obsessive quest for absolution that even she couldn't understand. But whatever the outcome of their arguments, Maddie still had that form back in London and she knew she could use it whenever she was ready. For now, she decided to acquiesce: "I know you do."

There was an eloquent silence, before Maddie spoke again in a rush: "Mother, my phone card's running out, so I'll have to go now."

"When are you coming up to visit?"

"I don't know. I really can't say."

"Will you call me on Sunday?"

"Yes O.K."

"Have you rung Eva yet?"

"Who?"

"Eva. You know. Your cousin. I told you about her and gave you her telephone number. She lives in Bristol, and you said you'd visit her while you're there. It would be so nice for you to meet--"

"Yes, all right. I've got her number. I'll call her if I get the chance. But I'm always so busy."

"Do try, dear. I know she works as a solicitor so you probably don't think you'd have much in common but she's terribly cultured and interested in the theatre. Perhaps you could invite her to a performance--"

"Yes, yes, yes. I've got to go now. No more money. Bye."

"Goodb--" The voice on the other line was abruptly cut off. Maddie smashed down the receiver. She was trembling all over, but not from the cold. She let herself out of the phone box and emerged into the crowded street, feeling disorientated, her mind in turmoil. Her head throbbed all over, feeling thick and oppressively heavy, like a football that's been kicked all over the pitch.

As she staggered through the crowd of busy shoppers, she heard the bells from a nearby church chime twice and she realized that she was already late for her jazz dance class, which began at two and would take at least ten minutes to reach by foot. She began to hurry, now weaving her way in and out of the paths of other people in an effort to avoid collisions, irritated with them for getting in her way. It had just started to rain and large cold drops cascaded on to her bare shoulders. The nylon rucksack containing her dance gear bumped against her back as she walked, and it seemed to attack her with the sharp edge of one shoe. But she hadn't time to stop and rearrange the bag more comfortably.

It was while she was walking like this - quickly and impatiently with her eyes fixed on her destination and a look of preoccupied determination on her face - that a hand roughly nudged her shoulder. At first she thought somebody had bumped into her accidentally and she almost ignored it. But when she heard her name, she turned to see the grinning face of Alan.

"I thought it was you. Where are you going to, beautiful?"

It was his stock phrase, the one he had used when first picking her up and which had appeared so attractive at the time.

"Going to a class," she replied simply.

He stared at her as if expecting her to give a longer explanation or to want to make more conversation. "Oh. Right. You're in a hurry, are you?"

"Yes, I am actually. I'll see you some other time, O.K.?" Maddie spoke quickly and without expression, not unfriendly but indifferent. What surprised her was that she actually felt indifferent, totally indifferent, to his supposed charms. In fact, looking at him now and his rather ordinary face, she couldn't imagine why she'd been so besotted with him or why she had allowed him to make her suffer so.

"Oh. Right" Alan said again, and gave her a little wave and a sheepish smile, as if he was so unused to this situation that he didn't know how to respond.

"Bye then."

And the next moment, Maddie was gone and on her way again down the street. She didn't even feel triumphant at her rebuff of him. They say revenge is sweet but it had come too late for her. Now she simply no longer cared.

CHAPTER NINE

WITH HER FOREFINGERS and thumbs, she stretched her tight mini skirt down over the tops of her thighs, wishing she'd worn something longer. What was it her agent had mentioned about the part she was auditioning for? *A middle-class Estate Agent who works in an office.* Perhaps a short skirt was not the correct attire, but wanting to dress smartly, Maddie had donned the only businesslike suit she possessed - a tight-fitting two-piece in vivid blue cotton and lycra mix, jacket with padded shoulders and a low V-neck and fringed with army-style brass buttons. Maddie's nylon tights kept her thighs too warm and sticky in the heat of the day, but they gave a nice sheen to her legs and covered the downy fair hairs on her calves of which she felt ashamed.

Maddie had attempted a friendly smile at the girl sitting opposite - who currently had her head buried in a copy of *The Stage* - in a conspiratorial, us-against-them manner when her rival entered the waiting room, but the other girl preferred to maintain her demeanor of stony indifference to the world in general. She was rather plain - thought Maddie, as she sized up the possible competition by glancing at her surreptitiously from time to time - with long straight dark hair and a fringe which fell into her eyes, a square jawline with the hint of a double chin and a thick neck on broad shoulders. Maddie considered that - on the basis of looks alone - she stood a good chance of beating the other girl, unless the casting director were deliberately seeking a female less attractive than the star of the show to take this rather small part.

Nevertheless, Maddie was gratified even to have reached interview stage. She had never done any television work before - although she'd been seen by numerous casting directors and had made it to the last two for a leading role in a period drama once - and the show being cast was a popular soap opera with much prestige value for the actors involved. The part of the Estate Agent - although only a couple of scenes in the next episode - was, as Maddie's agent had pointed out with enthusiasm, almost certain to lead to a regular part in the series. Plus, it was a coup to meet the particular casting director concerned, who was notoriously difficult to entice with new talent, preferring to use people he already knew or had recently seen working. He had been invited to see *Puttin' on the Ritz* several times by Maddie's agent, but had never attended a performance, even though his office was literally around the corner from the theatre.

Maddie's thumping heart confirmed that she was more than usually nervous about this interview. None of the auguries had been good, and Maddie - in common with many of her colleagues in show business - was deeply superstitious in this regard. She had forgotten to wear her lucky charm, the birthstone which a close friend had given her for her sixteenth birthday and which normally accompanied her to interviews and auditions; the date was not a good one, being the 13th of the month; she had missed the bus by a hair and been forced to wait twenty minutes for the next one, making her almost late; the other interviewee had been unfriendly and so had the man at reception on the ground floor of the building. And now, she couldn't even be sure she'd worn the right thing. Her confidence was ebbing away from her by slow degrees, until she started to feel so negative that she wondered why she'd bothered coming at all.

She gazed at the stark walls of the little waiting room where they sat, with its mustard colored wallpaper, and at the few desultory pot plants which looked in need of water, trying not to eavesdrop as the sounds of the prior interviewee emanated from the room to her left. She could hear the girl's rather strident tones as she read from the script in a voice that was (in Maddie's opinion) far too bright for the laid-back quality of the character, and then gave a laugh of forced bonhomie at some joke the director had made, which Maddie didn't catch. The sound of another auditionee failing to impress did nothing to console Maddie. If anything, it made her feel worse than ever.

Suddenly, the door swung open and the victim herself emerged, blushing slightly and smiling in that way Maddie knew well - defiantly vivacious in the face of defeat. She had curly blonde hair and rather too much eye-makeup, and she shook the director's hand warmly as she made her departure, not even gracing Maddie and the other girl with a glance. The director - or perhaps it was the casting director - hesitated at the doorway uncertain which of the two girls was the next attendee and then, plumping for Maddie's rival who was sitting up now and smiling as if her mouth would break, said in a jolly voice: "Maddie, delighted to meet you. I'm Des, the casting director for *Up Your Street*. Do come through."

The other girl - in her keenness having failed to grasp the fact that Des had selected the wrong person - leapt out of her seat, flinging the paper down and grabbing her jacket from the chair. She had almost gone into the interview room before Maddie had a chance to declare: "Hang on. I'm Maddie Cambay."

The casting director looked momentarily baffled and gawped at the other girl, who covered her mouth with one hand and giggled: "Terribly sorry. Did you say Maddie? I didn't even hear...I'm Jane Stimson - for 12.30."

"So sorry" echoed Des. "I'm not wearing my contact lenses today, so everything's a bit of a blur." Jane giggled again and Maddie tried not to look as affronted as she felt. Des turned to Maddie. "So you're Maddie Cambay, are you? Do come through and meet Jeremy. We'll see you a bit later, Jane."

Maddie followed him into the little interview room and was introduced to the director, Jeremy Coultairn, a smallish man with a round bald head and wire-rimmed glasses. "Do take a seat...er...Maddie. We're not actually going to ask you to read for this part, we just wanted to meet you. I can usually tell whether somebody's right, when it's a fairly minor role such as this. Also, we're running out of time actually." He spoke in a breathy, sibilant voice and smiled frequently, pushing his glasses up the bridge of his pointy nose as he did so.

Maddie tried to conceal her disappointment at not being asked to read. She knew she was able to give a better account of herself when acting a role than just sitting "being herself". It seemed unfair that the previous girl had been given the chance to prove herself, just because she'd been interviewed before Maddie, and before Des and Jeremy had no doubt looked at their watches and begun anticipating their lunch break. Maddie gave her most winning smile and crossed her legs, pulling down her skimpy skirt and determining not to mind, although her already low confidence level sank an extra notch.

Jeremy proceeded to tell her a bit about the program and the current storyline, then added: "I assume you watch *Up Your Street*, by the way."

"Well, no. I'm not much of a soap fan, actually" Maddie admitted, then instantly regretted her words. It was always a good idea to pretend total enthusiasm for whatever project you were being auditioned for. But she was in such a negative frame of mind today that she was forgetting all her usual precepts. Perhaps part of her didn't even want to be offered the role. Perhaps the idea of having to remain in Bristol after her contract at the theatre had ended to do some filming for television didn't really appeal, because in the back of her mind she couldn't quell a desperate urge to run back to London as soon as possible, away from the site of her current problems.

"Never mind" continued Jeremy. "I'll tell you a bit more about what's just happened, then. If we offer you the part, you would be playing opposite Candy, who's just gone into the Estate Agent's office to talk about buying a house with her boyfriend..."

Maddie compelled herself not to ponder on her anxieties during the interview, and to smile at Des and Jeremy and appear positive and even bubbly. But at times when Jeremy was explaining the progress of the plot, Maddie almost didn't hear his words at all, so busy was she in trying to maintain an image of herself as relaxed and confident. She even had to ask him to repeat certain information - an embarrassing giveaway that her concentration was wavering - when he asked her if she'd be available for the filming dates.

When the interview was abruptly terminated by Des exclaiming that he and Jeremy were already running late and had two more people to see before lunch, Maddie felt completely sure that she had blown it. Even if they didn't choose her because she was genuinely not the right "type" that they were looking for, she knew she should have come across better generally, she should have tried to make a better impression. She wished she were back in London, on her own territory, and with none of the recent traumatic experiences behind her, where she could be her usual confident and lively self.

But - she reflected bitterly as Des showed her out of the room, and she noticed that three other girls had already gathered in the waiting room to be seen - there was no point dwelling on her failures now. It was too late to turn back or to wipe out recent events.

She decided to complain to her agent that the interview was too short, that the director was seeing loads of people, that they hadn't even given her the chance to read for the part. And she prayed that somehow - soon - she could put the past behind her and bounce back.

———∿∾⊙⊱⊙⊰⊙∽∿———

Gabriel always listened to the radio while he prepared his lunch. As he didn't work on Tuesdays he'd been doing some weeding in the garden, and he had to rinse the soil off his hands under the tap in the kitchen sink. It was a large old-fashioned aluminum sink with a single cold-water tap, which suited Gabriel perfectly. He had no need for modern conveniences like constant hot water, and he was quite prepared to boil a kettle for a shave or the washing up.

When the telephone rang, he expected it to be Rex - who often called on Tuesdays when he knew Gabriel would be at home, to check on the progress of his vegetable garden - and so was surprised to hear a warm female voice on the other end of the line. It was a voice he recognized, and it filled him with tender memories.

"Is that you, K...Kate?"

"Yes, it is. I'm flattered you remember my voice after all this time. It has been a long time, hasn't it?"

"Must be t...twenty years."

"I expect the others told you I've come home."

Gabriel laughed softly. "You still c...call it home?"

"Well, you know, I was very happy in Scotland but it's not quite the same is it? Home is where you're born, where your family comes from. You understand."

"I do."

"I thought it would be nice to see you again."

"Yes, it w...would be nice."

"I'm sure we've both changed, grown older, but..."

"I'm sure you're just as p...pretty." Gabriel had a sudden recollection of Kate in a flowered dress on a summer's day. That was the image he conjured when he thought of her, a laughing English rose in her twenties. He couldn't picture her matronly with grey hair, although he supposed she must be by now.

"You flatterer." Kate giggled, girlishly.

"You certainly s...sound just the same."

"Do you still like the theatre?"

"The th...theatre? I haven't been for years."

"Then maybe we should go. You used to love that amateur group from the church, those Shakespeare plays, don't you remember?"

"I d...don't even know what's playing."

"Neither do I. But it doesn't matter. I could come to you."

"To Bristol?"

"Yes, Tom would give me a lift into town. He has to come in anyway. Tomorrow evening?"

"T...tomorrow it is then."

"Tom can take me to your house for tea, and then we can walk over to the theatre and buy tickets for the show."

Kate had always made plans for them both, a decisive quality which Gabriel didn't mind. To him, it contributed to her charm. "I'll look f...forward to seeing you."

The two old friends said goodbye and Gabriel hung up the phone with a lighter heart than he'd possessed in days. He hummed softly to himself - *Ticket to Ride*, a tune remembered from the early 60's - with only half an ear on the local radio news broadcast, which he played mainly for the companionable sound of another human voice.

But, catching the tail end of a current story, something about it interested him: he halted his singing and turned up the volume.

"...was discovered in the river near the Clifton Suspension Bridge on Sunday, by a local girl on a climbing trip. Dental records have identified the body as that of Darren Webster, 23, from Cardiff. The young man is believed to have drowned, but as his skull was badly cracked, police are treating the case as a murder enquiry. Bristol police are asking anybody who might have seen Darren shortly before his death and can throw any light on the case to come forward. The number to contact is..."

Gabriel switched off the radio, not needing to hear more. He was certain the young man they were talking about was the one he'd seen falling into the water. Facts were irrelevant. He knew because it was Fate - his fate to see the death unfold, his fate to fail to tell anybody about it, his fate to be constantly reminded of his inadequacy, as others around him tried to piece together the jigsaw of which only *he* had the full picture. He felt almost angry. Why had he been chosen to shoulder this burden? He'd never asked for it. All he'd ever sought was a quiet life, with family, close friends and brief memories of love. And then this thing had happened, crashing in upon his cloistered life with harsh reality, exposing him to the cruelties of everyday existence that he'd tried so hard to avoid.

Even if he wanted to do anything about it, it was too late now. It would have been hard enough to contact the police just after the incident, but now? Not only would he be forced to tell what he'd seen over and over in statements to the police, but they would ask why he hadn't spoken up before, prod him with questions, fluster him and make him feel that *he* was the guilty party. And then there would be the trial. To stand up in Court in a roomful of strangers and let them all see him and hear his humiliation, the stammer that blocked his words...

He heard Helen's voice in his ear, so loud and insistent, it was almost like she stood in the room with him: *"I'm disappointed in you, Gabe. I didn't know you were so weak."* His own voice replied, tried vainly to defend himself: *"I'm not weak...it's just...it's j...just...I c...can't do it. Anything else, but not th...that."* She'd never really understood.

He looked up at the wall, where her photograph hung in a decorative wooden frame. It was the photograph he had taken of her in Nepal when they'd been happy together, and the one he loved the best. The sight brought still-painful memories flooding back.

[Her head is thrown slightly back and she regards the camera confidently with a wide smile.]

Gabriel stood in shock, the sun blazing in his eyes and almost blinding him.

"Help me, Gabe, help me!" Helen pleaded, as she knelt down beside the elderly man. "We've got to stop the blood. Have you got anything?"

"N...N...No...I..." Gabriel stood by like a helpless child, feeling stupid and ineffectual. He was still reacting to the previous event. He had only just taken his eyes from a young boy in flight - now halfway down the street - the one who had stabbed the blind beggar with a ruthless swipe of his penknife and run off with his box of coins. Gabriel

had taken a few faltering steps in pursuit of the boy before being alerted by Helen's cries to do something to help the old man who was bleeding in front of them.

The couple was on a dusty path leading up to Bodnath - a famous stupa that had been enthused about by a fellow traveler. There seemed to be no one else within hailing distance. The whole thing had happened so quickly that Gabriel still felt stunned. But Helen's reactions had been immediate, and she had dropped to the ground by the man's side, desperate to help him.

It was obvious from the old man's vacant gaze that the notice by his side proclaiming his blindness was not a lie to extract sympathy from passers by. He sat motionless, staring straight ahead of him with a stupefied air, as if such things happened to him all the time and were only to be expected. He seemed unaware or at any rate unconcerned about the blood gushing from his arm and the pain it must have been causing him.

"Can't you use your shirt?" Helen begged, looking at Gabriel.

"What?"

"Your shirt. Rip it up. Oh, look!" Before he could stop her, Helen dragged her shawl from around her shoulders - the beautiful one he'd bought for her - and, tearing it desperately with her teeth, ripped off a swathe of the brilliantly-colored silk. This she used as a bandage, which she bound tightly round the old man's arm, stemming the tide of blood surprisingly effectively. When she had finished, the old man mumbled something in Nepali and brought his hands together in a gesture of prayer, shaking his head from side to side. He was smiling.

"I think he's thanking us," said Helen. "Or blessing us. I don't know."

Gabriel was relieved at Helen having helped the old man successfully, if saddened that she had used her precious shawl to do it, but his relief was not to last long. It was only a few moments later that a fierce argument ensued, connected as ever with Helen's contempt for what she regarded as Gabriel's weakness. The two Westerners towered over the little, hunched man, their voices gradually rising to a crescendo - Helen's strident and Gabriel's plaintive - discussing him in a way that he couldn't possibly have been aware of.

Gabriel said that he was happy to search for a local doctor to attend to the old man's wounded arm, and to pay for him to be taken to the hospital. But he refused to go to the police station and make a statement about what they had seen.

"But what that boy did was wrong. He should be brought to justice," stormed Helen.

"We don't know anything about their j...justice. They might s...sentence him to life imp...prisonment, or anything. Just for stealing a few c...coins. That wouldn't be f...fair, would it?"

"Oh, don't be ridiculous!" Helen almost stamped her foot. It was surprising how she lost her bohemian demeanor when angry, and started behaving like the middle-class English girl she had been brought up to be.

"Wasn't it evil of that boy, to stab a defenseless blind beggar and steal his coins, his only few coins?" she protested.

"We don't know about the b...boy's life, do we? He may be p...poor and starving. He may have a f...family, brothers and sisters to f...feed."

Gabriel knew, even as he put forward these rather spurious arguments, that Helen was aware of his real motives for inaction. Perhaps she couldn't bring herself to say the words, but she knew Gabriel was afraid. Afraid of authority, afraid of involvement, afraid of consequences. He could cloak his fear in rational argument, but she saw the little boy inside who didn't want to stand out from the crowd. Perhaps because she realized that whatever she said would make no difference, she clamped her mouth shut and refused to discuss it any further.

Gabriel sat and stared at the photograph, and thought of how much he had loved Helen. Their time together had been so short, in comparison with the rest of his life, but his recollections of her never seemed to fade. It was as if her every word and expression were a precious jewel, which he took out and dusted from time to time and gazed at, longing in vain for the love he had lost.

He knew it was the incident with the blind man that had begun the change in their relationship. Things were never the same after that. Although they were able to talk, share jokes and make love just as before, both of them knew that something of their old affection was lost forever.

Gabriel recalled the time, several weeks later, when they were on the last leg of their journey and Helen had insisted they revisit Bodnath, to see if the old man was still there. To Gabriel's surprise, he had been. Despite a large red scar on his right arm he sat unperturbed, in the same position, with the same sign announcing his blindness and another box of coins on his lap.

Helen went up to him and tried to ask him some questions in English but with a few Nepali words she had picked up thrown in: "Does your arm still hurt? Did you get your money back? Did they catch the boy?"

The pair could make little sense of his replies, spoken as they were in a high-pitched voice with much smiling and nodding of the head. It was apparent, though, that the old man - despite his blindness and lack of English - knew who they were. When Helen lightly touched his wounded arm with her fingers his gabble became more fervent, his eyes lit up and from his pocket he drew a slip of material and held it out to them with a radiant smile.

"It's the shawl! My bit of shawl!" Helen exclaimed delightedly. "Oh no, but he must keep it. You must keep it," she said to the old man, trying to press the material into his fingers.

"I th...think he wants us to h...have it." said Gabriel thoughtfully, and as if responding, the old man nodded and handed the silken cloth to Gabriel.

Gabriel knelt down beside the man and took the cloth from him, saying the Nepali word for thank you - Dharanya. The old man repeated it joyfully, Dharanya, and Gabriel smiled as he slipped the piece of silk into his trouser pocket.

Gabriel still had the slip of cloth. He kept it in a drawer under his photographs and diaries, out of the light, so that the colors were still as vivid as his memories.

CHAPTER TEN

W HEN THE FRONT doorbell rang Maddie didn't hear it, hard at work in her room following the exercise routine of a Jane Fonda Aerobics Workout with the accompanying tape blaring out disco music. She liked to warm up for the matinee show at 2 p.m., an activity she preferred to conduct in the privacy of her own room rather than at the theatre. It was satisfying to be able to concentrate on the movement and stretch of a limb or the pain of a fully-tautened muscle without any extraneous distractions, physical exertion being the one thing that could liberate Maddie's mind from unwelcome thoughts. Perhaps it was the almost trance-like state she had successfully induced which caused her to flinch suddenly at the sound of an unexpected knock on her door. Or perhaps it was her generally nervous state of mind.

At any rate Maddie was irritated at having her routine disturbed, and she grumbled inwardly, wondering what was important enough to warrant this interruption. She switched off her tape recorder with a sigh and flung open the door to see Bella's father - still in his gardening coat and wellies, a sprinkling of soil on his hands - facing her with an anxious expression. He was a wizened little nut of a man, with dark eyes and a brownish face that had once been handsome. Seemingly perpetually in an apologetic state - whether towards Bella's mother who dominated the household, Bella herself or one of her equally large and imposing sisters - Maddie would have found his manner the object of amusement if she hadn't secretly rather pitied him. Now he stood in the corridor wringing his hands while he attempted a placatory smile, appearing to be even more harassed than usual.

"Oh Maddie my dear, so sorry to disturb you, but er..." He halted, seeming to be at a loss for words. Maddie looked beyond him at the two men in uniform hovering on the stairs regarding her with stony faces, and gathered at once the reason for Mr. Marconi's embarrassment. A wave of fear passed over her like a hot flush, making her fingers and toes tingle with apprehension, as she realized the significance of their visit.

Bella's father attempted a wan smile which seemed curiously inappropriate to Maddie, and, waving an arm at the men behind him, introduced them with a formality that made him look gauche: "This is Detective Inspector Grundy and Detective Sergeant Lionel from Temple Meads CID. They would like to have a few words with you, if you don't mind." His expression offered a mute apology, as if disclaiming any responsibility for inviting such men into the house. "Would you like to talk in the living room?" he enquired delicately, taking in Maddie's casual attire and recollecting the small size of her bedroom.

It was a question addressed to the general assembly, but the taller of the two uniformed men replied first: "Yes, that would be convenient. Could you join us downstairs, Miss Cambay?"

Maddie nodded dumbly and followed them down the stairs, feeling vulnerable in her Lycra leotard and bare feet. The strength she'd derived from her exercising evaporated with every step, and her stomach seemed to flutter with a thousand butterflies' wings.

Once in the living room Bella's dad dithered, still wringing his hands, reluctant to leave and uncertain how to proceed. His customary habit was to leave unpleasant circumstances for his female cohabitants to deal with - whose instinct guided them smoothly through any crisis - but since he and Maddie were alone in the house, the dilemma of how to cope with this uncommon and nerve-wracking situation had fallen squarely on his shoulders. His halfhearted offer to make a pot of tea was refused by the policemen and when Maddie also shook her head silently, Mr. Marconi took this as his cue to vanish with evident relief and return to his uncomplicated flowerbeds.

Maddie positioned herself on the sofa and hunched her body against the sudden chill of an unheated room. The older and larger of the two policemen - who Bella's father had introduced as Grundy - remained standing, his back to the gas fire, his feet a little apart, giving him an air of solidity and the impression of a ninepin that has no intention of being bowled over. He appeared to be in his fifties, with a lined, swarthy complexion and a fine thatch of wiry grey hair. Maddie was reminded briefly of police dramas from the television - the kind of program she detested - where rugged, invincible cops face cringing criminals with the consequences of their sins. Except she didn't consider herself a criminal. The Inspector - or whatever he was - was regarding her with an uncomfortably steely gaze, and the look of one who'd already made up his mind that Maddie was guilty of an offence. Or perhaps that was just his normal mode of behavior. Perhaps - Maddie reflected - she was falling prey to paranoia. She breathed deeply and maintained her expression of calm expectance.

"We're sorry to disturb you, Miss Cambay. We'd just like to ask you a few questions." The policeman's voice was polite but cold as a block of ice.

"Yes, of course" replied Maddie, attempting to echo his politeness and banish the tremulousness from her voice.

She turned to view the other policeman, who was standing with his back to the bay window, partially blocking the light. He was younger and shorter, a black man with curly hair and a wide, boyish face. His facial expression was unclear to Maddie because he was standing with the light behind him, but his posture was less erect than his companion, and his bearing less threatening. The younger officer held his hands in his pockets, and fidgeted every now and then with a bunch of keys in his right hand, jingling them as if he were impatient to leave. Being of inferior rank, he seemed content to let his partner do most of the talking, while he remained composed and silent, letting his gaze drift around the objects in the room.

Wasting no time on pleasantries, Grundy came straight to the point: "I understand you attended a party here on Saturday night the second of June" he began.

"That's right" Maddie assented.

"Mr. Marconi told us that his wife and himself were on holiday when his daughter held the party here." Grundy paused, as if waiting for Maddie to make a connection.

"Why are you...?"

"We're talking to everyone who attended, in order to investigate a murder enquiry."

"Oh! Who...?" Maddie swallowed hard. Her expression of alarm didn't need to be feigned. "Who was it who...?" She broke off, unable to make herself complete the sentence.

The officer was happy to oblige: "Young chap called Darren Webster. His body was discovered in the river here at the weekend... I'm sorry. It's rather a gruesome thing to have to discuss, I know."

Having spotted the look of horror on Maddie's face, he misread it as a young girl's revulsion at the mention of a corpse.

Maddie cleared her throat. "It's all right. Carry on."

Sergeant Lionel took a couple of steps towards her, then seemed to think better of it and placed himself at the arm of a chair. Now that he'd come out of the sunlight, Maddie could see him more clearly. He flashed her a smile that was almost sympathetic, and she felt her heart lighten. Perhaps this questioning was merely routine, after all, and the police had no particular suspicions of her.

The Inspector continued: "This young chap Webster, he didn't just fall into the water and drown, he was hit on the head as well, which is why it's important for us to investigate." His tone was arrogant and defensive, almost as if he expected her to accuse him of a fault, or to lash out at him with some protest. But Maddie regarded him silently, her body still and tense. "As we have gathered from his friend Ted Bown, the last place that Darren was seen alive was at the party here."

"He was here?"

"Yes." Grundy's expression was scornful. He seemed to disbelieve Maddie's attitude of surprise.

Now Sergeant Lionel took up the story: "That's why we need to speak to everybody who came to the party. We want to try and find out where he can have gone to when he left." His tone was patient, almost patronizing, as if explaining these details of police procedure to a rather backward child. At another time, Maddie might have resented his condescension. But at the present moment she was grateful.

Grundy returned to basics: "It seems that Webster fell into the river sometime in the early hours of Sunday morning."

Maddie judged that she was expected to contribute at this point. "I see." She paused in reflection for a few moments, looking down but feeling the gaze of the two men upon her. After a few seconds had elapsed she turned up her face to meet their eyes and asserted: "I don't remember meeting anyone called Darren".

"Did you know everyone at the party?" That was the sergeant, who darted her an enquiring but not unfriendly look.

"Well, no, I..."

"You might have met him but not found out his name" the older man suggested. "Did you only talk to people that you knew? Or did you meet other people at the party who were strangers to you?"

Maddie considered it best to be as honest as possible - up to a point. Certain facts could be corroborated by others. "Mostly I talked to people from the theatre, that I knew already. But I did...meet other people as well. I suppose I must have done."

The Inspector handed her a rather crumpled photograph. Maddie immediately recognized the young man she had danced with. Although the picture had been taken some time before and Darren looked much younger, he had the same cocky grin and self-assured stance. She felt a stab of shock, of familiarity, as the photograph cemented the reality of what had occurred. But she managed to hide her feelings from the two policemen.

"Did you see him at the party?" asked Grundy.

"Erm..." She paused, caught between potential explanations. "Yes, I think I did. It's rather difficult to tell, of course. The lights were dim and I'd drunk a bit and it was a few days ago, but I think so."

"Did you talk to him?"

"I might have done."

"Do you remember when? Was it at the beginning of the party? Or more towards the end?"

"Quite early on, I think," she said, honestly. "Because later I was singing songs with the cast and I don't remember noticing anyone I didn't know then."

"So you met him and talked to him a little at the beginning of the party?"

"Yes."

"And you didn't find out his name? Did you find out anything about him? Where he lived? Where he might have been going after the party?"

"No."

"And what did you talk about?" The older man seemed to be deliberately provoking Maddie with the hostile tone of his question, but she was determined not to be goaded.

"What about? I really can't remember. We didn't have a long conversation or anything, just party talk."

"What time did you leave the party?" asked the Inspector.

"It must have been about five o'clock because it was light. Bella made me some coffee and I walked home," Maddie volunteered.

Grundy stuck his hands in his pockets and looked at Lionel, who nodded as if to confirm that the interview was at an end. "Well, thank you very much for your help, Miss Cambay. Sorry to have disturbed you. We'll contact you, should we need your assistance again. We'll see ourselves out, thank you."

Maddie peered through the curtains as the policemen got into an unmarked car and drove away, wanting to make sure they didn't hang around outside the house waiting to catch her doing something suspicious. Feeling paranoia begin to creep up on her, she consciously fought it off, returned to her room, lay down on the bed and tried to command her beating heart to slow down. The tension of the experience had left her whole body trembling. It was quarter to one and she would have to leave in fifteen minutes to get to the theatre for the half, but she had to try and calm down first.

She had not lied. Throughout the whole ordeal, she had not told one actual lie. Except of course, for lies of omission.

She wished she could have revealed everything. She wished she could tell someone, to take what had become an unbearable burden from her heart and her conscience. Because she wasn't a murderer. What had happened had been a terrible accident, a moment of panic, an action of pure self-defense.

But it was too late to admit anything now. To confess now would make her appear guilty of a far more heinous sin than she'd actually committed. If she told the police now, her story of an attempted rape would look like pure fabrication for the sake of reducing her sentence. So it was wiser to keep quiet.

All Maddie could do was fervently, desperately hope and believe that there was no physical evidence to place her on the bridge with Darren Webster. Of course, there was the old man who had seen her. He had seen everything that had happened, including the knife Darren had held to her throat. He couldn't have told the police anything - not yet at least. Perhaps he didn't intend to. Perhaps he had seen Darren attempting to rape her and felt some sympathy for her. Or perhaps he was merely waiting, for some warped reason of his own, until the day when he would emerge from the woodwork.

Maddie couldn't escape from her thoughts: they kept batting about in her head like tennis balls over a net, back and forth, back and forth. Her brain was going round and round in circles so much; she no longer knew what to believe. She felt she would burst if she didn't talk to someone, anyone.

If Bella had been in the house, Maddie would probably have confided in her at that moment. But this time, Bella wasn't there to turn to. On an impulse, Maddie strode into Bella's bedroom, picked up the telephone extension next to the bed and dialed a familiar number.

"Hello. 6958. Can I help you?"

On hearing her adoptive mother's voice, Maddie went cold and sat rigid on the bed, the receiver in her hand, unable to speak.

"Hello? Who's there? Hello?"

She couldn't imagine what her mother's response would be, or how she could possibly phrase it delicately: *Hello mum, a few days ago I killed a man. It was an accident, but the police have called at the house, they already know it's me. What should I do?* When had her mother ever given her useful advice, or even been supportive and sympathetic? Certainly not when Maddie was in trouble. All she would get was reproving words, a voice full of reproach and condemnation.

Maddie put the phone down. She felt sick. Her watch said quarter past one and she was going to be late for a show for the first time in her life.

CHAPTER ELEVEN

"MERLIN'S CAVE" WAS a tiny shop with no windows and a glass front that formed part of a parade of such shops in an enclosed walkway beside an old church. It - along with the others adjacent - catered for the young and inquisitive, New Age customer, with its rows of books on the occult and mysticism, wind chimes from California and hand knitted cardigans from Peru. Maddie often came into "Merlin's Cave" purely to browse and enjoy herself poking about amongst its curiosities, but on this particular afternoon she was intending to purchase a specific item. She had plenty of time to kill, as it was at least two hours before the evening show and the theatre lay only a stone's throw down the street.

The music playing in the shop - Maddie recognized it as the *Enigma* record currently popular, a mixture of Gregorian chants, haunting pan pipes and synthesized drones - induced an atmosphere of calm contemplation, which was suddenly broken for Maddie as she felt a hand on her shoulder and heard an unexpected voice in her ear, saying her name.

She shivered slightly and turned to see Paul - the Bristol Old Vic's resident lighting operator - standing behind her, beaming in delighted recognition. "I thought it was you" he enthused. "Funny I never bumped into you before, 'cos I'm often walking about round here before the show. What you buying?"

"Oh. Nothing in particular. Just having a look, you know." Maddie wished she hadn't been recognized, especially by someone from the theatre, where gossip spread like wildfire. But she had no cause to be cross with Paul, who was consistently kind and pleasant to her.

She stood with the object she had just been examining clutched guiltily in her hands. It was an aromatherapy burner, quite large, in blue-glazed terracotta and with geometric designs cut out of the sides to let out the aromas. She'd wanted to find a burner exactly like Bella's birthday present, but as none of the others on display were a perfect match, this one was the nearest equivalent.

Paul regarded the burner with interest. "Bella got you one of those for your birthday, didn't she?" he said. "Did you break it or something?"

"No, of course not" Maddie replied, hiding a blush at her lie as she replaced the burner on the shelf and wished Paul weren't so perceptive. "I was just wondering how much she'd paid for it."

Paul laughed: "Checking up on her generosity, eh? I see." He suddenly looked apologetic. "Listen, I'm sorry I never got you anything."

"Oh that's O.K."

"No, I want to make it up to you."

"There's no need." Maddie - having practically forgotten the occasion already - couldn't understand why he was making a fuss about her birthday.

"I said I want to. How about dinner with me tonight?"

"Tonight?" Maddie raised her eyebrows. "I'm on stage."

"Afterwards, silly. We could sneak off and grab a Chinese. I know a great restaurant. What do you say?"

Maddie hesitated for a moment, but she could think of no reason not to accept his offer, and in truth she was flattered by it. It suddenly dawned on her that Paul had always shown a keenness for her company. In fact she might have accepted Paul's advances if she hadn't met Alan and fallen for his laid-back manner and roguish charm. Perhaps - she reflected briefly - if she'd chosen the reliable Paul instead of Alan with his moods and his carelessness of her feelings, the ensuing events might never have happened.

Still, she knew it was fruitless to speculate on what might have been. She couldn't change her personality, nor her fatal attraction for men who caused her heartache.

She decided that she may as well enjoy a free meal and some pleasant company. Although she had to admit that Paul didn't attract her sexually, her ego was sorely in need of a boost. Plus, he was one of the few men she found it easy to talk to openly. He had a kindly face, an appealingly gauche and ingenuous manner and large gentle hands that were often used to push unruly hair back from his eyes in a shy gesture.

"All right. You're on. Come round to the stage door about half past ten and I'll be there."

When Paul had sauntered away, Maddie returned her attention to the burner. She was sure Bella had purchased her burner in this shop, but there wasn't another precisely

127

the same. She would have to keep searching. She needed one near enough the original for Bella not to notice. She could have mended her present but not well enough to disguise the cracks, and she didn't relish answering awkward questions about how and when it had been so thoroughly broken.

—⁓∽◦◦◯◯◦◦∽⁓—

"Dad - can I have an ice cream? Dad - I want an ice cream. Dad. Dad!" The little boy - who was about seven years old in Gabriel's estimation - pulled at the cuff of the man's shirt, his voice growing increasingly loud with the effort to claim his father's attention.

"Just wait a minute, Mark" replied the man absentmindedly, as he surveyed the rack of postcards and selected a picture of the river by night to add to the small collection he held in his left hand.

"Dad" insisted the child, pointing to the freezer compartment by the window, "They've got a Space Bomber."

"What on earth's that?" queried the man, with a quick glance at Gabriel - who wore a benign expression as he waited from behind his counter for the pair to make their purchase - at the same time raising his eyes to heaven in a meaningful gesture as if to say *What will kids be wanting next?*

"Choc-lit...with...vah-nil-la...cen-tah..." chanted the boy peering into the compartment and slowly reading the label. Growing impatient, the lad slid open the lid of the compartment, slamming the glass door in his hurry, and reached inside to claim his prize.

"Hang on, Mark. I haven't said you can have it yet," admonished the father, striding over to his son and seizing the child's offending hand. "Does your mother let you have ice-creams?"

"Yes" asserted the boy with a fervent nod of his head, which caused his tousled black curls to bob up and down. "Whenever we come here. She always buys me one. She always lets me have ice cream."

"All right then, I suppose one ice cream can't do too much harm" relented the father with a sigh. "Just one though" he added, as the boy - testing his luck - had already started to reach into the compartment for a second Space Bomber. The man took the sweet from his son and carried it over to the counter. "How much is this please?" he asked Gabriel.

"S...seventy pence" Gabriel replied "Plus twenty five for the p...postcard." The man paid him then gave the ice-cream to the boy, who grabbed it without ceremony.

"Say thank you" chided the father.

"Thanks dad."

"Happy now?" The boy didn't reply but tore the wrapper off his treat and began sucking vigorously at its garish orange tip.

"D...did you want a...anything else?" asked Gabriel, with a smile at the man, as he handed over his change.

"Just to see upstairs. I don't think Joe's seen it before, have you?" The boy shook his head wordlessly, his eyes widening. "It is open, isn't it?"

Gabriel nodded. "I w...was going to w...wait for more c...customers, but I don't think th...there'll be any more n...now for a while. C...come on up." He stepped out from behind the counter and led the way up the steep and winding stairs with the man and his son bringing up the rear.

"Why does that man talk funny?" asked the child of his father in a loud voice.

"Ssh" chastised the man. "Don't be rude." Then he added softly but loud enough for Gabriel to hear: "I'll tell you later."

Gabriel - accustomed to having his affliction commented upon by children too young to have learnt discretion - took little heed of this interchange. When the little group reached the top landing, Gabriel pushed open the door and ushered them into the small circular room, which was the focus of the building.

"It's dark in here" complained the lad as they entered. "I can't see anything."

"You'll soon get used to it" reassured his parent. "Take my hand, if you like."

"The only l...light is from a h...hole in the ceiling," explained Gabriel. "Do you s...see it?" He pointed upwards at the ceiling. "It's that l...light that forms the i...image."

"What do you mean?" The boy had now lost his bravura and was shy of this new experience, and of talking directly to the man with the "funny" voice.

"C...come here. You'll see." Gabriel gave a kindly smile and waved them into the center of the room.

Father and son stood beside the stone slab, as Gabriel swung a heavy wooden lever into position. "The l...light is refracted through a l...lens at the top, so that it th...throws an image on to the s...slab of what's h...happening outside. At the s...same time as it's h...happening."

"Wow" exclaimed the boy, seeing an image of the bridge appear on the stone as if by magic. "There's the bridge. That's where we was before, dad."

"That's right."

"It's like television!"

"Well, s...sort of. Except that th...this is a very p... primitive c...camera."

"Where's the camera?" asked the boy, scouring the room with his eyes.

"This whole r...room *is* the camera. You're i...inside it. We're a...all inside it."

"We're inside a camera?" echoed the boy, perplexed.

"Yes, because essentially a camera's just a box" described the father, delighted to appear knowledgeable in front of his son. "Except that in this case the images won't be captured on paper, but we're seeing them real time, as they happen."

"Th...that's right."

The boy looked again at the slab, as Gabriel swung the lever and a different angle came into view, this time of the green lawn outside the building and the path leading down to the bridge. A young couple stood kissing by some bushes, oblivious of the fact that they were being watched from above. "Can those people see us like we can see them?" quizzed the child.

"No, that's the great thing you see," replied his father. "We can see them but they can't see us. It's just like *Candid Camera*."

"What?"

"You know - that program on the television where people don't know they're being watched and they do funny things. "That pair down there for example, they might...I don't know...do something they wouldn't want us to see--"

"He might have a pee!" suggested the boy with a giggle.

"Yes, and we'd catch him at it."

"And we could laugh at him." The boy jumped up and down with glee at the notion of the stranger's imminent embarrassment: "We can see you, we can see you!" he taunted.

Gabriel swung the lever away from the couple, so that now they were looking at innocuous blue sky and clouds. He remembered that other couple, the girl and youth he had witnessed who had not realized they were overlooked. That was a scene he wished with all his heart he could have avoided. But there was no escaping the memory of that moment and the guilt it had caused him. He shielded his eyes with one hand and wished the man and boy would leave soon.

The child noticed his action and regarded Gabriel with a wondering expression. "Are you here all the time?"

"Not a...all the time. M...most days, though."

"Have you lived here all your life?"

Gabriel laughed gently. "I d...don't live here. And I h...haven't been h...here all my life, no. B...but I have been l...looking after this b...building for a long time. Probably l...longer than you've been a...alive."

The boy digested this for a few moments then turned to his father: "I'm still hungry, dad."

CHAPTER TWELVE

A S THE FINAL notes of her ballad diminished and faded away into silence, Maddie could feel the wellspring of the audience's emotion burst into an avalanche of applause. She stood - as she always did - her face uplifted, arms held stiffly at her sides and a little away from her torso, in a posture of open acceptance.

The curtain fell with a slow swish and the lights simultaneously dimmed, until Maddie remained standing alone on stage, for a few seconds in utter darkness but still aware of the enthusiastic clapping from the auditorium. She always loved this moment best of all: it made sense of her reasons for being in the show, for her having chosen to be a performer at all. All the waiting weeks out of work, the agonizing in rehearsals and the pre-show nerves and strain were worth it, to be able to recreate this instant.

After a short while, the backstage lights were brought up and she could hear the audience begin to chatter and shuffle in their seats, prior to their departure to the theatre bar or the powder rooms. Maddie always took delight in gazing around her briefly at the empty set, before leaving the stage. Now stripped of performers or special lighting effects, the bare boards seemed faintly whimsical, without the glamour bestowed on them by a show. You could see now that the staircase leading to the bridge was made of chipboard, not marble, and that the greenery surrounding it had been painted on, cleverly assuming the three-dimensional appearance of real fronds and leaves. Maddie enjoyed the knowledge that she and the audience were jointly participating in an illusion: everybody knew it wasn't real, but they derived pleasure from it anyway. And it meant something to them - or she believed it did.

When Maddie had first broached the subject of her desire to be an actress, while she was still at secondary school, her adoptive parents had failed to understand her motives. The teachers had castigated her for not making use of her obvious academic gifts by studying for a more worthwhile profession. Maddie wasn't able to offer a rational explanation to any of her detractors as to why she believed so strongly that artistic expression was important, as important as making money or having a family or the myriad things that were expected to fill up a person's life. She didn't know why she instinctively felt this with such conviction; just that it was as true as the talents she'd been gifted with.

As Maddie passed into the wings, Richard - the A.S.M. who was "on the book" - poked his head around the curtain and smiled. He was a pretty boy of nineteen or so, with blonde hair and a small moustache. "That was really good tonight" he enthused.

"Thanks. You mean you're not bored with it yet?"

"Oh no. I always listen to your song. You do it really well."

Maddie smiled, slightly embarrassed by the compliment, and exited to the corridor. The other performers had all gone to their dressing rooms, and a low murmur of conversation could be heard, spiced with laughter as some of the chorus girls in the large room on the ground floor changed into their second act costumes. Maddie ascended the stairs to the second floor, holding her long dress up in front of her so that she wouldn't trip.

As she rounded the corner at the top of the stairs, Maddie was disconcerted to spot an unfamiliar man standing outside her dressing room, in animated conversation with Bella. He was tall with a distinguished bearing, thick grey hair and owlish spectacles in large frames. She caught snatches of what he was saying, and his voice was low and deep, with an educated accent. When he heard Maddie's steps along the corridor, he swiveled and beamed widely at her, showing two rows of neat white teeth. "Ah, so this is the girl herself! I'm delighted to meet you, Miss Cambay." He proffered a hand to shake and Maddie took it, smiling in return but not quite sure how to respond to this effusion.

Bella came to Maddie's aid by making the introductions: "This is Piers Dalton - he's from the *Bristol Herald*. Saw the first half of the show." Maddie couldn't be certain, but she thought she caught a wink from Bella as her friend said this.

"I absolutely loved it, it really was fabulous." The gentleman was now clasping Maddie's right hand in both of his, and leaning in towards her with an intense expression. There was a faint hint of alcohol on his breath. "I thought your solo in particular was superb."

"Well...thank you." Maddie murmured in embarrassment, bowing her head slightly.

"So sorry I can't stay for the second half, but you know how it is. A critic's work is never done" he quipped, to Maddie's relief releasing her hand from his grasp. Bella chuckled loudly. "See you both again, I hope. Goodbye." With a wave of his hand, he departed and strode away down the corridor.

Maddie slipped into the dressing room and shut the door. After one look at Bella, both girls collapsed into giggles. "I think he's fairly taken with us," gasped Maddie.

"With you, you mean," added Bella, without a touch of envy. "He was raving about you before you came in."

"Great, well I hope he gives us a good review," replied Maddie, beginning to change her costume.

"He will. You can add it to your collection."

"It's just the role, you know. You'd have to be pretty bad not to shine with that solo."

"Stop being so modest" said Bella. "You do it really well."

"It's a good part for me" Maddie admitted. "I'm very lucky."

"Yeah, well, enjoy it while it lasts. You never know when you'll have another chance, in this business." Bella rose from the dressing table and filled the kettle with enough water for two cups of tea. She didn't need to ask Maddie whether she wanted any: the enforced companionship of sharing a dressing room for several weeks had brought the girls so close that they were intimately acquainted with each other's habits.

Maddie dressed quickly in her second act costume and noticed from the clock on the wall that there was ten minutes to go before her next entrance, so she took the opportunity of sitting with her legs propped up on the dressing table, to take the weight off her tired feet and enjoy a moment of relaxation. She sometimes considered that intervals were her favorite time of the day, being the only time when she wasn't busy preparing to do a show or coming down from the excitement of having finished one. It was the only moment of their daily routine when she and Bella sat and relaxed and had a quiet chat about nothing in particular.

"Have you got anything lined up for afterwards?" It was the standard question Maddie asked near the end of a job, when she was starting to worry about the next one.

"No, fat chance. Have you?"

"No. Did a television interview yesterday, though."

"Really?" Bella turned, surprised, and halted briefly from pouring the boiling water into cups. "You didn't tell me. What was it for?"

"Oh, it was one of those last minute things. My agent rang in the morning and told me to go along in the afternoon - I thought I mentioned it. But I was really crap. I can't believe I did so badly."

"What did you have to do?"

"Just talk to them. The sort of thing I usually handle well. But I really blew it."

"I bet you weren't as bad as you think." Bella placed Maddie's mug of tea on the dressing table in front of her.

"No, I was all over the place. I kept asking stupid questions. I don't know what got into me."

"Asking questions doesn't matter. If they liked you, they liked you."

"They didn't like me," asserted Maddie.

All at once, Bella shot her friend an enigmatic look, part slyly curious and part anxiously concerned: "Have you been worried about anything lately?"

Maddie, flustered by the question, kept her head down and pretended to be very involved in blowing on her hot tea till it was the right temperature. "No, not particularly. I usually get a bit...jumpy about this time in the middle of a run. Start wondering if I'm ever going to work again." She gave a little breath of laughter.

"I know what you mean." Bella had stopped studying Maddie and her face was turned away from her colleague now.

Maddie gave an inward sigh of relief that her excuse had evidently been believed. Part of her was longing to confide in Bella. And now that Bella had seen there was something wrong, it was as if she'd opened the door of disclosure a little chink and all Maddie had to do was throw it open wide. Only her fear and distrust stopped her. There was a moment of silence between the two girls, and Maddie began to wonder if this wasn't the ideal opportunity to blurt out her problems to her friend. She gave an intake of breath and it was on the tip of her tongue to initiate her confession - then something happened which blasted it right out of her mind.

There was a buzz on the intercom, and Bella answered it. "All right, send 'em up if you must" she said.

"Who is it?" Maddie asked. She suddenly had butterflies in her stomach, as if from some premonition that Bella's reply would disturb her.

"I can't make head or tail of what that Jones says," said Bella, sitting down again heavily in her seat. "He seemed to say coppers. But what the hell would they want with us? And right now, for heaven's sake."

Maddie was afraid to reply.

A few seconds later, there was a knock at the door which Bella answered and two men with whom Maddie had been dreading another encounter, faced her in the corridor. It was Inspector Grundy and Sergeant Lionel, the policemen who had questioned Maddie at Bella's house the day before.

Maddie had chosen not to mention her interview with the policemen to Bella, nor had Mr. Marconi spoken about them, not wishing to distress his family, so Bella was still unaware of the incident and of the significance of this, the officers' second visit to her friend in as many days. Maddie had been praying that Grundy and Lionel's interview with her the day before would be the end of her association with them. One visit from the police could be construed as simply routine, but a second visit - and while she was at work - indicated that they might have cause for a deeper interest in her affairs.

Maddie's heart was thumping so loudly she was amazed that nobody else heard it, that Bella didn't point it out: *"Hey, Maddie, could you stop that pounding, I can't hear myself think!"*

However, the officers seemed at first to be mainly interested in Bella. Grundy expressed regret that he'd missed her at her home the previous day, saying as he had to Maddie that they were speaking to everyone who might have seen Webster just prior to his death and assuring her that this was purely a routine interview to ascertain how much she knew about the dead boy who'd attended her party. Bella, although mildly surprised that neither her father nor Maddie had mentioned the police's earlier visit, was not averse to answering a few questions while changing into her Second Act costume.

Grundy and Lionel asked a few standard questions, and seemed to accept without demur Bella's assertions that she'd never heard of Darren Webster before that moment, she didn't remember seeing him at the party, and yes, although she was the hostess, there had been several gatecrashers in attendance whom she'd not actually invited but who knew of the event through friends of friends, her parties being notorious amongst the staff at the theatre as wild affairs and open to all comers.

To Maddie's surprise and discomfiture, instead of departing promptly when they had finished interviewing Bella, the police officers turned their attention to her. Grundy again took the lead: "I'm sorry if it's not convenient, Miss Cambay, but we would like to have a few words with you also."

Bella looked at Maddie and shrugged her shoulders as if to say she'd done her bit, retreated to her side of the dressing room and began removing her bodice, blithely unconcerned at the fact that - as she never wore a bra beneath her costume - her naked breasts were in full view of the police officers. The Detective Inspector swung his eyes away from Bella - his modesty more affronted than hers - and faced Maddie.

His sidekick, Sergeant Lionel, was smiling at Maddie as if they were old friends. Maddie was confused by their attitude towards her and the mixture of signals - sometimes hostile, sometimes approachable - that she received from the two men. She'd never had any dealings with the police before, so had no idea what kind of treatment to expect. But, looking at the pair of them now, she couldn't help thinking that they resembled all the copper double acts she'd seen in drama series' on the television, standing there with stiff and formal postures that were distinctly out of place in the casual atmosphere of the theatre.

Maddie knew that to answer even a few questions now would set her nerves on edge, and she wanted to give an especially good performance tonight, as her agent was in the audience. "I'm sorry, I can't really talk to you right now. We're just about to go on stage."

"It is very important..." began the Detective Inspector.

"Look, I've literally got five minutes before I have to go back on stage. Isn't there some other time..." Maddie started to feel affronted at the insensitivity of these policemen - *didn't they know better than to disturb someone in the middle of their work? How would they feel in her shoes? Did they think acting wasn't proper work anyway so it didn't matter?* - but she fought down her anger and quelled the bitter words that were on her tongue. She knew instinctively that it would be unwise to lose her temper with them.

Bella stayed uncharacteristically silent throughout their exchange, but she still managed to make her disapproval of the policemen's continued presence apparent. It was impossible to ignore her large frame as she flung her First Act skirt on to a hanger, her every movement indicating impatience and annoyance.

Grundy appeared to concede, although he was unabashed at his snub by the two girls: "In that case, Sergeant Lionel and I will pay another visit to your residence, if it would be more convenient. Say - 10 o'clock tomorrow morning? We can talk to you then."

"Erm...I suppose so. All right". Maddie, discomfited, had no better answer. It hadn't occurred to her that Grundy would leap in so quickly with another suggested appointment. She had hoped, rather optimistically she now realized, to stall him and Lionel for longer. She detested the policemen's formal way of putting things: *your residence.* But there was no way she could refuse to see them again.

The two police officers made polite but icy goodbyes and walked away down the corridor, the sound of their heavy boots echoing on the cold stone floors. In an effort to regain her composure, Maddie began to dab at her cheeks with unnecessary powder, pretending that the policemen's visit had already been cast from her mind.

"What idiots" remarked Bella, when she'd waited long enough for the two men to be out of earshot. "This is no time for a social call," she added playfully, adopting a Southern American accent like something out of a Tennessee Williams play. She swiveled her head towards Maddie and demanded: "They've interviewed you about this Darren bloke already, haven't they? What more do they want with you?"

"I...don't know" Maddie spluttered.

"This is a lot of fuss to make over a parking ticket" Bella replied, jovially. Then she noticed the look on her friend's face: "Hey, there's no need to be so upset. These coppers, they'll get their knickers in a twist over the stupidest things. You know what, I had them come round to me once, really grilling me and making me feel like a criminal and I didn't know what the hell I'd done. Turns out, some bloody friend of mine - if you can call him that - had been growing dope in his back garden, told them he'd been stashing the stuff at my place. Well, that was a lie of course, to save his skin. I might have taken a little packet off him once but I certainly wasn't a dealer. But they had to check me out anyway."

Maddie had managed to control her trembling now, and she attempted a rather wan smile at her friend. "Was it really horrible?" she asked in order to say something, not really caring about the answer.

"Oh yeah, but I got over it. There wasn't enough evidence for them to charge me with anything, so it was O.K." Bella patted Maddie on the arm. "Don't worry, love. You'll be fine. I'm sure it's nothing serious."

Maddie loved Bella at that moment. She knew she'd be eternally grateful to her friend for believing in her. It was obvious that the possibility of Maddie's having committed a grave offence had never even entered Bella's head.

———

"I hope you've bought us seats near the front. I'm afraid my hearing's not too good these days."

"Yes of c...course. They were a b...bit more expensive, but I thought it was w...worth it. After all, it's not that o... often I have an evening out."

"Let me give you something towards it" Kate offered, reaching into her purse.

"No, n...no. I wouldn't h...hear of it."

Kate squeezed Gabriel's hand affectionately. "You're a good man. You may not believe this, but I've missed you all these years."

Gabriel moved away, too embarrassed to reply. "Let's look at the photographs of the cast," he suggested.

Kate smiled knowingly and joined her friend by the display board in the theatre foyer, on which could be seen photographs of highlights from the current production of *Puttin' on the Ritz*. The couple gazed at a group shot of the entire cast assembled for the final chorus number, in which about thirty people stood in three rows, all with their arms raised and their mouths open in song; a photograph of a dramatic moment as two of the male members of the cast who played gangsters engaged in a gunfight; and a photograph of a girl standing in a pool of light on a darkened stage, clad in a long silk dress which emphasized the slimness of her body, her long blonde curls falling to her waist.

"What wonderful hair. Do you think it's real?" pondered Kate.

"I don't know. She's a p...pretty girl" commented Gabriel. "I d...don't think much of these ph...photographs, though. They're so s...static. They were obviously t...taken out of c...context, not while the sh...show was going on, or in reh...hearsals."

"You know, I think you could do a better job. Why don't you do something like this, Gabriel?" Kate suggested.

"What? Take pub...blicity photographs for the th... theatre? Oh no." He laughed briefly and waved his hands, as if to brush away the suggestion. "I w...wouldn't have the exp...perience" he continued with modesty.

"You might take better pictures than this man's done."

"Oh well. I have my w...work at the Camera Obs... scura. I don't have the t...time. Shall we go to the r... restaurant now?"

"Certainly." Kate put her arm through his in a gesture of comfortable familiarity, and the couple stepped out of the foyer and into the street. The evening was warm and fine, and the late sun sent ripples of golden light on to the pavement as they walked.

"I'm looking forward to seeing this show. It must have been years since I last went to the theatre," remarked Kate.

"Me too" agreed Gabriel.

"Do you know much about it? It's a new musical, isn't it?"

"Yes, written by a l...local man. It's had g...good reviews in the p...papers, I believe."

"Rex said you used to work for the local paper."

"That's right. The *Bristol Herald*, as a ph...photo journalist. Until I got t...too old and decided to s...settle for a part time j...job."

"It must have been so interesting, being involved in the media." Kate made it sound as if Gabriel had lead a dramatic life, full of excitement and glamour.

Gabriel was keen to paint a truer picture: "Oh, not really. We just c...covered stories of l...local interest, you know - agric...cultural shows and tr...trade fairs, that sort of thing. I enj...joyed it, mind."

"So now you're semi-retired?" Kate kept her eyes on Gabriel as she talked to him. She had a knack of making casual conversation seem intimate, by focusing all her warm attention on the person she was addressing.

"Yes. Although I always have a lot to o...occupy me. I keep a...active." Gabriel reflected that it had been a long time since he'd been able to converse so naturally with a woman, one who wasn't part of his family.

"I'm sure you do. You always did." Kate was going to add that, with no wife and children to care for, Gabriel must have a need to occupy himself more than most men with his activities, but she didn't want to appear tactless or open any old wounds. She was enjoying just strolling along with this man, the childhood friend whom she was now getting to know all over again in her twilight years, and coming to realize how much she appreciated his quiet companionship.

She had not spoken of missing Gabriel purely out of flattery or a desire to placate what may have been his ruffled pride. She'd never regretted her decision to marry Hamish and move to Scotland: Hamish had been a good husband to her and provided the children she'd always wanted. But always in the back of her mind she had wondered what life might have been like if she'd stayed at home and waited for the gentle Gabriel to claim her. Perhaps now - she concluded - she'd been donated a second chance to give him the love and friendship he so obviously lacked.

And this time, she wouldn't throw that chance away.

———ﾟﾟﾟﾟﾟﾟﾟﾟ———

Maddie had completely forgotten her promised meal with Paul, as she hurried out of the theatre that night. When she saw him waiting expectantly for her at the stage door she almost demanded why he was there, but fortunately recollected their earlier meeting just in time to save her from rudeness.

Paul put a protective arm around her shoulders and escorted her to his car, a dull brown colored Vauxhall parked a few yards down the street. He was friendly and more chatty than usual, and Maddie was relieved to let him make most of the conversation, as he drove them to a small Chinese restaurant he knew in an out-of-the-way corner of Bristol.

When they entered the restaurant, the head waiter greeted Paul like an old friend and shook Maddie's hand warmly, saying: "I've heard so much about you". Maddie wondered whether Paul had been eulogizing about her or whether the waiter had simply chanced to read her glowing reviews in the papers. At any rate, she was a little embarrassed although secretly flattered when Paul insisted on repeating to his restaurateur friend Maddie's most admiring review, published in *The Times* at the start of the run. Paul trotted out the phrases that had been said about her with evident pride and as if they were well known to him: *"A truly poignant quality", "...this newcomer with the remarkable voice..."*

The waiter continued to be extremely solicitous, and appeared to Maddie to be favoring her and Paul with far more attention than his other customers. Leading the couple to a secluded candlelit table at the back of the restaurant, he rallied a bevy of other, eager black-suited waiters around them, who insisted on fulfilling their every whim.

All this ministration was very flattering to Maddie's ego, and, partly because she had not anticipated the evening turning out so pleasantly, she found both her meal and the conversation with Paul delightful. He could be very charming company, not because he told a lot of jokes and anecdotes himself, but for the way he appreciated Maddie's stories, listening to her as he did with undivided concentration, gazing at her with his mouth shaped into a warm smile, his head cocked to the side or resting on one hand.

Maddie consumed more of the delicious food than she'd intended, washing it down with copious amounts of Chinese tea. Although Paul was keen for her to share the wine he had ordered, she refused, choosing this evening to refrain from hazarding the potential hypoglycemic attack that imbibing alcohol always meant for her. There were times when a rebellious instinct caused her to flout the normal precautions she took on account of her diabetic condition and drink as much alcohol as she liked, unconcerned at the possible outcome. Feeling bitter at being twenty-five and unable to let her hair down like other people of her age, rebellion had been her mood on the night of Bella's party. But, aware of how disastrously that had ended for her, tonight she was in a different frame of mind, more cautious and sensible than was her usual wont. Maddie was amused to notice Paul's evident disappointment: perhaps he had been hoping that in an inebriated state she would be more inclined to accept his advances.

Towards the end of the evening - when Maddie and Paul had been seated at their table for over two hours and the restaurant was otherwise deserted, waiters discreetly clearing away plates to the low drone of taped Chinese music - the couple's conversation became more serious and Paul's expression more intense. Maddie's mood having mellowed, she was more open than she might have been on another occasion. With a sigh, she admitted to Paul that she had decided to return to London as soon as the run of the show finished at the end of that week, and not stay on in Bristol.

"But I thought you said you liked Bristol" Paul complained, as if Maddie had insulted him personally by declaring his hometown not good enough for her.

"I do like Bristol. It's not that." Maddie hoped that Paul wouldn't pry any further, as she didn't wish to divulge her real reasons for escaping so abruptly back to the metropolis.

"What is it, then?"

Maddie paused, smiling slightly, but feeling her mellow mood begin to evaporate: "Well, London's my home..."

"Oh come on, you've got no family there, you've only lived in London for a couple of years anyway you said. You could just as easily make Bristol your home." Paul's tone and expression were more defensive than Maddie had seen ever them before.

"What would I *do* here?" blurted Maddie, beginning to feel a little irritated at having her decisions judged unacceptable.

"Just the same as you do in London, of course. We've got a theatre, we've got nightclubs where you can sing, even a television station." Paul seemed to be prepared with all his answers, as if he'd been giving the subject some thought.

Maddie sighed, wondering how to explain more clearly: "I know there's a cultural life here, but it's just not the same. London is at the center of things. It always will be. And I've got to be where the work is, it's important for my career."

"What about what you were saying last week about how grotty it is in London, and how unfriendly?"

"I know, I know, it is grotty and unfriendly but I have to put up with those things..."

"That's not what you said before. You said you'd rather live somewhere pleasant, where people talked to each other in the street and--"

"Yeah, O.K., well I've changed my mind."

"Why?" demanded Paul.

Maddie hesitated before replying. "No particular reason. I've just thought about it more and I've decided I...don't want to stay."

There was silence for a few seconds as Paul lowered his head and contemplated his empty dessert plate, seeming to deliberate on a reply. Maddie waited till he raised his head and gazed at her steadily: "So does that mean it's no go for us?"

Maddie looked away briefly in embarrassment at his presumption, then shrugged and suggested: "We can still be friends, can't we?"

"You know it never works out that way" Paul replied in a low voice. "People always say they'll keep in touch but they never do."

He seemed sulky and discontented now. They made desultory conversation for a few minutes, as if neither wanted to admit that the evening had ended on a sour note. Paul asked a nearby waiter for the bill - his friend having disappeared some time ago into the kitchens - and the couple talked about things unimportant to them both, in order to avoid looking at each other.

"Cambay's an unusual surname. Where's it from? Is it your real name?"

"No, it isn't actually. My real name's Wetherby, but there was another Madeleine Wetherby in Equity so I had to change it."

"Why did you choose Cambay?"

"I wanted to think of something a bit different, but which wouldn't tie me to playing any particular nationality. So, Cambay was a place in India that my auntie was fond of. She used to talk about it a lot. I liked the sound of it, sort of romantic and exotic but not particularly Indian. I thought it would suit me as well as any other name."

"Yes, it suits you pretty well in fact."

"What about you? Have your family always lived in Bristol?"

"Yes."

After this, Paul's answers became more and more curt and monosyllabic, and eventually the conversation lapsed into near silence, the pauses between sentences getting further and further extended until they were uncomfortable.

When the waiter finally returned to their table with the bill, Maddie inwardly gave a sigh of relief that the now awkward encounter with Paul was soon to end. Maddie tried to foot her half of the cost, attempting to place her credit card on the saucer before Paul could object. But she soon realized that Paul would only take this as a further humiliation, being a tacit acknowledgment that she earned a lot more money from the theatre than him. So at his insistence, she agreed to let him treat her to the meal as a late birthday present.

Nevertheless, Maddie's guilt was subtly increased by this act: she knew she hadn't done what was expected of her in the circumstances, hadn't paid her dues by agreeing to sleep with him.

But although she felt pity for Paul and a little sadness that their relationship hadn't blossomed into something more serious, she wasn't regretful. Maybe if they had come at another time, she would have been able to reciprocate Paul's attentions. But he had been unfortunate with his timing. Just now, the mere thought of involvement with another man - so soon after the disaster with Alan and the ensuing horrifying events that were still fresh in her memory - was anathema to her.

Liquorice's ears twitched. The slow tick of the grandfather clock in the hall had woken her from a sleep dream-filled with birds and tree chases enjoyed in younger and livelier days. She opened one sleepy eye and blinked at Gabriel. He was seated in the armchair that he invariably occupied - although the fire wasn't lit, the weather being mild this evening - which afforded a good view of his extensive garden through the bay window. He would have seen little now, though, even if his eyes had been open, because it was past 10 o'clock and the evening dusk had settled in.

A half-finished tumbler of sherry was placed on the small round occasional table by his side, and on his lap - which moved softly up and down to the rhythm of his peaceful breathing - lay one of the photograph albums which were Gabriel's most treasured possessions. He had been surveying them more frequently of late. This particular album - which was part of the gilt edged set of five normally resident at the top of the glass-fronted bookshelf in the living room - had left its customary position for the first time in several years, and now lay open on Gabriel's' knees. One of his arms hung down over the side of the armchair where it had fallen in slumber, and his right hand rested on the album, with the index finger almost caressing the corner of one of the photographs. This was a black and white snapshot - with crinkled edges, as was the custom in the 1960's - and the two people shown in it were the same pair who featured in virtually all the pictures in the book.

[The younger Gabriel - looking flushed and happy and as if he has just managed to reach the spot after a hurry - smiles back at the camera, his hand clutching his partner's. She too looks happy, though rather more subdued, her tanned legs crossed, her left arm (the one not taken by Gabriel) slightly raised as if just about to point something out to the photographer and her lips parted as if in mid-speech. She is dressed in a sari, which appears somewhat incongruous next to her very Western face and the sixties hairstyle of loose, straight, long locks. He is in the ubiquitous shorts and t-shirt and he has a camera case slung over one shoulder. They are seated on

a low stone wall and behind them - obviously the reason for the picture - is a stunningly ornate temple, its colors partly bleached by the bright sunshine but the beauty of its design clearly visible.

Other tourists surround them, frozen in mid-stride by the camera, as they walk up to or away from the historic monument.]

Gabriel took his camera back and thanked the American gentleman in the large Stetson. He and Helen had given up asking Indian children to take their pictures because they always expected money, and after four weeks on the road they had little left to spare. Gabriel exhorted Helen to start exploring the temple with him, but she shook her head: "No, it's all right Gabe, you go on ahead. I'm beat."

"Are you t...tired? I'll s..sit with you then."

It was the middle of the day and the sun was scorching, but Helen never seemed to feel the heat. She sat with her eyes closed and her face lifted, for the time being not interested in conversation. Gabriel was thirsty and he opened the flask of water they'd brought with them. It was one of the most useful things they had thought to pack when leaving England. He knew their holiday was nearly over and he was already starting to feel bereft, as if he knew that the beauty of this trip couldn't be captured and kept forever. Maybe that was what made him feel so romantic that day and so desperate to pour out his heart. At any rate, he said the thing suddenly and without premeditation, as if the words had escaped from his mouth before he could stop them. "Should we get married?" He *was surprised at himself for saying it. Even the stutter wasn't there.*

Slowly, Helen opened her eyes and turned her head to his. She looked mildly shocked, and Gabriel felt foolish.

She replied kindly, though. "You're a dark horse. I thought you didn't believe in marriage."

"I only said that b...because you said it."

Helen laughed and patted Gabriel's knee affectionately. "You nutcase. I meant it. You should say what you mean, not what you think I want to hear."

"I l...love you. I want to be with you."

"I love you too. You're a fab guy. But I'm not the marrying type." Helen turned her face to the sun. "I told you that before. You should accept it."

"M...marriage isn't so bad, if you l...love each other" Gabriel said softly.

"Sure" she replied, "Sure, if it's what you want, it's not bad at all." She took his hand and gently eased him off the wall. "Let's walk. I'm not so tired now."

Gabriel followed her reluctantly as they made their way up the pathway to the temple. "But what about ch... children? Don't you want any?" he asked.

Helen came to an abrupt halt and looked at him suspiciously. "How did you know?" she demanded.

Gabriel didn't understand. "What do you mean?"

Other people were walking past them, irritated at having the pathway momentarily blocked. Helen started walking and didn't speak to Gabriel again until they got into the cool of the temple doorway. "I wasn't going to tell you yet, but...I'm pregnant."

Gabriel gasped a little in response. "How do you kn... know?"

"I saw a doctor in Gujerat. When you had your tummy bug."

"But..."

Helen spoke in a fierce whisper. "I've made up my mind, Gabe, so don't try to talk me out of it. I don't want the baby. I know it's yours as well, but it's mainly me who'd have to put up with having it and I don't want it. Do you understand?"

Gabriel could only shake his head sadly.

"I've always wanted to be free. It's a big thing with me. I know you don't dig that sort of thing, you're different from me, we're different. It doesn't mean I don't love you. But we can't stay together forever, it wouldn't work. Anyway, I don't want that with anyone. And I don't want to start having babies and being a mother and all that, it's just not my scene. How can you be free with a baby hanging round your neck?"

Gabriel found his voice and spoke loudly, breaking the hushed silence of the temple and making heads turn. He didn't notice. "But what about the child? Our ch... child? You want to kill it?"

"Don't be melodramatic. It's not born yet, so how would I be killing it? Can't you understand - I wanted to be different, to be free. I don't want to be shackled by an outdated moral code or family values that mean nothing. Oh, I knew you weren't going to dig this, that's why I didn't want to tell you."

"You don't make sense." Gabriel thought that Helen's words were not her own, that they'd come from a book

she'd read. He couldn't believe she meant what she said. But she spoke with such a passionate intensity that it was evident she was convinced of the validity of her argument.

"O.K. I don't expect you to understand, why should you? But please, Gabriel, if you love me like you say you do, just accept it and let me be. Let me do what I want to do with my life."

It was the first time she'd ever called him by his full name. She'd always said she hated the name Gabriel, that it sounded like some prissy angel from a bible story, so she'd dubbed him with a nickname she preferred. But there was a formality in her expression now, a distance, that Gabriel had never seen before.

CHAPTER THIRTEEN

THIS TIME WHEN the two police officers came to call on Maddie at Bella's house she was prepared for them, and she answered the door almost before the bell had finished sounding. Wishing to imbue herself with courage to face the interview, she had taken care to dress more formally than on the previous occasion, in pressed grey slacks and a plain blue shirt, with her hair pulled back from her face in a thick ponytail.

Inspector Grundy and Sergeant Lionel followed Maddie into the front room without any attempt at softening their entrance with pleasantries, both men arranging themselves on the sofa with their backs to the window to sit facing her with grim countenances. Maddie took up a solo position on the armchair, her spine erect and her hands folded neatly in her lap in an attitude of mute expectation.

"Right then, we're sorry to have to bother you again Miss Cambay." The Inspector stalled briefly while he consulted his notepad, then added: "It is Cambay, is it?" He looked up at her with a slight frown creasing his brow.

"Yes. That's my stage name" Maddie attempted to answer politely, moistening her dry lips with her tongue and regretting the timbre of her voice which had come out tight and small.

"Your stage name" Grundy repeated in confirmation, writing something down in his book and pronouncing the word *stage* as if it were some sort of perversion. "So that must be why your doctor referred to you by another name - Madeleine Wetherby. Is that correct?"

"My doctor?" Maddie echoed stupidly, feeling a twinge of shock. *Why had the police contacted Dr. Chen?* Hiding her discomfiture, she attempted to explain further: "Wetherby's my real name. There was another Madeleine Wetherby in Equity, so I had to change my name."

"I see. So Wetherby is your family name," the Inspector reiterated, seeming not to expect an answer from Maddie.

"Family name. Well, yes, sort of. It's my adoptive parents' name."

The Inspector glanced at Maddie, an unspoken question in his eyes.

"I'm adopted, you see" Maddie elucidated.

Grundy glanced momentarily at Lionel with an unreadable expression, hesitated for a second or two, then scribbled down something else. "I see. Your doctor didn't in fact mention that, but it's not particularly relevant in any case."

"Thank you for telling us" added Lionel.

Maddie gave a nod of acknowledgment, feeling like a schoolchild who's just been patted on the back by her teacher.

"All right. I'll come straight to the point Miss, er... Wetherby. When we visited you at home a couple of days ago, you told us that..." Grundy consulted his notes to find the exact words: "you remember seeing and talking to someone of Darren Webster's description at Bella Marconi's party on June 2nd. Is that true?"

"Yes."

"You say you chatted to him briefly at the beginning of the party, that was all you did, and you don't remember seeing him at all later on?"

"No...er, yes."

"Since our first interview with you, some further information has been brought to our attention. A young chap called Ted Bown came into the station yesterday - he was a friend of Darren's. He was able to give us a very accurate description of you and he's absolutely sure that he saw you and Darren dancing together at the party."

"And it was quite late in the evening, he says" added Lionel. "Not early, which was the only time you had any contact with Darren, according to you."

There was a silence as Maddie prepared her reply and the two officers waited expectantly for her response. Grundy's expression was accusing, with a hint of triumph in it, like a busy spider pleased to have trapped an unwary fly in his web.

"Well...I'm not sure, I can't remember. I suppose I might have danced with him," Maddie declared, feeling her face grow hot with mortification. "I never said I didn't dance with him. But I don't think it was late in the evening. No. Because I was singing later on. Ted must have...remembered it wrongly...made a mistake." Her voice had a plaintive edge to it, and the hands which had laid calmly in her lap moments before were now twisting around each other in distress.

"At what time did you dance with Darren, then?" demanded Inspector Grundy.

"I...I don't remember exactly" Maddie stuttered.

"Before midnight? After midnight?"

"I don't know. I don't wear a watch. I wasn't aware of the time." Maddie felt frustration and helplessness begin to possess her. *How do they expect me to remember details like that?* - she asked herself.

The Inspector examined her with his chin slightly lowered and eyes raised, as if he didn't believe her assertions but he wasn't prepared to argue the point. Maddie noticed now that every word they had just uttered had been recorded by Sergeant Lionel who was busy scribbling in a small black notebook. Lionel looked up sensing a lull in the conversation, and gazed at Maddie, his young face placid and untroubled.

"So. Do you wish to change your statement now, to say that you not only talked to Darren Webster, but you danced with him as well?" interrogated Grundy.

"Erm... I suppose so. Yes" Maddie replied, feeling that she'd better co-operate, although she was disquieted by the way he'd referred to her earlier comments in interview as a *statement*.

Inspector Grundy paused for a few seconds while he added something on his notepad. Lionel's long legs were crossed and one foot tapped on the carpet in a staccato rhythm that Maddie found irritating out of all proportion. She breathed in and out deeply in an effort to calm herself.

Grundy continued: "Ted also told us he was under the impression that Darren was going home with you."

"He got it wrong" Maddie replied quickly, conviction giving her voice more confidence. "I don't know what Darren said to Ted, but we never went home together. Never. I told you that the other day. Bella will tell you. Ask her."

"We did ask her and she supports your story" Lionel interjected. "But I'm afraid it's still her word against Ted's, and as she's your friend we would expect her to side with you." His sympathetic expression, so out of keeping with his words, gave him an ironic edge that Maddie was only now aware of. She suddenly distrusted the apparent friendliness that had encouraged her before, and wondered what sort of a game he was playing with her, they both were playing - a sort of cat-and-mouse gamble where they pressed certain buttons confident of eliciting known responses from her.

Maddie resolved to be firm from now on: "I walked home on my own at 5 o'clock" she reiterated.

"Perhaps Darren wanted to come home with you and you said no? Is that it?" Grundy suggested.

"No. He never said anything like that. I told you. I hardly knew him. I only talked to him for a little...hardly at all. I danced with him, at the beginning of the party, and then I didn't see him again. I swear, that's the truth."

There was only one lie in her story and it was a lie of omission. Maddie's self-defense, therefore, was spoken with a passionate conviction that made it hard to doubt her words.

But Grundy was not a man to be easily convinced: "Why do you think Ted was under the impression that

Darren was going home with you? Did he follow you perhaps? Without you realizing - or wanting him to?"

Maddie bowed her head and shook it slowly from side to side, feigning annoyance at their refusal to believe her: "No. No."

"Thank you then, for your assistance. We'll be going now." The policemen got to their feet.

To Maddie's great relief and surprise, Grundy and Lionel seemed disinclined to pursue the matter further, having accepted as true the one lie she had told during the interview.

"We may need to speak with you again. But that will be all for the time being."

Maddie rose and showed them to the door: "I'll see you out, then."

When Lionel smiled at her on his way out of the house, Maddie didn't return the compliment. She no longer set any store by his kindly demeanor. And she had a sneaking feeling she'd not seen the last of the two men.

CHAPTER FOURTEEN

W HEN THE HOUSE lights came up for the interval, Gabriel turned to Kate sitting beside him and touched her hand gently. "Did you want an ice c...cream or something?"

"No, it's all right. I don't like pushing my way through the crowds." Kate smiled warmly. "Are you glad we came?"

"Oh yes. V...very."

Kate had bought a copy of the program, which lingered on her lap. "Can I see?" asked Gabriel, indicating the booklet.

"Yes, of course" Kate replied.

As Gabriel leafed through the pages, Kate drank in the atmosphere of the theatre, relishing the chance to survey the ornate golden ceiling and the lively to and fro of people as they made their way to the bar or the cloakrooms, discussing the performance with one another. Even when three people on their row pushed past and she had to move her knees to the side to make room for them, her countenance didn't lose its contented and beatific expression. This was an experience she savored, one she hadn't had in years, and while Hamish had been alive, never expected to have again. Unlike Gabriel, her late husband had never inclined towards cultural outings.

Kate glanced at the friend from her childhood days, and marveled at how little he'd changed since a young man. Certainly, the years had given him a few wrinkles and turned his black hair white, but it was mostly his demeanor, which hadn't changed. Maybe because he'd never had a family or had to bear the responsibilities of fatherhood - she mused - Gabriel retained an air of youthful enthusiasm and sincerity uncommon in a man his age, which she found just as endearing as when she had first known him. His life of lonely bachelorhood might have turned another man bitter, but Gabriel kept that aspect of angelic sweetness for which he'd been named as a baby, a quality of placid acceptance of the world as it was.

Noticing that he was gazing at a particular photograph in the program, Kate gently moved Gabriel's fingers to reveal what interested him. "Maddie Cambay" she said, reading aloud the name under the photograph. "Oh, it says she plays Henrietta. Isn't that the girl who sang that last song? She did have a lovely voice."

"Yes" Gabriel agreed. "There's a b...biography of her here. She's only y...young, but she's already done quite a l...lot of things."

"So she has. It's not a very good photograph. It doesn't look at all like her, does it?" remarked Kate.

"I th...think she wears a w...wig in the play. She's not really b...blonde."

"Of course. How silly of me."

"B...but you're right. It's not a good ph...photograph."

"Oh yes, you told me the other night. You used to work as a photographer, didn't you? Do you still take any pictures?"

Gabriel nodded. "Only of the family now." There was a note of longing and sadness in his voice which Kate hadn't heard before, and all at once she wondered if he was satisfied with what he'd achieved in life. So many people she knew - herself included - had dreams that had never quite been realized, but most stopped dreaming when they reached a certain age, content to fill the gap with material comforts.

"Did you ever study photography? I can't remember. You seem to know a lot about it."

"No, I just p...picked it up through my w...work on the p...paper." He pointed at the program: "B...but I can tell you what's wrong with this photograph - it's sort of too p...posed and false, you see. It doesn't capture any of the girl's...p...personality."

"What, you mean, a photograph should tell you something about a person's inside as well as their outside?" enquired Kate.

Gabriel looked at her in surprise. "Y...yes, exactly. That's ex...xactly right."

Kate smiled. "Well, she's very pretty anyway, you can certainly tell that." She took the program back from Gabriel. "Could I look at it for a moment? I wanted to read about the history of the period. I do like to have a bit of background."

Gabriel fell silent for a few moments as Kate read, and seemed to be deep in contemplation or building up to saying something that was on his mind. When he did speak, the words blurted out in a rush: "D'you know why I was l...looking at th...that picture? The one of the g...girl?"

Kate shook her head and looked at Gabriel with an interested expression, glad that he had chosen to grant her an unprompted confidence.

"She reminds me of s...someone."

"Oh really?" Kate responded, intrigued. "Who is that?"

"You remember that g...girl I told you about th...the other night, when we were at the r...restaurant? The one I almost m...married?"

"Helen."

"Th...that's right. The girl reminds me of h...her."

Kate suddenly realized that this was something Gabriel had been preparing to get off his chest ever since showing her the photograph. She wished to find out more about the story behind his admission and help him if she could, without appearing pushy or prying. "Helen must have been very beautiful" she assayed. Gabriel nodded silently, his lips closed. "Do you still see her?" she asked, gently enticing him to reveal more.

"Oh no" Gabriel replied in an expressionless voice, his face slightly averted from hers.

"What a shame you never married."

"I w...would have done. Sh...she didn't want to" he confessed.

"Why ever not?" asked Kate sympathetically.

"She h...had her reasons." There was a brief pause. "She had a ch...child, you know. A d...daughter - her p... parents told me. I know it was m...mine. B...but sh...she didn't want to s...see me. They t...told me she didn't w... want to see me."

Kate stroked his arm gently with her hand. "I'm sorry," she murmured. His face was still averted, but she could see his Adam's apple bobbing up and down in his throat in an attempt to contain his emotion. "You know" she said softly, "your daughter might want to get to know you. After all, you are her father. Have you ever tried to contact her?"

Gabriel shook his head mournfully. "It didn't seem f... fair to Helen. After she asked me n... not to."

"But this all happened over twenty years ago, didn't it? What about *your* feelings? And what about your daughter's feelings? She'll be a young woman now, with her own opinions. I think you owe it to yourself, and to her, at least to try."

As the lights in the auditorium dimmed and the Second Act music began, Kate realized she'd been so wrapped up in Gabriel's problems that she'd completely forgotten about the play they'd come to see. Now the interval was over, she held his hand in the darkened theatre and hoped he would enjoy the rest of the performance. She'd had no idea of the pain and loneliness he must have suffered these past twenty-five years while she'd been living in Scotland. It wasn't something his family would ever speak about, even to good friends.

Somehow, she'd always imagined that Gabriel had wanted to remain a bachelor, had chosen to live alone. At least, she thought, there was still time for her to be his consolation and support during his remaining years. She never doubted for one second that he would wish this as much as her.

Maddie had hurried around Bristol's shopping center that afternoon, looking for appropriate goodbye cards to give to the director and the rest of the cast. She'd had to search long and hard, to find a picture on each card, which would inspire a suitably apt and witty comment about the show. And then she had to choose how many of the cast members to grace with cards: should she include on her list the two understudies, the orchestra musicians and the stage management team? She finally opted for the ten principal cast members, the understudies (whom she hardly knew but pitied, especially Sharon her understudy, who made the best of a two-line part in the chorus and had never been offered the opportunity to perform the greatly coveted starring role, due to Maddie's robust good health), the musical director and the pianist.

The most expensive card of all was of course reserved for the director, as Maddie was not above currying favor if it meant the chance of a part in his next production. The director - the young son of a theatrical impresario who, it was widely suspected, owed his success more to nepotism than any particular artistic flair - was expected to attend the last night cast party, even though he hadn't shown his face since opening night. Rumors circulated that he was secretly directing another show in London simultaneously, and that this was the reason for his frequent absence at rehearsals and his apparent lack of interest in their show once it had started the run.

Since her second interview with the police officers the day before, Maddie had made a determined effort to put the whole Darren Webster affair out of her mind. She kept reassuring herself that she only had one day left - one matinee and one evening show - before she could quit Bristol and return to London. And London had suddenly become her lodestar. She felt illogically certain that once she arrived back in the metropolis she would be safe, and the whole nightmare of that morning on the bridge would evaporate. Like a runner approaching the finishing line, she willed herself to hold out for those few extra yards, those few remaining hours, after which everything would be miraculously settled.

Perhaps if she hadn't been in such a heightened emotional state, she could have admitted to herself how irrational she was being. She knew in her heart of hearts that if the police suspected her of murder they would come after her, and find her, wherever she was. But she was in such a panicky condition; her only salvation was to cling to her belief that the worst would never happen. Her mind was in turmoil, there was no one she could turn to for advice, she had to maintain her composure enough to perform for the last few occasions, and this was her only strategy for coping.

Accordingly, in addition to buying last night cards, she did all the other things she would normally do to prepare for ending a run and going home. She rang the lodgers in her flat and arranged a time when they would be in to hand her back the keys. She packed most of her belongings at Bella's into a big suitcase, just leaving out the few essentials she would need the next day. She telephoned her agent to see if there would be any auditions for her in London the following week, and was disappointed to hear that there was nothing on the horizon. Her agent also informed her - sweetening the news with the encouraging phrases to which she inevitably resorted: *They really liked you, anyway, and they'll bear you in mind for other things in the future* - that Jeremy Coultairn hadn't offered Maddie the part of the estate agent in the television program, which came as no surprise to her. Maddie collected her final pay packet - with holiday pay - from the Company Stage Manager. And for her final chore, she made the usual duty call to her mother, merely telling her that the show had been an unqualified success and that she'd received some excellent reviews.

Maddie snatched a few brief minutes in her dressing room during the second half of the show, while she had a break before her reappearance in the final scene, to write the trite messages on her goodbye cards that she'd been preparing in her head. She was intending to distribute them the following evening, just before the very last performance.

Maddie could hear over the tannoy Bella's voice booming out the familiar lyrics of her popular belt number, and she couldn't resist a smile as she remembered the ruder version that she and Bella had concocted during rehearsals. The orchestra played the finishing chords of the song, and as the last notes died away the audience broke into tumultuous applause. The house was exceptionally good tonight, as it had been for most of the week. Maddie suspected that the final week of any show drew better than average audiences, because people often waited until it was their last opportunity to see the production.

As the dialogue of the penultimate scene drew to a close, Maddie stuffed the cards she'd been writing into her bag along with her biro, checked her appearance in the mirror and smoothed her blonde wig with practiced hands. Richard's soft voice over the tannoy announced: "Mr. Cooper, Mr. Denbigh, Miss Arnold, Miss Cambay, this is your call for the final scene. Please make your way to the stage for the final scene."

Maddie grabbed her jacket from the clothes rail and slung it round her shoulders, reflecting that this would be the last but one time she would perform this specific action, and that forty-eight hours from now she would be sitting in her bedsit flat in London, already feeling that the world of show business was a million miles away. There were always mixed feelings of relief and regret at the end of a show. Relief that all the little niggles that had been part of that particular show would no longer have to be endured, relief at being able to enjoy the comfort and privacy of home. Regret at losing contact with friends, at not having a regular working routine, at being thrown back into the whirlpool of rejection letters and auditions with disappointing outcomes and casting directors with empty promises to bear you in mind for the future. Ordinarily, the regret strongly outweighed the relief. But this time, the situation was different.

As Maddie turned to leave the room, she noticed a slip of white paper under the doorframe, and wondered when it could have got there and why she hadn't seen it before. Surely - she thought - she would have heard somebody slipping paper under the door while she'd sat in the dressing room writing her cards. And yet, as far as she could remember, it hadn't been there when she'd come in.

Her curiosity aroused, she picked up the paper and unfolded it. The words were made up of letters cut out from newspapers, more in an attempt at melodrama than anonymity:

Maddie Cambay.
I know you done it.

She stood in shocked silence holding the paper, feeling the blood rush to her head. When the second tannoy announcement came, this time singling out her name as the only one who hadn't yet reached the wings, she hardly heard it.

Maddie refolded the paper with trembling fingers and slid it into a pocket of her handbag, well out of sight. She dusted her pink, flushed face with white powder and hurried down the stairs.

Afterwards, people said she gave the best performance of the entire run that night.

The next morning, the more Gabriel tried to distract himself with occupations which he usually found pleasurable and fulfilling - such as gardening or developing a new set of photographs - the more he failed to erase from his mind the image of the girl he had seen at the theatre. Her face kept coming back to haunt him, sometimes blending into the face of the young Helen. And he remembered Kate's words and her exhortations to at least try and find his daughter. He felt driven to lay the ghost once and for all.

Gabriel possessed an old address book, which contained Helen's parents' address in York, the place to which he had sent a hundred letters that had never elicited a reply. It was pointless trying to contact the Blandfords: they would have been in their eighties by now if they were still alive, besides which they had never been particularly well disposed towards Helen's much older suitor.

But there was another name in the address book. Carol Thewliss was a friend of Helen's who had also participated in the anti-Vietnam demonstration in 1968 at which he and Helen had met. Carol had been living in London when he and Helen took their trip to the Far East in the summer of that year, and she had given them her address and telephone number in case they needed a place to stay when they returned to England. In the event they hadn't needed it, as neither of them had chosen to stay in London after all, Helen returning immediately to York and Gabriel to Bristol. But perhaps - he pondered to himself - Carol and Helen had kept in touch or remained friends for a while. It was a long shot but it was worth a try.

Gabriel took a deep breath and rang the telephone number in his book. The first time he tried, there was only an ansaphone message saying that "Donald and Joan are out at the moment." As Gabriel didn't like leaving a message in the circumstances, he was glad that on the second try - a couple of hours later - somebody answered, a middle-aged man with a rather plummy voice. To Gabriel's disappointment he said he'd never heard of a Carol Thewliss, although he and his family had been living in that flat for 15 years. He said he'd ask his wife and contact Gabriel if she had any ideas. As luck would have it, Joan rang back later to say that she *had* heard of a Carol Thewliss, though she was called Carol Parker now and living in Leicester. Carol was the daughter of the previous owners of the flat, and Joan was able to supply Gabriel with their number.

When he rang Carol's parents they seemed rather suspicious of his reasons for contacting their daughter, especially as he was secretive about revealing his reasons for wanting to speak to her. But when he mentioned that he'd also been a friend of Helen Blandford, they relented - having been fond of Carol's erstwhile schoolmate - and they gave him Carol's current telephone number in Leicester.

A few minutes later, Gabriel rang the number he'd been given and asked for Carol Parker. A woman with a flat Northern voice answered that it was she who was speaking. Gabriel explained how he'd known Helen and had met her, Carol, briefly on a march in London.

"Oh yes, I did use to do a lot of protesting in them days. Helen dragged me to all those demos. I didn't know what it was about really, just thought I might meet some boys." She gave a hearty laugh. "And I met you there, d'you say?"

"Yes. You gave me your ad...dress."

"I did, did I?" She laughed again. "That would have been typical."

"We went to the Far East together, H...Helen and I. You to...told us we could st..stay with you when we c... came back."

"Oh, I remember you now. Gabriel. But she used to call you Gabe, didn't she?"

"Th...that's right. She didn't like my full name."

"Gabe, yes. You went away for a few months, didn't you?"

"It was only supposed to be a few weeks, but we stayed s...six months."

"Quite a trip. And you never did come to stay with me?"

"No. Helen was p...pregnant when we came back. She w...went home to her p...parents."

"Pregnant, eh? She never told me about that."

"So you kept in touch?"

"Oh yeah, didn't see each other much, 'cos we were always living in different parts of the country, or she was off traveling somewhere. Sent Christmas cards though, that sort of thing."

"But...did she have the child, a child? Did she ever...?"

"Helen? Oh no, she never had any children. I remember that much."

"Are you sure?"

"Oh yes, positive. I think she would have told me something like that! No, Helen wasn't the children type, marriage and all that, what was it she used to say? Not my bag. We used to say some daft expressions didn't we, when we were young? She meant it, though."

"But, what happened to the b...baby?"

"She probably had it aborted, love. That would have been her style. Didn't want to be tied down, did she?"

"She was t...too far gone. When we got h...home. She was already the...three and a half months. Her parents t...told me she h...had the baby. That it was a g...girl."

"I don't know, love. Maybe she had it adopted. Or it died. Who can say? She certainly didn't tell me. Doesn't matter now though, does it? It's all too long ago. All water under the bridge, as they say."

Gabriel said goodbye and rang off, wishing he'd never phoned. All these years he'd been living with the illusion that somewhere out there, was the child that Helen had conceived with him - *his* child too - and hoping that one day he might meet the person who was a part of him. But now it seemed his dreams had been a miasma.

He'd wanted so much for it to be true - that by some miracle his daughter had wandered into his life, that Maddie Cambay was Helen's child - he had convinced himself it was possible. But what a ridiculous fantasy! Coincidences like that just didn't happen. In ludicrously sentimental American films maybe, but not in real life. There must be thousands of girls in the world who resembled Helen. She wasn't so unusual looking, and anyway how true to life was his memory of her? It was kept alive only by photographs in an album. Ridiculous to assume that, just because some girl bore a passing resemblance to his long lost love, she must be the child he'd been searching for - consciously or unconsciously - all these years.

Besides, Carol was absolutely right. It wasn't in Helen's nature to be a mother or a wife. That had been what drove them apart, as it *was* in his nature to be a father and husband. Perhaps that was why she hadn't responded to his letters - pathetically, as he could see it now, asking after the welfare of their child - not wanting to hurt his feelings by admitting that she'd had the baby adopted, when she knew how much it meant to him. In which case, there was even less chance of him ever finding out what had happened to her.

It was pointless to even try, he thought. He remonstrated with himself for his years of fruitless longing for what could never be. He told himself to forget the whole thing, concentrate on the present not the past, and accept life as it was.

CHAPTER FIFTEEN

M ADDIE HAD JUST completed packing a final few items into her overnight bag, when she heard Bella in the hallway downstairs calling her name. She assumed that Bella - impatient to leave for the theatre, having stated her intention not to be tardy for the final matinee performance - was checking whether Maddie's suitcase was ready to be stowed in the back of her car. Consequently, Maddie didn't bother to respond immediately to her friend but glanced round her little bedroom to confirm she hadn't forgotten anything, lugged the suitcase - heavy with recently acquired presents for friends back home - out on to the landing and hung her head over the bannister rail to give Bella the good news that she was finally primed to go, although she needed somebody's aid in getting the suitcase down the stairs. To her surprise and dismay, however, she was greeted not by Bella's cheerful demeanor but by the figures of two men, standing below her by the front door, which were becoming uncomfortably familiar.

The Detective Inspector, not having heard Maddie leave her room, was studying a trio of colorful china heads - made by Bella's artistic friend in lieu of the ubiquitous ducks - which were arranged to fly up the wall in the hallway, his hands clasped behind his back. The Detective Sergeant had his head lowered over his notebook and was humming to himself, following a popular tune which could be heard from Bella's radio in the kitchen.

Maddie took a deep breath as she watched the police officers, stifling her initial desire to run or hide, and steeled herself for the encounter. She knew there was no option but to face them.

Thinking to elicit some sympathy, she grabbed the handle of the suitcase and dragged it slowly after her down the stairs. It bumped unwillingly behind her, knocking painfully against her feet, which were clad only in thin jazz shoes, and the two policemen looked up on hearing Maddie's approach.

Maddie feigned mild surprise at noticing Grundy and Lionel. "Oh! I didn't realize you were here again. We're just leaving, actually."

"Yes, as Miss Marconi told us..." commenced Grundy.

At that moment, Bella - looking harassed - swept into the hallway from the kitchen: "I'm sorry for being rude earlier, but we're a bit pushed for time. Can I offer you chaps some tea or coffee?" she suggested brightly.

"No thank you, that won't be necessary" Grundy declined.

"We apologize if this visit is inconvenient," added Lionel.

"That's O.K. I'm sure you're only doing your job" replied Bella, before exiting again darting Maddie an encouraging glance, which seemed to say *I'm here if you need me.*

"So, what do you want?" demanded Maddie, failing to keep the bite of impatience from her voice.

"I'm afraid I'm going to have to ask you to accompany us to the station" Grundy said, maintaining his uncompromising stance with legs slightly apart and hands behind his back, while holding her eyes with a steely stare.

"What - now?" flustered Maddie, still grasping the handle of her suitcase as if it were a lifeline.

"I'm afraid so, yes."

There was a pause as Maddie looked at the police officers in turn, then gave a short exhalation of disbelief. "But...I'm going out. We're on our way to the theatre to do the matinee. I can't come *now*. Can't you see?"

"I am aware of that, Miss Wetherby, but this is a very urgent matter. I'm afraid you're not going to be able to conduct your business just yet."

Maddie hated Grundy at that moment, as he stood in the position of bulwark against which she would have no hope of prevailing. All the wheedling pleas, persuasive arguments, attempts to charm with flattery that she was contemplating died on her lips as she regarded his stony expression, utterly devoid of sympathy or understanding. Desperately, she turned to Sergeant Lionel, but his erstwhile friendliness had disappeared and his face was averted from hers in an attitude of indifference. She felt as if she'd unaccountably lost an ally in the younger policeman, but she didn't know how or why. There was nothing to do but accede to their demands.

The horrible cold sensation in her stomach which overwhelmed her - as if an iron door had closed upon her and she was already suffocating in a dark prison - persisted, as Maddie nodded mutely, dropped the handle she was clutching and let the suitcase fall to the ground with a thump and allowed the policemen to escort her to their waiting car. To her relief, they didn't consider it necessary to bind her wrists in handcuffs, but simply walked either side of their captive until they reached the vehicle.

Maddie - seeming smaller than usual sandwiched between the two large men - stumbled out of the house staring straight ahead of her, without even the will to look back or attempt to explain to Bella and her parents why she was departing without a word. Her suitcase remained in the middle of the hallway, like some forgotten baggage from the *Marie Celeste*.

As Maddie entered the car and took up her place in the back seat behind the two officers, she was aware of hearing - seeming to come from a great distance, as in some sort of nightmare - the crackling of their car radio issuing mysterious instructions. Grundy put the car into gear and they moved off, driving quickly through the residential streets towards the police station in the center of Bristol, the two policemen talking casually to each other and leaving Maddie to stare forlornly out of the window, feeling sick and desolate.

How differently this day had turned out from her expectations on rising that morning, full of energy and cheerful high spirits. She had been looking forward to doing the final two performances and afterwards to enjoying a meal with the cast at an expensive restaurant selected and paid for by the director, as the fitting finale to a very successful run. She'd been anticipating her departure from Bristol with mounting excitement, thinking of the friends she'd visit on her arrival back in London, the pleasure of having all her evenings free for social events and - most of all - the end of the nightmare that had started with Bella's party.

Now she knew and had to accept that none of those things were going to happen. She'd been living in Cloud Cuckoo Land, allowing herself to believe that she could escape so easily from the consequences of her actions. Maddie realized with a sinking heart that Grundy and Lionel must have some very strong motive for dragging her back to the police station at such short notice. She dreaded finding out what that motive was. Perhaps some new evidence had come to light that pointed the finger definitely at her. Perhaps the old man who'd witnessed the incident had suddenly had a change of heart and spoken out after all. Perhaps he hadn't seen the young man attacking her, but only appeared on the scene at the moment when Darren's body was hurled into the water, thus receiving the impression that Maddie was the aggressor. Maddie couldn't even remember now exactly when the old man had arrived, nor could she remember his expression as he'd looked at her for those few seconds before she ran away. Her memories had become hazy: she'd pushed the whole nightmarish incident so far down into her subconscious in an effort to forget it that retrieving those memories with any clarity was now virtually impossible.

Maddie could feel her fighting spirit beginning to evaporate, at the thought that the police might have acquired some irrefutable evidence. She asked herself now whether it would be better to confess the truth and reveal the whole story - tell them that, yes, she had been responsible for hitting Darren so that he fell to his death, but she had good reasons for it, he'd been attacking her and she'd acted in self-defense. Perhaps they would confound all her expectations and believe her. Perhaps she wouldn't, after all, face a murder charge, once they were aware of all the circumstances. Perhaps she should have just told the truth in the first place. But she had been too afraid then, and blindly certain that she'd never find herself in this position.

The voices of the police officers were low and serious. Maddie wondered if these men ever laughed together, played stupid pranks or larked about like children. They were so unlike herself and her thespian friends, to whom life was there to be enjoyed and crammed with as much fun and play as possible. She pondered what kind of person would be drawn to police work: probably - she assumed - somebody who took life seriously, who was never frivolous or lighthearted. Maddie often exercised her actor's muscles by imagining herself in another life, with a different job, a different set of priorities, a different background. So now she mentally tried on the role of police officer, like a new coat in a clothing store. But it was hard to place herself in their mindset, there being so few parallels between herself and them. They were people with whom she had nothing in common, no ties of experience or attitude.

She had no friends in this place or the place where she was going. And she had never felt so isolated.

The car pulled up at the police station - a grim, brick building in the industrial heart of the town - and Maddie was ushered into a waiting room, where she sat alone to attend her destiny. She had little to do but wrap her hands around each other in anxious contemplation and stare at the plain, white-faced clock on the wall - resembling something from an old-fashioned schoolroom - which proclaimed the time as ten minutes past three.

D.S. Lionel had informed Maddie on their arrival at the station that she had a right to demand the presence of her solicitor during the interview, and now she racked her brains to think of someone. Never having needed such a thing before this moment, the names of no potential solicitors to represent her came to her mind. But as she waited on her black plastic chair to be called into the interview room, a thought occurred to her. She had a vague recollection of her mother mentioning a relative who lived in Bristol, a cousin who worked for a firm of solicitors. She remembered her mother enclosing the phone number of this woman in one of her many letters, exhorting Maddie to call on her while she was in Bristol. But being too preoccupied with her own affairs and busy with her friends, Maddie had never taken up her mother's proposal. Maddie wished fervently that she'd bothered to call her relative before now, or that she'd had the presence of mind to bring her Filofax with her, which contained her cousin's telephone number hastily scribbled in one of the back pages.

She jumped up from her seat and spoke to the Desk Sergeant, managing to keep her voice quite calm as she informed him that she wished to have a solicitor present during her interview.

"You can call him from here" replied the young officer, indicating a black telephone on the desk to his

right, in a bored and offhand manner. He gave the merest glance in Maddie's direction before turning promptly to attend to a member of the public who had just entered the front door of the police station.

"Her. And the problem is--" began Maddie.

"What?" The Desk Sergeant swiveled his eyes and frowned back at Maddie, as if accusing her of deliberately causing him aggravation.

"The problem is that I don't know her telephone number."

"What's the name?" the young man barked, ducking under the desk to search for an object beneath it.

"Eva...erm... I can't remember. Eva..." Maddie felt foolish but her brain was refusing to co-operate. Her mind had gone a complete blank on her cousin's second name. She screwed up her face and scoured her memory to recall it. *What was Eva's last name?* It was something a bit peculiar, foreign sounding, beginning with D, or was it G... "Look - I can't remember her last name. But she's a relation of mine, a distant relation. I've got her telephone number in my Filofax, but that's in my shoulder bag at my friend's house. I should have brought it with me but I didn't have time, I mean, I didn't think about it. Couldn't I just ring...my mother in York and ask her. She'll have a note of it, you see."

"You're only allowed one phone call," snapped the Desk Sergeant, as his head bobbed back up. "Hang on a minute" he barked to the fraught looking middle-aged man who had approached the desk and was now hovering impatiently beside Maddie. "Trevor" he boomed into a room behind him in a voice that had never known inhibition: "Have you got that register of local solicitors, mate?"

"Yep" came the response, and in a few seconds an A4 sized black folder was flung unceremoniously on to his desk.

"Do you know what firm she works for?" the young man demanded, not looking at Maddie as he opened the folder.

"Erm...No I don't, I'm afraid."

The Desk Sergeant graced Maddie with a look of withering contempt and thrust the folder under her nose. "Here you'll have to look for yourself, while I deal with this man. Can I help you, sir?" He turned his attention to the older man.

Maddie thumbed through the pages, feeling more and more stupid, as the names swam in alien formations before her eyes. Looking up in despair, Maddie scanned the room wildly, before her gaze came to rest on a gold watch adorning the wrist of the man next to her. His tanned arm was beating the desk in anger as he explained that his car had been clamped and towed away in error. Then it came to her in a flash. Goldstein. Eva Goldstein. That was her cousin's name. Hurriedly, Maddie returned to the register and flipped through the alphabetical index, quickly locating her cousin's name listed under a firm of solicitors who had an office in the center of Bristol.

"I've found the number," she announced triumphantly to the Desk Sergeant. "Could I make my telephone call, please?"

Without replying, the young man pushed the black telephone towards her, and Maddie punched out the number with quivering fingers and a thumping heart. As Maddie made her connection, the middle-aged man stormed away, and she noticed the Desk Sergeant turn his attention back to her, now following her constantly with his eyes and obviously intending to eavesdrop on her conversation. Feeling his gaze boring into her as she spoke into the mouthpiece, Maddie wanted to remind him bitterly that she wasn't a hardened criminal willing to spend her life on the run, just an unlucky girl who'd acted foolishly and now was being made to pay for it.

"Can I speak to Eva Goldstein, please?" It seemed to take an age for the receptionist to put her through. Meanwhile, the Desk Sergeant's eyes kept flicking back to Maddie, and she noticed that her officers - Grundy and Lionel - were both in the corridor now, waiting outside the interview room with impatient expressions. But she turned her back on them and clung to the line, not intending to be harassed into having an interview with no solicitor present if she could possibly help it. The relief she felt when the phone was finally answered - by a pleasant and sympathetic sounding woman with an educated voice - was enormous.

"Hello. My name's Madeleine Wetherby. My mother gave me your number. She thought maybe we could get together while I'm in Bristol."

"Oh yes, Madeleine, I remember. Your mother told me you might call. How nice to hear from you. Are you going to be in Bristol for long?"

"No, well actually...the thing is, I'm really sorry I've left it so long to call you, but I'm in a bit of a fix at the moment and I wondered if you could help me."

"I'll certainly try."

"Mum said that you were a solicitor, and I need a solicitor."

"I see." The temperature of the voice changed, from warm and lighthearted to more serious, though not unfriendly. "What's the problem?"

"Well...it's rather awkward to tell you over the phone. I wondered if you could come here. I'm at the police station, the big one in the middle of town. I don't know the address exactly..."

"It's all right, I know the address. Have the police brought you in for questioning?"

"Yes, that's right." The fact that Eva had so quickly divined the situation filled Maddie with a welcome sense of comfort. Here at last was someone she could confide in.

"In that case, I'll be over there as soon as I can. Don't worry; it won't take me long, I don't live too far away. Just sit tight and insist they wait till I get there. O.K.?"

"Yes. Thank you, Eva. Thank you."

"Don't mention it. I'm glad to help. I'll see you soon."

Maddie put the phone down, realizing only now how close to tears she'd been throughout the conversation. Having to explain her predicament to a stranger had brought all her emotions bubbling to the surface. But now she felt an enormous release of her burden, to have Eva coming to help her. At last, she would have someone sympathetic with whom she could share the truth.

Maddie asked the Desk Sergeant to inform Grundy and Lionel - who had now disappeared from the corridor - that she wasn't prepared to be interviewed until her solicitor arrived. Then she returned to the waiting room and resumed her seat beneath the schoolroom clock.

She waited there for twenty minutes, counting each one as it ticked by. There were magazines to read, spread out on a low table, but she was far too nervous to contemplate looking at them. She could see through the open door of the room as people in uniform scurried past, chattering together with an unknown purpose, and calling to each other across corridors or through double doors. At one point, a sullen looking young man wearing handcuffs was led past her by a fresh-faced W.P.C. He threw Maddie a quick, envious glance. But he was the only person to take notice of her.

Maddie tried to concentrate on character exercises, to take her mind off her anxiety. For every person that walked past, she concocted a history. She built up a picture of their family background, what sort of house they lived in, whether they were married, what they liked to eat for breakfast. Maddie always enjoyed this game; in fact her mind was so preoccupied with it that she didn't hear her name being called out by the Desk Sergeant until he'd repeated it three times. With a start that made her heart race - realizing that Eva must have arrived - Maddie rose from her chair and passed through into the entrance.

Sure enough, a woman in her early forties stood at the front desk, and she smiled warmly at Maddie as she noticed her approach and extended her hand. "Hello, you must be Madeleine. I'm Eva Goldstein. Very pleased to meet you. I'm sorry it's in such inauspicious circumstances." Eva had a frizzy mop of dark hair, slightly greying at the temples, and was dressed in a smart black suit and white shirt. Her eyes were large and grey and slightly staring, but with a genuine warmth and compassion in their expression.

Maddie decided at once that she liked her, and she regretted not having got in touch with her before, when she could have been a friend rather than a relative beseeching a favor. Maddie's instant reaction to strangers was based on intuitive feeling, and as something about Eva reminded Maddie of a favorite aunt of hers who had died, perhaps that accounted for her immediate trust of the unknown woman.

Eva took charge of things quite naturally, and informed the Desk Sergeant that she was going to have a word with "her client" for a few minutes, before Maddie's interview with Grundy and Lionel. Then she and Maddie returned to the empty waiting room for a speedy consultation. It was all flashing past Maddie too quickly: she wanted to explain everything to Eva in great detail, to tell her not only the events but all the emotions surrounding them. But Eva wanted to concentrate purely on the facts - just for the time being, she assured Maddie - and as she scribbled rapidly in a neat little hand on her large notebook, she looked up from time to time to encourage her client to continue with the exposition.

Ten minutes later, the two women were shown into the interview room, where Grundy already sat in attendance. Maddie noticed to her surprise that Sergeant Lionel wasn't there, but instead a young W.P.C. was placed in the corner taking notes. The Detective Inspector silently motioned Maddie to a chair behind a small desk and positioned himself opposite her, his head bowed initially in thought. A tape recorder lay on the desk between them, which Grundy switched on as soon as he commenced speaking. Eva occupied the chair beside Maddie. Before starting the interview, Grundy gave Maddie the usual caution and stated the time and date in a forceful voice, bending his head into the tape recorder's microphone.

Incongruously, it seemed to Maddie, she could hear the cheep of birds outside, through the small high window with the bars across it, and that comforted her and reminded her that there was still a real, normal world where things like this didn't happen. Maddie fought the confusion that filled her head with cotton wool. She commanded herself to get a grip on her emotions and make a clear decision on how much of the truth to tell the police. But everything was happening so swiftly that she felt completely passive, like a pawn in somebody else's chess game. Her mind was crammed with thoughts and possible decisions that buzzed around like flies, never settling long enough for her to grasp them. She had forgotten all about the last night meal or the fact that the understudy would be going on for her for the matinee performance and possibly for the final evening performance as well. By the time the interview began, Maddie felt almost paralyzed with fear, her voice barely audible.

Firstly, the Detective Inspector went over with Maddie all the statements she had made to him and Lionel during their first two interviews with her at Bella's house. He checked and re-checked every minute detail, all of which he or Lionel had recorded in a notebook. The more Maddie heard the things she'd said before repeated back to her, the more nervous she became. She'd forgotten half of the things she'd said, and now it all sounded contradictory and false and she could no longer be sure how much of it was true. When Grundy came to the part of her story where she talked about walking home from Bella's party, he altered tack slightly:

"You say you walked home at about 5 o'clock in the morning and you were entirely alone?"

"Yes."

"Tell me again the route you took from Bella Marconi's house to your digs."

Maddie described in detail the exact route she'd taken.

"So you walked across the bridge at about 5.30 a.m.?"

"Yes."

"And you didn't see anyone else on the bridge?"

"No."

"You didn't see Darren Webster on the bridge?"

Maddie replied before Eva had a chance to confer with her: "No."

"Because Darren Webster fell from the bridge at some time in the early hours of that morning. When his body was found he had a severe head injury, a blow to the left side of his skull from a heavy object. Somebody must have knocked Darren pretty damn hard with something, so that he lost his balance and fell into the water." The Detective Inspector glared at Maddie, awaiting her response, but she kept her head down and said nothing.

"You met Darren at Bella's party the night before. You danced with him. He even kissed you. His friend Ted said he was under the impression that Darren was going home with you. You were on the bridge - on your way home - at about the same time that Darren was killed. And you still maintain that you didn't see him there? That you were alone?"

Maddie gave a monosyllabic reply that was too soft to hear. Eva leaned in and whispered something in her ear.

Grundy ordered Maddie to repeat her response, loudly enough for the tape and the W.P.C. with the notebook to record it.

"I was alone when I reached the bridge."

With a heavy sigh, Grundy produced an object from his pocket, which he placed on the table between him and Maddie: "Do you know what this is?"

Maddie stared at it and nodded.

"Please give us a spoken reply, Miss Wetherby."

"Yes."

"Could you tell us what it is?"

"A diabetic pen."

"And who does the pen belong to?"

There was no denying it. She recognized the familiar and distinctive shape of the object. Her name was printed on the side in colored Dymotape letters. She knew that without looking. "To me."

"Somebody found this pen on the bridge on June 3rd. Do you remember losing it?"

"Yes."

"Where did you lose it?"

Maddie hesitated. "I don't remember."

"Do you remember the circumstances of how you lost it?"

Maddie shook her head. "No." She would deny everything. That was the safest way. She would mask herself in a cloak of amnesia.

"Did you carry it in your bag?"

"Yes."

"So it must have fallen out of your bag."

"Yes."

"How did it fall out of your bag?"

"I don't remember."

"You don't remember" the D.I. echoed wearily. "Could it have fallen out of your bag when you swung your bag like this?" He demonstrated the motion that Maddie had surely made when she had hit Darren. She wondered helplessly if they had spoken to the witness. Why were they playing cat and mouse with her if they knew everything anyway? How could they guess - otherwise - what had happened? She stared at him dumbly and said nothing.

While Grundy waited for her response, Eva leaned in to Maddie again and whispered: "He's making suppositions, he's got no witnesses or he'd have brought them up. Don't admit to anything."

Maddie breathed deeply and continued to stare at the Inspector, refusing to respond to his goading.

"My client has no comment," declared Eva.

Finally, Grundy sighed and seemed to make his mind up. He said, in a sonorous tone: "Madeleine Wetherby, I am arresting you on suspicion of the murder of Darren Webster. You do not have to say anything but anything you do say..."

"Now, look here--" began Eva, but her words were drowned out by Maddie.

"No! No! No!" she practically screamed. "I didn't kill him! It wasn't murder! It wasn't like that! You don't understand!" Then Maddie broke down and wept, the tears coming out in great gasping sobs, a welcome release from the tension of the previous hour.

The W.P.C. brought her a box of paper hankies and supplied cups of tea all round. Meanwhile, the Detective

Inspector switched off the tape recorder and drew thoughtfully on a cigarette, hardly taking his eyes from Maddie.

When Maddie had recovered sufficiently, Grundy asked if she wished to change her story and make a revised statement. After seeking Eva's advice, Maddie agreed to do this. She found that the relief of confession was sweeter than she'd imagined. This time, she told the D.I. everything. The complete truth and the whole story with no facts altered or missing. How Darren had bothered her at the party and she had tried to avoid him after their initial dance. How he had followed her home and caught up with her at the bridge. How he had tried to rape her and brought out a knife from his pocket. How she had hit him - in self defense - with her bag, not meaning to kill him, not meaning for him to fall, just intending to stun him briefly so she could get away. She apologized for not having told the truth straight away, explaining that she'd been afraid no one would believe her.

Grundy seemed most concerned about the knife: "You say Darren held a knife to your throat. Do you know what happened to the knife when Darren fell into the river? Was he still holding it? Could it have been thrown from his hand into the street?"

"I don't know. I really don't know," said Maddie, shaking her head miserably.

"No knife has been reported as found, and we did search the area after the pen was brought to us..."

"There was a witness. He would have seen the knife" Maddie interjected. Suddenly, the old man seemed to her more of a potential ally than a foe. So long as she hadn't

196

been arrested for Darren's killing, a witness who could verify her presence at the scene of the crime was a threat. But now that she'd been arrested anyway and had told the police everything, a witness could confirm her story of what really happened that morning. The old man may have seen her struggling. And surely, she judged, if he arrived at the bridge soon enough to see Darren attacking her, he must have spotted the knife as well and realized the implications.

He hadn't attempted to rescue her from Darren, but he was an old man and events had moved so quickly there probably hadn't been time. All at once, Maddie wished she had tried before now to contact him, to win him to her side or at least make sure he understood. She'd acted like such a fool, burying her head in the sand and pretending everything would be all right if she just ignored it. If only - she wished - she had dared to confide in someone and take their advice; they might have suggested a more sensible course of action. But as usual she'd been too proud and rebellious, too scared of opening her heart to anyone. And this time, her reticence had proved disastrous.

The Detective Inspector questioned Maddie about this witness, and she told Grundy all she could truthfully remember. But she knew so little about the old man, beyond the flash of his face on her memory and the knowledge that he'd been at the bridge for a few seconds. Grundy regarded Maddie with evident suspicion, as if he believed the old man to be a convenient figment of her imagination, appearing in her story just in the nick of time. But Maddie privately resolved to enlist Eva's aid in finding the witness, realizing now how essential it was that they persuade the old man to speak in her defense.

When her confession and interview were completed, Grundy asked a junior police officer to lead Maddie away to a cell. Ironically, now that she was a prisoner officially under arrest, the people at the police station treated Maddie with more consideration. The young P.C. who guided her to the cell, told Maddie that, before being incarcerated for the night, she was allowed to telephone anyone she wished.

To Maddie's surprise, the person she wanted most to speak to at that moment was Paul. She felt that he was the least likely person to judge or criticize and the most likely to offer support. Eva reassured Maddie as best she could, telling her not to worry and that she would find her the best possible defense lawyer. The solicitor promised to telephone or visit the police station every day to let Maddie know the progress of events. She assured Maddie that she would do her utmost to procure a reasonable bail arrangement, so that Maddie wouldn't have to spend long in jail. And, to Maddie's sincere gratitude, Eva offered to ring her mother and explain, as delicately as she could, what had happened.

Once alone in her cell, with the worst behind her, Maddie thought of the theatre for the first time in hours, remembering that it was the final night of *Puttin' on the Ritz*. The world of show business seemed a million miles away now. Maddie wondered how the others were coping without her and whether chaos was currently ensuing backstage at the Bristol Old Vic. She thought of her suitcase, lying where she had left it in the middle of Bella's hallway, and she wondered idly if Bella's dad had shifted it into a cupboard somewhere. She thought of Bella and Peter and Nigel and wondered what they would be thinking now and what they would be saying to each other. She imagined she could almost hear their voices.

———⌒⌒⌒⌒⌒⌒———

At about that time, chaos *was* ensuing backstage at the Bristol Old Vic. On realizing that Maddie had left with the two police officers, the first thing Bella had done was ring the police station to find out what was going on. Despite Bella's protestations to the Desk Sergeant that it was essential Ms. Cambay were released to do the matinee, the man in question was singularly unhelpful. He refused to tell her when the police might be finished with Maddie. He wouldn't even let Bella speak to her friend. He told Bella she was welcome to call back later if she wished, but he could offer no guarantee that Maddie would be released in time to do the matinee or the evening show, if at all.

The only thing Bella could do was inform the Company Stage Manager that Maddie would be off for the matinee and possibly that night as well and tell him to prepare the understudy to go on in her place. Bella arrived at the theatre alone, in an uncharacteristically subdued mood. When Peter and Nigel popped by for their usual cup of tea before the half, she had to tell them what had happened, and the shock and dismay on their faces only made her feel worse. The last night present she had bought for her friend lay forlornly on Maddie's side of the dressing table, along with the cards sent up from other members of the cast as yet unaware of Maddie's disappearance.

Between the matinee and the evening performance, Bella rang the police station again, and this time was told that Maddie definitely wouldn't be released, as she'd been arrested on suspicion of murder. At least, this time, Bella was allowed to speak to Maddie on the telephone. Maddie sounded so dejected that her normally bubbly voice was almost unrecognizable. Bella - usually so optimistic and good at showing people the positive side of the coin - hardly knew what to say to console her friend.

"Look - it's a mistake, isn't it? They must have made a mistake. They can't really think that you would...that you could..."

"Bella..." Maddie bit her lip to stop it from trembling. "They haven't made a mistake. It's just that...I just...it's not as bad as they think. I mean, I didn't intend what...I didn't intend anything..." Maddie couldn't speak any further for a few seconds, but sat breathing deeply and staring down at the floor, feeling her heart beat like a drum in her chest.

"Take your time, love" soothed Bella. "Tell me what happened. Why didn't you tell me before? You must have been keeping this to yourself, all this time. It must have been terrible. You should have told me."

"I know I should. I almost did. But it was just too difficult, you know?"

"Sure. Well don't worry now. I just wish I could have helped you."

There was silence for a few moments, then Bella continued. "Was that why those police officers who came round to the theatre wanted to grill you again?"

"Yes."

"Dad mentioned something about them coming to the house, the day before yesterday wasn't it, asking you about the party. I was feeling paranoid, after that hassle I had with them before, remember? I asked Jono if he'd left any spliffs in the living room, and he said no, but I don't think he'd remember anyway." Bella gave a short laugh, trying to lighten the mood of the conversation.

"It's a bit worse than that, isn't it?" Maddie breathed, in a small voice.

"Yeah. Do you want to tell me about it?"

After a pause, Maddie said: "O.K. I was dancing with this bloke at the party, I don't know if you saw him..."

"When was that? After you had your tiff with Alan?"

"Yeah, after."

"I don't remember. I was probably too far gone, or in the kitchen or something."

"Anyway, I was just dancing with him, you know. I wasn't leading him on or anything, we didn't even kiss... well, he tried to but I pushed him off. I wasn't in the mood, not after the thing with Alan."

"Sure."

"I don't know if he...thought that I...Well anyway, I'd forgotten all about him when I left your house--"

"You walked home, didn't you--"?

"Yeah. Anyway, he must have followed me."

"I knew you should have taken a taxi. I should have insisted..."

"Come on, Bella. It's not your fault."

"The little creep. So, what did he do?"

"I don't know why, maybe I was in a daydream, but I didn't hear him following me till I got to the bridge. The suspension bridge, you know?"

"Yeah."

"All of a sudden he was just there, and he was walking behind me and he wouldn't leave me alone..."

In the pause that followed, Bella guessed what Maddie was driving at: "Did he...did he attack you?"

"Yes he did. I know he was small and everything, but it was the shock, you know? He took me by surprise; I wasn't expecting him to leap on me like that. Anyway, one minute he was behind me and the next minute he was...pushing me back against the wall and he was trying to...you know..."

"He was trying to rape you?"

"Yeah."

"Shit. The bastard."

"I just wanted to get him off me. I just wanted to...stop him. I never meant to..."

"What did you do? Did you hit him?"

"Yeah. With my handbag."

"Good for you."

"And it had that aromatherapy burner in it that you'd given me for my birthday. I'd forgotten it was in there, but it must have been that that hit him on the head, because..."

"It knocked him out, did it?"

"Not just out. It knocked him over. Over the bridge."

"Into the river?"

"Yeah."

Bella let out a sigh of relief. "But that's an accident, my love. A stupid accident. You didn't mean to kill him, did you?"

"No, but..."

"Surely they'll understand that. Why are they saying it's a murder charge? You were just defending yourself against a rapist."

"I should have told them in the first place. Then they might have believed me. But I thought they wouldn't find out. So I kept quiet."

"Still, that shouldn't--"

"If I'd told them immediately they might have believed it was just self-defense. But I didn't..."

"You were frightened--"

"I know, but now they think I've got something to hide. Because I lied to them earlier on they think I'm lying now." Maddie moaned. "Why didn't I just tell them? I'm so stupid. I've ruined everything..."

"Don't be daft. Have you got yourself a good lawyer?"

"I've got a solicitor called Eva Goldstein. She's really nice. She's a cousin of mine I've never met before..."

"And is she going to get you a good defense barrister? I can recommend someone if--"

"I'm sure she'll do her best for me. She's on my side."

"So she should be. Oh, you poor thing. I'm so sorry, Maddie. I wish you'd confided in me earlier..."

"So do I" said Maddie miserably.

"Anyway, don't worry. Everything's going to be fine. Things are in a right mess here at the theatre, of course."

"Really?" Maddie giggled, glad to get on to lighter subjects and indulge in a bit of gossip. "I guess Sharon's going on for me tonight. How's she taking it?"

"Bloody hell, she's not nearly ready. You should have seen her at the matinee! I felt sorry for the audience who'd paid to see you and got her instead--"

"Well, it probably wasn't just me they came to see--"

"She really cocked up the big number, it was so embarrassing. Peter's taking her through the music again now. He's pissed off at having to rehearse on the last afternoon. Good thing for her that Dexter didn't see the balls up she made, he isn't watching the show till tonight."

"I thought he said he was coming to the matinee as well. God, that man's a tosser!"

"Not too loudly, my dear. He may be a tosser, but he's one you'd like to work for again. Shit, this is such a drag that you can't do the last night. We're going to have a great party--oh, sorry, I don't want to make you feel bad..."

"That's O.K. Say hi to everyone from me, won't you."

"Of course I will, my love. We're all behind you - well, apart from Sharon, she's pretty thrilled to finally get her big moment, not that she's a patch on you of course. But look, I'm going to have to dash now or I'll be late--"

"That'll make a change."

"Don't be cheeky. No, listen, I'll phone you again tomorrow or whenever."

"Great."

"And remember, if you need anything, I'm here for you."

"Thanks, Bella. You're a pal."

"Keep your chin up, girl. Everything's going to be fine. You'll see."

Maddie wished she could believe her.

CHAPTER SIXTEEN

THE BRIDE WAS a short dumpy girl in her early twenties. The dress she had chosen looked vaguely ridiculous, emphasizing as it did her stout little figure with yards of stiff white taffeta trimmed with cream silk. But her smile was radiant, as she stood outside the church in its somewhat overgrown graveyard, clutching her new husband proudly by the hand. Her name was Tina and she was one of Gabriel's many nieces.

Gabriel - who had been persuaded to take the photographs, as he nearly always did at family weddings - ushered the surrounding relations into neat little family groups around the bride and her groom. He didn't shout "smile please" or "ready" as many photographers do when about to take a picture, but simply raised his left arm in a significant gesture, as if ordering his troops into battle. Fortunately, everybody had been primed to his methods, and donned their smiles accordingly.

Funnily enough, however, the best photographs from these occasions were invariably the ones when Gabriel *hadn't* raised his arm, the ones which captured a private look or gesture or a guest in mid-conversation. Gabriel's photographs were renowned for their natural, unposed quality, and the reason was that - as photography was his passion not his job - he took many more pictures than he'd been asked to, for the sheer enjoyment of perfecting his craft.

Gabriel was unperturbed by the bustle and the buzz of conversation, which became increasingly raucous as the guests wandered about the grounds longing for the promised champagne and sandwiches of the reception. He possessed the type of mind that could cut out unwanted distractions and focus with absolute concentration on the taking of photographs. So he was now, moving the people around like pawns on a chessboard, arranging them in neat configurations to suit his artistic taste. He enjoyed being the photographer at weddings because it gave him a particular function and kept him from having to make small talk with strangers - something he abhorred. He was less pleased than the other guests, therefore, when the photographs had all been taken, the bride and groom had been driven off in their horse and cart (complete with a rather bored looking liveried footman, a special treat paid for by the bride's mother) and it was time to wander 500 yards down the road to the school hall where the reception was being held.

Long trestle tables had been laid out and names allocated to each place. Gabriel was glad to find himself seated at a table with his brother, sister-in-law and nephew. There was only one person at his table whom Gabriel didn't know, and that was Charlie, an old school friend of his nephew's who had travelled over from America for the occasion. Charlie had "made good" running his own pizza business in Chicago, and he'd been out there so long that his once gentle Bristolian lilt had been replaced by an abrasive mid-Atlantic twang. Not only that, but his personality too, had taken on a rather aggressive American edge, which Gabriel found disconcerting and unpleasant.

Charlie insisted on asking Gabriel questions of a personal nature, which the other people sitting at the table would have known better than to attempt. When the conversation drifted quite naturally to the increasingly young age at which people were marrying these days and the large percentage of those marriages which ended in divorce, Charlie blurted out: "Didn't you ever get married, Gabriel?" And in response to Gabriel's mortified shake of the head, he continued unabashed, "Why ever not?"

Unfortunately for Gabriel, the other duologues around the table had stilled and everybody fell silent, seemingly awaiting his response. There was no option but to tell the truth: "I n...nearly did once."

"Oh, ho, ho - you're a dark horse! Who was that, then?"

"A girl I u...used to know. Called H...Helen."

To Gabriel's great relief, at that moment there was a loud bang from nearby, and one of the guests on the top table - whom Gabriel recognized as the bride's father - clapped his hands together and called out: "Silence, everybody, it's time for the speeches."

There was a general coughing and rustling of expectation as Stuart - the Best Man, who was also seated at the top table - rose to his feet. Stuart's perspiring face was buried in a sheaf of notes written on postcards, which he clutched in his hand. "Erm...I've never actually done this before but...I'm very glad that Robin chose me as his best man because..." He broke off and cleared his throat.

"We can't hear you. Speak up!" came a strident voice from the back, and Gabriel turned to see a rather overweight woman clad in a loudly clashing striped dress, who was rather tipsily clutching a glass of champagne.

Stuart coughed into his right fist and raised his voice a fraction, as he repeated: "I'm glad Robin chose me as his best man because, I believe I'm going to be allowed to accompany the happy couple on their honeymoon in Jamaica."

There was a ripple of laughter. "Isn't that right, Robin?" asked Stuart, addressing the groom, who was sitting adjacent to him. Robin's face was creased with amusement and he shook his head, wordless. His cheeks had gone bright pink. Gabriel noticed that the bride, sitting next to her new husband clutching his hand, was sporting a rather bewildered smile, as if she knew she should be laughing but wasn't sure why.

"Well, perhaps not..." continued Stuart. "Anyway, I wish them both well and I hope they have a wonderful holiday." He cleared his throat again and consulted the notes on his next postcard. "As some of you may know, I've been acquainted with Robin for quite some years. In fact, we're old school chums. So, erm...I've got ample evidence of his good character from an early age..."

The room fell silent, waiting for the inevitable embarrassing incidents to be related.

"Robin's always been a generous sort of chap. I remember the time when he very kindly passed on to me the German measles, which he'd contracted. In fact, I think he passed it on to the whole school, if I remember rightly..." This time, the laughter was more genuine. Robin smiled and nodded at his bride. "Still - I didn't mind too much, as it meant I could miss quite a few lessons...Erm... Now, I'm not at all surprised that Robin's ended up in the profession he's chosen, as a tax inspector, because from an early age he showed a natural tendency to enjoy poking about in other people's business..." Laughter greeted this observation, and some knowing looks from Robin's parents.

"Every year when we had the Easter Egg Hunt at Robin's house, Robin's mum - I don't know if you'll remember this..." He turned to the woman in question and she shook her head, unable to predict his next words. "Robin's mum used to spend hours hiding the hardboiled eggs which she'd decorated all over the garden, and we kids were supposed to find as many as we could. Now, we couldn't understand why our friend here..." He put his hand on the groom's shoulder for maximum comic effect. "Was always able to find many more eggs than the rest of us, until I realized one day, that he'd actually been standing at the upstairs window watching his mum hiding them."

A roar of laughter broke out. "The poor woman didn't stand a chance, did she?" Stuart looked flushed with success, having produced the hilarity he wanted from the listening audience. He waited until the mirth subsided, and then continued in the same vein.

Stuart's confidence increased after this, to such an extent that after a while he threw his notes down on to the table and carried on without them, having obviously learned his speech by rote anyway. When he sat down after ten minutes, many of the guests turned to each other and commented on how good they thought he'd been and how much better than they'd expected. After Stuart, it was the turn of the bride's father. He spoke in a loud booming voice with great authority and little humor, about the sanctity of marriage and how glad he was to see his only daughter wed to such a promising young man. During his pronouncements, there was an atmosphere of restlessness amongst the crowd, and a desire to get on with the next and more interesting part of the ritual.

Following the speeches, it was Gabriel's duty once more to act as paparazzo, and he gathered up his camera with alacrity and crept to the edge of the raised platform to snap the speakers. When he returned to his table for the wedding cake, he was relieved to find Charlie deep in earnest conversation with his old school chum.

There was to be a ceilidh that evening in the hall, and Gabriel was enjoined by the bride to continue taking photographs of that part of the occasion as well: "I'm sure you could take some funny pictures of this lot square dancing", she said with a tipsy giggle. The guests were required to leave the hall for a couple of hours, so that the tables could be cleared away ready for the dancing. In addition, the earlier clouds had lifted and it was a pleasantly sunny evening. Gabriel and his brother and sister-in-law elected to take a stroll in the balmy summer's air, his nephew and Charlie having gone back to the farm to get changed into less formal clothes.

Rex bought a local newspaper at the village shop, and the three family members sat on a bench by the green, under the shade of a large apple tree, its fruit just beginning to ripen. Rex read his paper, and Gabriel and Brenda sat watching the sun set in the distance with glorious colors, as it threw a red glow over the houses and trees, making them appear lit by the flames of a dying fire. Gabriel loved this time of day best of all - the mellow stillness of it and the light which seemed to illuminate everything and make features stand out like pictures from a child's storybook.

Gabriel's reverie was suddenly interrupted, when he heard his brother give a loud "humph!" from beside him. "Well I never!" Rex expostulated.

"What is it, my dear?" asked Brenda benignly.

"They found some young chap in the river last week - or, his body, I should say. Evidently, he'd been deliberately murdered."

Brenda looked at Gabriel, suppressing a smile behind her hand: "Most murder is deliberate, I would have thought."

"I h...heard about that on the radio" Gabriel chipped in.

"Oh yes, I think I did too" agreed Brenda. "Shocking, wasn't it? Wasn't he very young or something?"

"Twenty three, it says here", confirmed Rex, his nose still in the paper. "But nobody seems to know the motive. Listen to this: *Police have taken a girl in for questioning.* A girl! You wouldn't credit it, would you?"

"What was it, a jealous rage or something? A crime of passion?" Brenda's eyes glowed. She loved to watch crime thrillers on the television, and - unknown to her husband - was a secret fan of the more lurid crime novels.

"Might 'ave been, I suppose. Who knows what goes on in a woman's mind, eh, Gabriel?" He winked at his brother.

"D...do they say who the g...girl is?" Gabriel asked, in reply.

"Oh no, they're not allowed to give out the name, are they?"

"It's sub... what d'you call it," explained Brenda, proudly.

211

"Sub judice, she means," added Rex. "It says she's an actress, though. Now that doesn't surprise me. These theatricals get up to all sorts, don't they? Drugs, and I don't know what else."

"I would have thought it was mostly university students with the drugs," argued Brenda.

"What do you know about it anyway?" demanded Rex of his wife.

"Nothing" replied Brenda, compliant. "But in any event, I shouldn't say anything against theatricals in front of Gabriel. He loves the theatre, don't you? He went the other night with Kate."

"Did you now?" asked Rex. "Well, I hope you and Kate enjoyed yourselves. As for me, I wouldn't be seen dead in one of them places. All that prancing about in silly costumes, I can't see the attraction. But you always were different like that."

"I th...think Brenda's right. J...just because she's an actress, doesn't mean she's g...guilty." Gabriel felt his face grow hot, as he tried to defend the unknown girl. It occurred to him that he was sticking up for her mainly because of his own guilt at not having come forward as a witness to the event. And here he was with his brother and sister-in-law discussing the situation objectively, with them unable to understand the truth, not having been there to see it. But Gabriel didn't dare reveal that he knew far more than Rex and Brenda ever would about the incident.

"The young lad wasn't from Bristol, was he?" Brenda interjected, in an attempt to change the subject before there was an altercation.

"I don't know, it doesn't say. I bet you *she's* not from Bristol. This girl who killed him."

"We don't know if sh...she killed him, nothing's been p...proved yet" said Gabriel hotly, overlapping with Brenda asking what difference it made where the girl was from anyway.

"Well, they've arrested her anyway. So she won't be able to go around murdering anybody else," continued Rex, ignoring both of their protests. "Honestly, it's not safe to walk the streets any more with people like that about. This happened over on the Clifton Suspension Bridge, you know Gabriel. That's very near where you live. It could have been you she came after, did you think of that?"

"Don't be ridiculous! Who in the world would want to kill our Gabriel?" his wife interposed.

"You d...don't know anything about it" said Gabriel. "What if sh...she was being attacked by the young m... man? Wh...what if it was an accident, or s...self defense?" Gabriel saw in his mind's eye an image of a young girl in a red dress, the glint of a knife at her throat, the terrified look in her face. He wondered if the police had arrested the same girl, the girl he'd seen, and if so, if they had any evidence to prove she killed the boy. He felt confused and bewildered - would it help or mar her case if he were to come forward now as a witness?

"I doubt if it was an accident. She's an actress, remember. She'll probably say it was an accident, but then they're good at lying, these actresses" declared Rex.

"Oh, for heaven's sake!" Gabriel interjected suddenly, with a vehemence that surprised all three of them. Rex and Brenda regarded him in surprise. He didn't know what to say next, so he got up and took his camera out of the case, pretending to line up a shot of the house opposite with the sunset's glow on it. His mind was racing and he could hardly hold the camera steady enough to focus.

"Well, they've arrested her anyway" Rex said in a low voice to his wife, thinking his brother wouldn't overhear. "The police have. They *think* she killed him. And they should know."

"They don't know for sure though, do they" said his wife tactfully, whose glance at Gabriel's heated face had warned her to play diplomat. "We won't know till the trial and then the jury'll decide. Oh - I wonder if they'll call me! I've always wanted to do jury service, and do you know, they've never once asked me? Some people get asked several times, I know Mrs. Coates said that her daughter..."

To Gabriel's ears, Brenda's voice trailed off into meaningless gabble at this point. He didn't want to talk any more about the affair of the actress and the corpse in the river. It churned up too many bad memories for him. He felt very disquieted by the whole episode, knowing that he should have defended her more successfully against his brother's random accusations. Gabriel knew that she hadn't deliberately murdered the youth. At least, that was how it had looked to him.

He reasoned that, because of his unique knowledge, the girl was subtly his responsibility. But he didn't know what he could do now to help her. He just prayed that her fate was not in his, cowardly, hands.

CHAPTER SEVENTEEN

"AREN'T YOU GOING to invite me in?"

Maddie's mother stood on the doorstep, her chin pulled back into her neck in that way she had when disapproving of something. Maddie recognized the lime green suit her mother wore - unsuitably for a hotter than average July day - as the one she always sported on special occasions. To her surprise, Maddie intuited that her mother was nervous: the older woman's nylon blouse showed sweat stains seeping out from under the armpits and her gaze was leveled at Maddie's chest rather than directly into her eyes.

"Yes, of course. I didn't expect you so early." Maddie stood back to let her mother into the house, then closed the door behind her. She hadn't yet brushed her hair that morning, and her nose was pink from spending too long in the sun the day before.

"It took me less time than I expected. There was so little traffic leaving York at 6 a.m...."

"You left at six? I told you there was no need, that I'd be here all day--"

"I know but I like to be early. You know how I am."

"Yes I do." Maddie preceded her mother into the front room and waved at the settee. "Sit down if you like. D'you want some tea or coffee or something? Didn't you bring any bags?"

"Don't fire questions at me, dear" sighed the older woman, dusting a few crumbs from the sofa with her hand before seating herself. "Yes, I'd love some tea. Not too strong. My bags are in the car. I wasn't sure if I'd come to the right place."

"Haven't you ever been to Bristol before?" Maddie asked before disappearing into the kitchen without waiting for her mother to reply.

"No, and it's a confusing place to navigate in a car on your own..." Mrs. Wetherby looked around her at the small living room and noted with a frown the rows of dog-eared paperback books stacked against the walls, the rather worn three piece suite with its uniform beige color broken only by a few cushions in equally muted tones, the curtains with their bold striped pattern. There was nothing sentimental about the room and nothing extraneous. It was obviously the home of a bachelor.

Maddie returned with tea in a mug, which she placed on the occasional table by her mother's feet. "Oh!" Mrs. Wetherby exclaimed with a small moue of distaste, "It's rather chipped, isn't it. Doesn't Paul possess any cups?"

"Only some posh china ones" Maddie replied, sitting on the armchair facing her mother. "He keeps them locked in a cupboard. Only uses them for special occasions."

"I see," said Mrs. Wetherby with a sigh. "Still, it's quite a nice house, I suppose. At least your friend keeps things clean and tidy."

"I like it here." Maddie watched her mother as she delicately sipped the tea. The older woman's forehead was glowing with perspiration. "Why don't you take off your jacket?" Maddie suggested.

"I'm quite all right, thank you. Are you sure Paul doesn't mind you staying here till the trial? It's rather cramped, isn't it? I don't imagine there's much room for the two of you."

"Three of us. Paul's got a flatmate who also works at the theatre."

"Really? Dear me."

"But he's quite O.K. about me staying here. I help out round the house and he says he likes having me around." Maddie was petulant, sensing the implied criticism in her mother's tone.

"That's nice. Still, oughtn't you to pay him something?"

"What do you mean?"

"Well. Some rent money. Something for looking after you."

"He's not *looking after* me. I look after myself," Maddie declared hotly.

"You're living here in his house. How can you contribute to your...upkeep...food and things, if you're not working?"

"I've got some savings--"

"Would you like me to lend you a bit--"?

"You've done enough for me. You paid my bail."

"Well, I could hardly let my only daughter languish in jail, could I?" Maddie's mother pursed her lips and fingered her wedding ring.

After a pause, Maddie countered: "I told you before, mum. My friends would have helped me. I could have got the money somehow. You didn't have to--"

"Darling, it's not something you can ask *friends* to do for you, pay your bail. It's not as if you were...I don't know...borrowing the money to make the down payment on a flat or something. When you're in trouble, I'm the one you should come to. After all, I'm your relation, your guardian. I should take care of you..."

"I can take care of myself," Maddie stressed. Her chin jutted out defiantly and she held her knees with her arms in a self-protective gesture.

Mrs. Wetherby sighed and shook her head slowly. "There's no need to be so proud, Madeleine. You're so like..." She abandoned what she was going to say and sipped her tea, staring out of the window at the street dappled with sunshine.

"Like who?" Maddie asked. There was no reply. "Like who?" she persisted, "My mother? My real mother? Or my father, whoever he is?"

Mrs. Wetherby put her mug down onto the table with a clatter. "I was going to say you're like your aunt. She was always headstrong too. Couldn't bear to be told anything. Shall we get my bags from the car?" She rose from the settee, as if she'd already made up her mind.

Maddie had intended to make a bitter reply, but the words died on her lips. There was no point in starting a full-scale argument. She had made a pact with herself to keep calm in her mother's presence and not let herself be goaded.

Maddie sprang out of her chair and followed Mrs. Wetherby out to the car. Outside, the air was fresh and sweet, scented with the odor of summer roses from next door's garden. "How long can you stay for?"

"A couple of days. I have to go back to York on Thursday - there's a Women's Institute meeting in the evening I promised to attend. I could stay longer if you'd like me to--"

"No, it's O.K." Maddie pulled her mother's heavy suitcase out from the boot of the car, and then stumbled under its weight. "What have you got in here? Are you really only staying two days?"

"Nothing much" her mother replied with a small smile of embarrassment. "Just a few provisions."

Maddie smiled in return. She guessed the sort of thing her mother would have brought: home made jams, cakes and buns, a treacle tart, some lemon curd. "Thanks. Paul and Andy don't have a sweet tooth. I've been living on chocolate bars from the newsagents."

They walked back into the house, and Maddie dragged her mother's suitcase up the rather steep, narrow stairs. "My bedroom's up here. You can have the bed and I'll go on the floor for a couple of days. Do you want to come and see?"

"All right, dear."

It was a small bedroom, but quite tastefully decorated: the walls were papered with a cream pattern dotted with small flowers, and the bedclothes and curtains were in matching lemon. "The bathroom's across the hall if you want to freshen up" said Maddie, gratefully releasing the suitcase to the floor.

Mrs. Wetherby was beginning to appear more cheerful: "Would you like to go out for some lunch?" she volunteered, brightly. "I thought I could take you. As a treat."

Maddie shook her head. "I'd love to. Perhaps tomorrow. But today I've got to meet Reginald."

"Reginald?"

"Reginald Flowers. He's the QC - my defense barrister."

"I see. Someone Eva recommended?"

Maddie nodded. "She says he's wonderful. He's very experienced. And he defended a similar case last year, apparently, and got the girl off."

"Well, I suppose Eva must know what she's doing. Is he nice? Do you like him?"

"Yes I do. He's funny. Quite a character. He recites Shakespeare!"

"I hardly think that's appropriate--" Maddie's mother replied with a tut of disapproval.

"No, he knows his stuff. And I don't feel so nervous when I talk to him. I think he's the best man to plead my case, I really do."

"I hope you're right. When does the trial start?" Mrs. Wetherby stumbled over the word *trial*. She still couldn't believe that her daughter would have to go through something so ignominious.

"The date's been set for August 15th. More tea?" Maddie seemed unconcerned about her coming ordeal. But the truth was, to her the trial was like the opening night of a play. She knew she would be terrified when she had to go through with it, but until the day it actually happened her trial didn't seem real. So she'd pushed the prospective nightmare to the back of her mind while she got on with her life. It was the only way she could cope.

Gabriel was on his feet in the tiny bathroom downstairs, which he'd converted into a darkroom, developing some recent black and white photographs of Ian's children, when he heard the telephone ring. He frowned in puzzlement and looked at the illuminated dials of his watch. Rex always called on Saturdays, and Gabriel wasn't expecting anyone else to call. So who could be trying to reach him at 10 o'clock on a Wednesday morning? Gabriel's heart started to thump, as he considered the possibility that his attempts to find his daughter had somehow borne fruit - perhaps it was the woman he'd spoken to the other week, perhaps she'd suddenly remembered something about Helen that she'd forgotten to mention at the time.

The thought propelled Gabriel into action: hastily he dropped the photographic print back into the developing solution and shook the excess liquid from his hands as he squeezed himself through the narrow door and into the corridor, then he lunged for the phone on the hall table, just managing to gasp out "Hello" before the twentieth ring.

"Is that you, Gabriel?" It was a familiar voice, but for a few seconds Gabriel couldn't place it, he'd been so distracted by expecting someone else.

"Oh. K...Kate. Yes, it's me."

"I hope I didn't call at a bad time. You're not rushing out or anything, are you?"

"No, no. I was just d...developing some ph... photographs."

"How nice. The ones you took at the wedding? Have they come out well?"

"No, I sent those off to the l...lab to be p...processed. These are just s...some I took of the ch...children the other day. B...black and white ones."

"Yes, I think it's a good idea to keep a record of them as they grow up. I expect Ian and Sue wouldn't bother keeping photographs if you didn't take them. I know what it's like when you're a busy parent, you take them for granted a little...well, not exactly that but...you somehow never imagine that they're going to grow up one day and leave home. It's so lovely to have some photos to remind you of how they were when they were little. I felt that way, anyway." She laughed. "I'm sorry, I'm rambling on. I do tend to these days. Something to do with age I think."

"It's f...fine. I don't mind."

"Speaking of children...I don't mean to be nosy but I just wondered..." She paused, as if unsure whether to continue. "Did you manage to find out anything about your child? You know, you said there was someone you might call, who might know something?"

"I did c...call. I spoke to a w...woman. She had been a f...friend of H...Helen's. But she didn't know m...much. She said H...Helen never h...had a ch...child, to h...her knowledge." Gabriel's stutter was more pronounced than usual, and he coughed and struggled to control his mouth. "She th...thought the b...baby m...might have been ad...ad... adopted."

"Oh. I see. I'm sorry. What a shame."

"Yes."

"Well, at least you know now."

"Yes." There was a silence. Gabriel couldn't think of anything else to say.

"I'm sorry. I shouldn't have brought it up. It was tactless of me."

"No. That's all r...right."

Kate gave a swift intake of breath, as if she'd decided to change the subject to something brighter. "I didn't call about that anyway. I just rang to ask if you were free this evening, actually. My son Andrew has come down a couple of days to see me. He's studying medicine at University College in London. He's offered to take me out to a meal in Bristol and I wondered if you'd like to join us?"

"Yes. That would be l...lovely. Thank you."

"Good. I'd like you to meet him. He's a good boy."

"I'm s...sure he is."

"He's interested in photography too. But for him, it's more of a sideline. So, shall we pick you up in the car? Around eight o'clock?"

"Yes. All r...right then."

"I'll see you later. Goodbye."

"Goodbye, Kate."

Gabriel put the phone down with a sigh and closeted himself once more in his darkroom. Once inside, he had to wait for a few seconds until his eyes adjusted to the light. Then he studied the picture of little Lucy swinging from the apple tree, which was still lying in the developing fluid. It had been in the bath much too long and was therefore over developed, with tones that were much too dark. He would have to start all over again. Putting on his rubber gloves, he slid the print out of the bath and laid it to rest on the vinyl work surface adjoining the sink. Some earlier prints were pegged up to dry around the room and he studied them closely, feeling satisfied with the results.

As Gabriel worked, his mind wandered. Perhaps it was because he was developing photographs that he recollected the photograph of the girl in the theatre play, which had failed to capture her beauty and made her seem stiff and characterless. He wondered where that girl was now, along with all the rest of the cast of the show, which had seemed so magical to Kate and himself. Did they all live in London? And what did actors do when they weren't working? People always said that to be an actor must be a hard life, demanding total commitment, both mentally and physically. Not a life he could have chosen, even if he'd had the talent.

Gabriel mentally wished them all well, particularly the young girl with the beautiful voice, which had moved him almost to tears.

———

Maddie's defense counsel, QC Reginald Flowers, was a neat dapper little man who sported a trim moustache and had a tendency to hide outrageous ties under his barrister's robe. "So, tell me again - are you absolutely sure you didn't hear Darren walking behind you until just before you reached the bridge?"

"Oh how many times! I'm absolutely sure. I don't know why I didn't hear his footsteps but I didn't. I suppose I must have been wandering about in a world of my own or something - I do that sometimes when I'm walking. Don't you? I didn't think about anyone following me, it just never occurred to me. O.K.?"

"I'm sorry to badger you, Maddie, but you see this is exactly the sort of thing the prosecution barrister's going to ask you at the trial. And you've got to convince him and the jury of the truth of what you're saying."

"Yeah, yeah, I know." Maddie gave a long sigh. She seemed weary and dispirited.

"Want some coffee?" Eva volunteered. "I can go to the machine."

"Love some" Maddie admitted gratefully.

"Me too" said Reginald. "Black with two. Have you got any change?"

"We don't have to actually pay for that muck, do we?" complained Eva, with a grin, searching in her handbag.

"I'm afraid so. Company policy. Screw the clients for as much as possible," replied Reginald cheerfully. He fumbled in his pockets, then withdrew some coins. "You're in luck. Here's a couple of twenty pences."

"You're a generous man."

"I know."

Eva disappeared from the room, closing the door gently behind her, and Reginald swung round to face his client. "Better to have all this out now than at the trial. Don't you agree?"

"Yes, you're right," sighed Maddie, stretching her arms behind her back.

"Think of this as a rehearsal. *All the world's a stage, and all the people in it merely players...*" Reginald broke off his soliloquy when he saw Maddie wince. "Right then. Back to your statement." He perused the sheaf of paper in his hand. "I think your description of the rape scene is very plausible--"

"Thank you" Maddie interrupted dryly.

"But the trouble is, we've only got your word for what happened. That's the problem with rape cases, generally. It's the woman's word against the man's, with no other witnesses to prove it either way. Or in this instance, just the woman's word..."

"Hang on. There *was* a witness," said Maddie.

"There was? Did you mention that in your statement?"

"I think so. But the police asked me so many questions, I got all confused and I couldn't think straight. All I could think of was that I was innocent, that it was an accident. They seem to have forgotten about the witness and I must admit it slipped my mind too. What with all the aggro over how much bail I'd be given and then waiting for the trial date, you know."

"But this is very important, it could be a very relevant issue." Reginald seated himself in the black leather chair beside his desk and chewed the end of his fountain pen thoughtfully.

"Yeah, I suppose so. I did mention it to Eva, ages ago. I thought about trying to find the guy at first and then I gave up on the idea. I never thought we'd be able to locate him."

"Never give up on anything," advised Reginald, tapping his pen on the edge of the desk. "So who was this witness? Tell me all about it."

At that moment, Eva re-entered the room with the coffees and distributed them, then seated herself on the edge of Reginald's desk with her long legs swinging from it.

Maddie scratched her head as she tried to remember accurately the events of that morning in June. "He was an old man. It was just after I...just after Darren fell into the river. I turned round and saw him standing there."

"How much did he see?"

"I don't know. I don't know how long he'd been standing there."

"You weren't aware of him approaching?"

"Well, no. It must have been while Darren and I were struggling. I wasn't aware of anything else much at all. Perhaps...I was screaming...perhaps he heard my screams and came to see what was going on."

"So you're sure he wasn't there earlier? While you were walking along talking to Darren? Or when you were being followed? You would have noticed the old man then, wouldn't you?" Reginald was frantically scribbling in his notebook, a strange set of hieroglyphics that resembled shorthand.

"No, I'm sure he wasn't there earlier. At least, I don't think so. I certainly didn't see anyone else on the street before Darren attacked me."

"Did the old man say anything to you?" Eva interjected.

Maddie closed her eyes for a moment, attempting to recreate the scene in her mind. "No. Nothing. He just stood there and looked at me."

"And what did you do?" asked Reginald, looking up for a moment from his notes.

Maddie paused. "I...I looked back at him."

"I thought you ran away immediately" Eva interposed. She was staring intently at Maddie.

"Yes, that's right. You're right" Maddie replied helplessly. "I'm sorry. It's awful how things get jumbled up inside your head. Even only a few weeks after it happened."

"Don't worry" reassured Eva. "It happens to everybody. The human memory isn't a computer. Sometimes memories get forgotten, lost for a while, only to reappear suddenly later. Or you remember things in the wrong order. I've seen it lots of times."

"What a piece of work is man!" remarked Reginald in a declamatory voice.

Eva ignored him. "So, when did you notice the old man?"

"Just after I...just after Darren..."

"How much of the incident do you think he saw?" Reginald asked.

"It's hard to say. But he must have seen something."

"He *may* have seen something," commented Reginald. "Something that would be useful to us, anyway. One mustn't make any assumptions at this stage."

"It would surely be worth trying to contact him, though" asserted Eva.

"Certainly" Reginald agreed. "The timing here is crucial. If the old man arrived on the scene early enough to witness the struggle between Maddie and Darren with Darren's ensuing fall into the river, he may well be able to corroborate Maddie's story that Darren's death was an accident caused by her attempt to defend herself against him. In which case, he would be a very important witness for the defense. Very important indeed."

"And he might have seen the knife" Maddie pointed out. "He must have seen it."

"Exactly" replied Reginald.

"Do you think you'd be able to recognize him again?" Eva asked Maddie.

"I think so. He was about...I don't know, sixty years old. He had white hair. He was quite tall, medium build. He had a nice face. A kind face. I don't know why I remember that."

"We can try and trace him," suggested Eva, turning to Reginald. "He's probably a Bristol resident. We can ask the local press to put advertisements in the papers and the media, asking him to come forward. I wonder why he hasn't already."

"People don't like to get involved" Reginald said sagely. "Not unless they're more than usually public spirited."

"We'll do our best to find him, anyway" said Eva, with a smile at Maddie.

Reginald returned to his notebook and began scribbling again. "So he said nothing to you and you said nothing to him, is that right?"

"Yes, that's right."

"Then what did you do."

"I ran away, as fast as I could. I didn't even think about all the stuff that had fallen out of my bag when I swung it. I wish I had or my pen wouldn't have got lost. I went back to look for it later but somebody must have picked it up and handed it in to the police. So they used that to pinpoint me at the scene. What an idiot I was!"

"Don't worry about that now."

"I was afraid, you know? I was so afraid that I panicked and acted stupidly."

"It's a shame you didn't stress this witness more to the police," commented Eva.

"I think not," said Reginald. "It may be very useful for us to use him as a defense witness. Our last witness. Assuming we can find him, that is--"

"And that he saw enough--"

"And that he'll give evidence."

Bella flung her shoulder bag over the arm of a chair and slumped into the seat gratefully. She'd walked back from town to get some exercise after her sedentary day in the office and now she was grateful to take the weight off her feet. She fingered the little pile of letters on the table, extracting the three that were addressed to her rather than her parents. Of the three - a ballot paper from Equity, a postcard from a friend visiting Italy and a letter from the Crown Prosecution Service in a brown envelope bearing its distinctive logo - the latter interested her most, and she tore open the top of the envelope and drew out a sheet of thick vellum paper.

"Want some tea?" Terry offered, entering the kitchen. He was clutching a rolling pin in his right hand and his plastic overall was covered in flour from several recent attempts at pastry making.

Bella made a clucking noise with her tongue. "Think I need something stronger."

"Glass of wine?"

"Yeah, great." Bella didn't look up, but busily re-read the contents of her letter from the CPS.

Terry extracted a new bottle of white wine from the fridge, opened it and poured a glassful, adding a cube of ice from the freezer. He glanced at Bella's letter as he placed the glass on the table by her right hand. "Anything interesting?"

"It's from the Court."

"Oh yes." Terry, having returned to the work surface by the cooker now, started rolling out a thick wedge of pastry for his flan base.

"About Maddie's trial."

"When is it?"

"In a couple of weeks. Starts the 15th of August. They want me to give evidence."

"You'll be away, won't you?"

"We can always change the date of the holiday, you know. We'd only lose the deposit money."

Terry paused and looked sharply at Bella. "Do you have to give evidence?"

"Well, I don't know if they can force me. Maybe they can. But in any case, I think I should."

"What can you say that would help Maddie?"

Bella's voice was jaded. She and Terry had had this argument before, several times. "I'm just a character witness. I can say what she's like, what sort of a person she is."

"What difference does that make? You weren't there when...it happened. So how do you know anything?"

"I know she wouldn't kill anyone. I know that. I can tell them what I know about Maddie's character."

"It's not exactly proof of anything--"

Bella put her head in her hands. She felt drained from her day of temping in an office, and depressed because she hadn't heard from her agent about an acting job she'd felt certain to get. The last thing she needed right now was to go over all this old ground with Terry. "Look. I know you don't think she's innocent--"

"I never said that. I just said that neither of us knew for sure because we weren't there and we didn't see what happened." Terry rolled his pastry far more than was needed, slapping his rolling pin down on to the soft dough with a whacking sound.

"I *know*. I know Maddie couldn't possibly have killed a man in cold blood. It's not in her character..."

"He's dead, though. That's a fact, isn't it?"

"It was an accident. She told me she was trying to defend herself, and I believe her. I don't care what *you* believe." Bella's tone was belligerent. Terry came up behind her and put his big floury hands on her shoulders.

"I just don't like the idea of you getting involved in all this. That's all" he said softly, kneading her tensed shoulders and rubbing her neck with his thumbs.

"She's my friend. What else can I do? Somebody's got to stick up for her."

"There are other people, Bella love."

"No there aren't. She's got nobody. No proper family. Just a mother, an adoptive mother she doesn't even like very much."

Terry sighed. "O.K. If it's what you want."

Bella continued: "I mean if I don't help her nobody else will. It's not as if I'm being asked to lie for her or anything. I'm not going to perjure myself. I'll just stand up in Court and tell them that I don't believe my friend could do anything like that."

"Well. I hope it does some good." Terry patted her shoulders fondly and returned to his baking.

"So do I. I don't want to postpone our holiday for nothing."

"Don't worry. Malta's not going to sink into the sea over the next fortnight."

Bella sneaked up behind Terry and grabbed him around the waist, making him gasp as she squeezed him tight. "Well, lover. What you got cooking tonight?"

———◦◦◦◦◦◦———

When Gabriel arrived home from work on Thursday evening, he hung up his jacket on the coat stand in the hall, opened the back door to let Liquorice in from the garden and turned on the radio in the kitchen so that he could hear the local news while he made a pot of tea. He sighed and clicked his teeth as he heard about a gang of youths who'd ram-raided a large video store in the center of Bristol and stolen most of the merchandise. The kettle began its shrill whistle and Gabriel poured the boiling water into his teapot, performing the habitual actions with practiced ease, as he heard that the weather for the next few days was going to remain fine. He smiled at the thought that his new tomato plants were doing well and were almost ready to have their fruit picked. He thought about giving some to Kate, to thank her for the pleasant dinner he'd had the other evening with her and her son Andrew.

How different things might have been if Kate hadn't moved to Scotland...he didn't let himself dwell on the thought. Fate had ordained that he should live on his own, and he should be grateful to have her companionship now at least. Gabriel sat himself down on one of the carved oak chairs that had once belonged to his parents, its hard wooden seat softened by the addition of a cushion that Sue had covered for him, and poured some milk into a mug with a picture of the Prince and Princess of Wales on it, which was chipped and stained with many years of use. It was at about this time that some words on the radio caught his attention:

"Defense lawyers involved in the trial of Madeleine Wetherby - the young actress accused of killing Darren Webster - which is due to commence in just over a week, are appealing for a local witness to come forward and help in their enquiries. It is believed that there was a witness to the incident, who is described as being a man in his sixties, tall, medium build, with white hair. The incident occurred on Sunday June 3rd this year in the early hours of the morning at the Clifton Suspension Bridge in Bristol. Could anyone with any information regarding this please call our Helpline number on...."

Gabriel sat stunned. The witness was him!

He felt as if someone had just shone a spotlight on him and exposed his miserable little life, had come into his kitchen and called his name out loud. He actually glanced around furtively, to see if anyone else was in the room with him. Gabriel prayed that nobody who knew him would have heard the announcement. Although, when he considered the situation more calmly, it was quite ridiculous to be worried about that. There must be several hundred men in Bristol of about his age and height with white hair, and there was nothing remotely distinguishing in the description.

But the girl had seen him there. He felt almost as if *he* were the criminal running from the Law, not her. He hadn't wanted to get involved and so he hadn't reported the incident at first, hoping that somehow she wouldn't be implicated, wouldn't get caught. And now, *she* was looking for *him*. Why? Perhaps - Gabriel pondered - he had done something illegal by not coming forward before. Perhaps, when she had admitted to the police that there'd been a witness, they'd decided to try and find him so that they could prosecute him for withholding information or perverting the course of justice, or whatever crime it was, not to speak up.

Gabriel could feel his heart beating with real fear. Just the thought of going back to the police with his information, or of telephoning the helpline they'd mentioned (he hadn't even made a note of the number) or of going anywhere near the Court during the trial, filled him with panic. He couldn't do it. If he continued not to say anything, they would never know. They couldn't possibly find him. He gripped the edge of the table with his hands, as if he thought he might fall off his chair.

And then another thought struck him. On the report they'd said, "A young actress". That made it even more terrible. Gabriel remembered the near-argument he'd had with his brother Rex on the day of his niece's wedding, how Rex had denigrated theatrical people and Gabriel had lamely tried to defend the profession. To think that the girl he'd witnessed was one of those people who performed in the theatre, weaving magical spells that enchanted ordinary people like himself and Kate.

For the first time, it occurred to Gabriel that she might even have appeared in the show he and Kate had seen at the Bristol Old Vic. There had been several women in the cast who might truthfully be described as "young". Thinking of this made the girl seem closer to him, in a strange way, as if he partly knew her because he may have seen her performing on stage.

So now she wanted him to come forward. She wanted him to tell what he'd seen. She needed him...

He almost rose to get up from his chair, then he sank back down again. His legs felt weak and trembly.

He couldn't do it. They would make him give evidence in Court. He'd promised himself all those years ago that he would never again speak in the defense of another. The people would jeer at him when they heard his stutter, and humiliate him for being a fool. He couldn't face that.

CHAPTER EIGHTEEN

"Now THEN, MADDIE my girl. I want you to remember everything I've told you before. Hold your head up high, tell the truth and don't worry. It won't be any worse than first night nerves, you'll see." QC Reginald Flowers gave his client a couple of brisk pats on the shoulder, then seated himself on one of the large leather chairs, and began busily collecting his brief into an orderly pile before retying it with a red ribbon.

"But did you see the jury?" Maddie was pacing the room, her voice quivering with nerves. She felt as nauseous as if about to take the stage in an unfamiliar and starring role.

"Yes, I saw them. Quite a sympathetic bunch, I thought. Only two females, but that can't be helped. Men are human too, you know. *The quality of mercy is not strained.*"

"No, I mean did you take a good look at their faces, their expressions? When you questioned me before lunch I was looking at them, you know, to see if I could tell what they were thinking-"

"That's a mistake. You can never tell what a jury's thinking, they're the most unpredictable group of people

237

on earth. Don't try to prejudge them. You should be concentrating on giving your evidence and making the right impression."

"I couldn't help looking at them. And none of them had any sympathy for me - any empathy, or whatever. You know, when I'm acting, I often look out to the audience to try and gauge their reaction to me - to the character, I mean - and I can always tell if they like me--"

"Forget about the theatre, just for once." Flowers declared, with more firmness than he normally showed, lifting his head from the brief papers and fixing Maddie with his small blue eyes. "I know I said you have to make a good impression on them and come across well, but this is *you* we're talking about, not a character in a play and this is a Courtroom, not the theatre."

"But I thought you said I should use my experience as a performer..." Maddie interjected, feeling like a small child who'd been ticked off.

"Bear it in mind and use your skill, but never make the mistake of appearing false. The prosecution's going to leap on you if he thinks you're playing any actory tricks. I'm afraid you may suffer a bit from the - very unfair in my opinion, but then I'm a frustrated thespian anyway - prejudice the public have against actors. Prosecution will make a meal of your profession and hold it against you, if he can. So it's doubly important that you come across as sincere and genuine, someone who doesn't act offstage as well as on. The jury has got to believe in you, because - unfortunately, since we didn't manage to find your witness - it's only your word we've got to go on."

"But that's just it! They *don't* believe in me. I can feel it. I can keep telling the truth till I'm blue in the face. I've *been* telling the truth, haven't I? But whatever I say, they don't believe it. It's making me nervous. I don't think they're going to believe me any more this time than when you questioned me."

"Panicking isn't going to get you anywhere." Reginald Flowers took his client by the arms and held them, in a controlling gesture. "There's nothing to worry about. Nobody can force you to say anything incriminating, if you keep a calm attitude. Did you deliberately kill Darren?"

"No!" blurted Maddie.

"Are you innocent of the murder charge?"

"Yes!"

"There you are, then. You know it's the truth and you've convinced *me* that it's the truth. Essentially, that's the only thing the jury want to know for sure. They're people, not ogres. They're ordinary men and women who've been called up for jury service and probably can't wait for it all to be over. They're on your side potentially, as long as they can see things from your point of view. Just tell the truth and keep calm"

Maddie swallowed and looked down. "All right" she said meekly.

"And the most important thing is to control your temper, whatever prosecution says. Don't let him rile you, because that's what he'll try and do. Don't get angry with him or the judge."

"I'll try."

"It doesn't help. Maybe it's our English reserve but the public don't like to see someone who isn't in control of their emotions. It creates a bad image of you. If people see you flying off the handle, they think, *Oh dear, she gets cross easily doesn't she, maybe that's what happened with Darren Webster.* Which is exactly what the prosecution will be playing on. He'll wind you up on purpose. You've got to be strong enough not to let him break you down. Do you understand?"

Maddie didn't reply. She was doing her best to fight back the tears that had welled up in her eyes - tears of helplessness and frustration. But she knew that Flowers was right. For her own sake, she had to control her emotions and not let anyone see if she was becoming rattled. She knew how to control herself when she was on stage, how to desist from laughing at the wrong moment by thinking of something sad and how to feign confidence when she was paralyzed with nerves. So this ordeal would be the same, except that here the character she was playing was herself and she couldn't hide behind the comfortable mask of another personality or the security of lines already written and rehearsed.

"Now, I know how you feel about the jury. If you want my honest opinion, you have been unlucky there. Juries are supposed to be a representative sample, but there's no law to say it has to be exactly equal women for men. It's unfortunate that there are only two women, but we can work with that. Remember that the men there are people too. They've got wives, girlfriends, sisters. They can identify with you, if you can appeal to their sympathy. You know how to appeal to an audience, don't you? I know you do. I saw you do it in *Puttin' on the Ritz*. You were very affecting in your solo."

"It's different though. On stage I've got a character. This is just me. And when I feel things, I can't cut off from them and say it doesn't matter. If people say bad things about me, things that aren't true, it hurts."

"I realize that. But try and distance yourself from it. Just tell the truth - calmly - and you'll be fine."

"I'll do my best."

"I know you will." A bell outside sounded and Flowers gathered up his things. "Ah, *The clock upbraids me*...I'd better go now."

At the doorway, he winked. "See you in Court."

The prosecution counsel was a Mr. Taylor Coleridge, a name which sometimes caused hilarity amongst his colleagues but which he bore with the aplomb of a man convinced of his superiority in all matters. He was in his late forties, with steel grey hair pushed carelessly back from his forehead, and a plummy voice distinguished by a flat, nasal tone, giving him an air of ennui, which made him appear supremely indifferent to the course of events.

"You say you encountered Darren Webster on the Clifton Suspension Bridge at about 5.30 a.m. on the morning of June 3rd?"

"Yes."

"But he had, presumably, been following you since you left Turner Road" - here the barrister turned to elucidate to the jury - "That was the site of the party at Bella Marconi's house." He continued: "How long did it take you to walk from Turner Road to the bridge?"

"About...I don't know...about twenty minutes..."

"So it follows that Darren Webster must have been walking, quite closely behind you in order to see what direction you took, for twenty minutes, and yet you didn't notice him in all that time?"

"I don't know if he was walking closely behind me or not. I didn't see him."

"So when *did* you see him?"

"He called something out to me."

"When you got to the bridge?"

"Yes, about the time, or just before I got to the bridge, yes."

"What did he call out to you?"

"Erm..." Maddie gazed at a spot on the top left of the ceiling for a few seconds, in an effort to remember the exact words Darren had said. Her counsel had advised her to be as honest, clear and precise as possible, so Maddie endeavored to do so: she disregarded the emotions surrounding the events and just replayed them in her mind, like the progression of a film that had no subjective relevance for her. Now she could hear Darren's voice, calling: "Hang on. He shouted out to me to hang on a minute."

"And that caused you to notice him?"

"Well, I had heard his footsteps before that, but I didn't know who it was. I didn't know if I was being followed or not and I didn't dare turn round, but when he shouted out to me I thought I'd better turn round."

"So you turned around and you saw, not a stranger but a young man whom you had just met at a party."

"I hadn't just met him, it was a few hours before--"

"A few hours before, the evening before, at a party. But you did recognize him?"

"Oh yes."

"This was a young man who you had met, talked to, danced with and er...kissed, so I believe, a few hours before at a party."

"I hadn't kissed him--"

"You said in earlier evidence--"

"No, I said he'd tried to kiss me while we were dancing, but I hadn't wanted to."

Maddie - feeling annoyed by this line of questioning - looked up boldly, and happened to catch Paul's eye. He was sitting in the front row of the public gallery upstairs, watching the proceedings with intense concentration. She thought she saw a flicker of a smile cross his face but she couldn't be sure.

"Were you dancing with him for quite some time?"

"Oh...I don't' know...a couple of dances, three maybe."

"Fast dances? Slow dances?"

"Erm..." Maddie was still determined to be honest. "At first fast dances, but then we did a slow one later on. That was when he started getting too...intimate with me."

"So when you were doing the slow dance with Darren, were you dancing quite closely together?"

"Yes, I suppose so."

"You had your arms around each other, like such?" The barrister demonstrated. He looked ridiculous in his cloak, but Maddie had never felt less like laughing.

"Yes, we did."

"Would you say that it was...normal... I mean, natural, that a young man with whom you were dancing closely and with your arms around each other should feel emboldened to try and kiss you?"

"I don't know...maybe."

"Do you feel that, perhaps, you were giving the impression to this boy that you wanted him to kiss you - by dancing with him in this way?"

"No, I hadn't given any *impression*. I only danced with him."

"You could have refused to dance with him at the outset, if you weren't at all interested in him, couldn't you?"

"I could have done."

"So why didn't you just refuse to dance with him in the first place?"

"Well, I... I thought he looked quite nice, you know, and I... wanted to dance with him."

"So you're not denying that you found him nice looking, you found him attractive? Maybe just at first perhaps?"

"Well, fairly attractive, reasonably attractive. Anyway, I don't see any harm in dancing with people at parties. It's what people do."

Maddie looked up at the jury, hoping to see a young face that would seem to corroborate what she had just uttered, but all the countenances were inscrutable - blank or bent over pages of notes, young and old alike.

"Let's return to what happened later. You've said that you heard someone call out and you turned around. At that stage you recognized the person who had been following you as the young man you had danced with at the party. How did you feel?"

"How did I feel?"

"Well, were you frightened, angry, surprised?"

"I was frightened."

"Why were you frightened? Was he behaving threateningly to you in any way?"

"Not then, but--"

"Would it be fair to say that you were more *angry* than frightened?"

"No, I wasn't angry--"

"Here was a young man who had been following you (without your knowledge, so you assert), who possibly wanted to spend the night with you (or what was left of it anyway). Did his persistence not annoy you?"

"You make it sound like I *knew* he was following me. But I didn't. It was a shock, when I saw him there. I hadn't expected it."

"Even though you led him on at the party?"

"I *didn't* lead him on. I hadn't even seen him for hours. I didn't even know he was still at the party when I left. I'd forgotten all about him"

"So you'd forgotten all about him, but he, unfortunately" stressed Taylor Coleridge with a hint of irony, "hadn't forgotten about *you*."

"Apparently not."

"So you say you were frightened when you saw him. Frightened he might attack you, I presume?"

"Yes."

"How did this fear manifest itself?"

"What?"

"Did you run away when you saw him?"

"No. I thought that might make things worse."

"You thought he might chase you and catch up with you?"

"Yes."

"Even though he was rather the worse for wear, having drunk a lot of alcohol?"

"I didn't know that."

"Could he not have caught up with you before this, if he'd been able?"

"Maybe he didn't want to."

"Maybe he *did* catch up with you, before you reached the bridge even. Maybe he walked with you for most of your journey?"

"No. I told you. He followed me without my knowing."

"So you - when you saw him - in your fear, rather than run away, you stood your ground, is that right?"

"Yes" she replied slightly dubiously. The barrister had a way of stating things that were true, but in such a way that they implied something quite different from the truth.

"You let him catch up with you."

"I asked him why he was following me."

"And what was his reply?"

"He...he denied it."

"Did you ask him to leave you alone?"

"Yes, of course I did."

"But he didn't leave you alone?"

"No, he just kept on...walking behind me."

"And you allowed him to?"

"What was I supposed to do?" Maddie couldn't prevent her rising anger from flushing her cheeks.

Although Reginald Flowers had counseled her to remain calm at all times, her emotions were starting to get the better of her.

The prosecution barrister continued sedately, yet he had a glint of triumph in his eye, like a hunter scenting its quarry. "You made no attempt to get away from his, you say unwelcome, advances?"

"I've already told you, I thought running would make it worse. I asked him to go away but he wouldn't, so all I could do was walk," Maddie countered, hotly.

"And what did he do next? Leap on you out of the blue and attack you?" There was a definite smirk on Coleridge's face as he said this.

Maddie summoned all her strength to remain calm and not let fury at these inferences incite her to forget Reginald's warnings. "No, not right away. He kept following me and calling out to me. Then I got angry and I shouted at him."

"So you *were* angry."

"I was then. But I was frightened as well, angry and frightened." Maddie felt wrong-footed, though she didn't quite know why. She noticed the judge staring at her intently. His face wasn't unkindly and she suddenly wished she were explaining all this to him and in some private place, away from all this public scrutiny and the persistent questions that twisted and reshaped the words in her mouth.

The prosecution barrister drew breath and suddenly altered the course of his questioning. Maddie wasn't sure whether to be relieved or worried. "We've heard from Mr. Ted Bown, Darren Webster's friend, that Darren was quite a short young man, I think he said...5'6" tall." He read his notes. "Yes, 5'6", quite small and skinny, in Mr. Bown's words. So, not a big man. Not much of a threat, in fact. How tall are you, Miss Wetherby?"

"5 foot 6."

"So you're the same height as your supposed assailant. He was by all accounts of a small, slight build, hardly more than yourself, quite a girlish young man in fact. He was hardly Arnold Schwarzenegger, was he?"

There were titters from the watching crowd. Maddie didn't reply to what she supposed was a rhetorical question, having by now gathered what was to be the thrust of Coleridge's argument.

"And you are a dancer, are you not? Accustomed to exercise, to keeping fit?"

"Yes."

"So, can you really say that you were actually frightened of this young man?" The barrister always referred to Darren as a *young man*, as if that afforded him a vulnerability, which in Maddie's memory Darren had certainly not possessed.

Maddie was on the defensive now. "His size isn't the point. You can be small but still be aggressive, still know how to fight. And he had a knife."

"Ah yes, the knife. You've mentioned this before, in your second statement to the police. If I could just refresh your memory, Your Honor, members of the jury..." Mr. Coleridge searched through his sheaf of papers till he came upon the typed transcripts of Maddie's statement to Detective Inspector Grundy, taken when she'd been arrested. "On page 13 of Exhibit 1, the defendant's statement, which I think has been given to the jury...?"

The judge nodded: "That's correct. I also have a copy here."

"If I could just read out the relevant passage - *He had me pressed back against the wall of the bridge. I could see that he had a knife in his hand and he was threatening me with it* - now, apparently no knife has so far been recovered from the scene, has it, Miss Wetherby?"

"No. The police were looking for it but they couldn't find it. It must have fallen into the water."

"Be that as it may, I'm afraid that without actually retrieving the knife itself we have only your word that Darren did possess a knife and was threatening you with it."

"The witness saw the knife. He must have done."

"Witness?" The prosecution counsel, briefly nonplused, fell silent and addressed a mute query to the judge.

"The old man I spoke about in my statement. I only noticed him at the end, but he must have seen the knife" continued Maddie.

Hearing this, the judge halted the proceedings momentarily while he motioned for Reginald Flowers to come forward and the two men whispered together for a few seconds. Then the judge turned to Maddie and spoke aloud: "I'm afraid Miss Wetherby that we cannot consider this witness relevant to the case unless he comes forward and gives evidence for the defense. Members of the jury, you will please ignore the defendant's last comment. Please carry on, Mr. Coleridge."

Maddie felt disheartened when she looked at the faces of the jury members and saw no commiseration there, only curiosity, as if she were a character in a play they were watching. Strangely for her - who had played so many parts in the past - she wished they would view her as a real person, with feelings and weaknesses similar to their own. Maddie had a sudden urge to call out to them, touch them, make them understand. But the formality of the Court situation precluded any demonstrations of emotion. Meanwhile, the clock on the wall ticked remorselessly on; the Clerk of the Court stood stiffly in black robes like a guardian of justice; people occasionally walked in and out of the courtroom, bowing their heads to the judge as they did so - as if he were some kind of God - or speaking to each other in hushed and deferential whispers; the Court Usher answered the telephone's muffled bleep, cupping his hand over the receiver and speaking so softly that he was completely inaudible; members of the public stifled yawns or wrote assiduously in notebooks; the trial lumbered on.

The prosecution counsel took up his baton again and recommenced the fray. "After you shouted at Darren, you say that's when he attacked you?"

"Yes."

"Did you anticipate that he was going to attack you?"

"No. He grabbed me from behind."

"Wasn't it rather foolish of you to turn away from him if, as you say, you were frightened of him and you didn't know what he might do next?"

"Maybe it was. I didn't know what else to do."

"So you say he grabbed you from behind. Which bit of you exactly did he grab?"

"My...waist. He sort of pinned my arms behind my back." Maddie demonstrated this action.

"Couldn't you break free?"

"No...I...it happened too quickly. I was shocked."

"Did you not guess he was going to try something?"

"I didn't. I thought he might leave me alone after I'd shouted at him."

"What did he do next?"

"He sort of...spun me round and pushed me back."

"Back where?"

"Against the wall."

"Did you call for help?"

"Of course, but nobody heard me."

"There were houses quite nearby. Surely someone would have heard you if you'd screamed loud enough?"

"I don't know. I screamed as loud as I could. Nobody came, anyway."

"Did you try to escape?"

"Yes, yes, I struggled, but I couldn't get free. He wouldn't let go."

"You say you couldn't get free, and yet you did manage to swing your handbag at him. It says in the statement which you gave to the police: *He relaxed his body for a moment and I swung my handbag at him.*"

"Yes."

"Why did he relax his body just then?"

"I don't know. Perhaps he saw something. I'm not sure what he saw."

"So, at any rate, you got your right arm... was it your right arm?"

"Yes."

"You got your right arm free and you swung the bag. Were you aiming at his head? Or at any part of his body in particular?"

"No, I wasn't really thinking about aiming or anything. I just swung the bag in his general direction."

"So you swung the bag and it just happened to collide with his head, is that right?"

"Yes."

"Now, I have here the Coroner's report, your honor, if I could trouble the Court to listen for a moment, which outlines the damage to the young man's skull as a consequence of receiving this blow." Here, the barrister read out from a long typed paper for about five minutes. The medical jargon was rather incomprehensible to Maddie, but the gist of the comments was that the blow had done extensive damage to the skull.

"Is the Coroner able to say whether it was the blow to the head which was fatal, or whether death did not occur until the young man's descent into the river?" enquired the judge.

"No, he's not able to say for certain, your honor, but in his opinion the damage to the skull was such that the injury could have been a fatal one."

"It was certainly a very forceful impact, then?" asked the judge.

"It was, yes."

"Do continue, Mr. Coleridge. I'm sorry for having to interrupt you" apologized the judge.

Maddie thought it was bizarre how polite everyone was to each other in the Court room, when talking about bodies and fatal head wounds, as if they were discussing the inclement weather or the price of cup cakes.

The prosecution barrister continued: "So we have ascertained that the blow to the head was an extremely forceful one. If it did not in fact cause Darren's death, it can almost certainly account for his loss of consciousness at that moment which would have caused him to lose his balance and fall into the river to his death." He turned back to Maddie: "Was it your intention to knock him unconscious?"

"No, of course not?"

"What was your intention?"

"Well... to stun him."

"So, you wished to stun him, to knock him senseless in other words."

"Er...yes, I suppose so."

"Did it occur to you to consider that a blow to the head with a heavy object could cause a fatal injury?"

"No, I didn't think...I wasn't thinking clearly at the time."

"Was there anything else you could have done?"

"What do you mean?"

"Could you have had recourse to another method of escaping from him? If he relaxed his grip on you for a moment, as you say, could you not have taken that opportunity to break free and run away?"

Maddie paused for a moment, thinking hard. The atmosphere in the courtroom was tense and expectant, almost electric. "It's hard to say. And it happened so quickly, I can't really remember..."

"All I'd like to know is, Miss Wetherby, whether looking back on it now, you feel you could have taken some other course of action."

"I suppose I could have done."

"Are you saying you could have broken free from him at that point, while his grip on you was relaxed and his attention was diverted from you, just for that moment?"

"Maybe I could have done. I don't know."

"But you chose not to take that option."

"I was frightened. He had a knife to my throat. His hand could have slipped accidentally, anything."

"Yes, although you claim he had a knife to your throat we haven't actually got any evidence to prove that. So, for whatever reason, you swung your handbag at his head in order to stun him?"

"Yes" Maddie admitted, miserably.

"Was there somewhere in your mind at that moment a desire to hurt him for what he was doing to you?"

"No...I...I wanted to stop him...I wanted to get him off me..."

"You've already told this Court that you could have run away, if that was all you wanted to do. You say you were acting out of fear and panic and purely in self-defense. But wasn't there some anger mixed up in your feelings as well? Some residual anger about your boyfriend's treatment of you, earlier that evening?"

"I can't remember. Maybe I felt angry with him. I'm not sure."

"So you admit then, that you did feel angry?"

"He was attacking me. Of course I felt angry."

"No further questions, your honor."

All of a sudden - Maddie realized - the cross-examination was over, and the judge was ordering the jury to reconvene in the morning. She could hardly remember what she had just been saying, all her words and Coleridge's having meshed into one indistinct blur. She had a strong feeling she'd said something she shouldn't have, had made some fatal mistake or unwise admission. But she couldn't think how. She'd just told the truth.

Maddie shook her head and felt the tears well up in her eyes. She was led away from the witness box, like a dumb animal going to the slaughter, blindly following the usher to the little room at the back of the Court, in which she waited to be visited by Reginald Flowers and Eva Goldstein before she was allowed to go home.

———⁓⁓◦◦◦◦⁓⁓———

Gabriel had the fire stoked up in his front room, because it was unseasonably cold for a day in mid-August. Heavy rain pattered against the roof of his cottage, a sound that Gabriel had a special fondness for. Liquorice lay curled into a ball, on what seemed a precarious perch on the back of Gabriel's armchair, which was placed so as to get the maximum warmth from the fire.

Gabriel had just put his potatoes and homegrown carrots on to boil in his little kitchen, where a pork chop browned slowly under the grill, the edge of which had been chopped off and placed in the cat's bowl. Liquorice always expected a small portion of whatever Gabriel was eating.

Now, Gabriel came through to the front room - where the television was on with the sound turned down - and closed the shutters to stop any rain getting in and spattering his mahogany dining table. Then he went to the mantelpiece above the fireplace to wind up the clock (an antique which had been presented to his father on his retirement from the engineering firm to which he'd devoted all his working life), an activity he normally indulged in at precisely this hour, just before 7 p.m. and the local TV news.

There was only one item on the mantelpiece that hadn't had its residence there for a number of years, and this - partly because of its relative novelty value - Gabriel took down from the shelf and leafed through. It was the theatre program from *Puttin' on the Ritz* that he had seen several weeks before at the Bristol Old Vic. He turned to the cast biographies at the back of the program and looked once again at the small and muted picture of the young girl called Maddie Cambay who had played the juvenile lead in the show and had sung so memorably sweetly.

At that moment, the clock dutifully struck 7 o'clock and Gabriel - almost automatically because of force of habit - went to the television to turn up the volume.

It was one of those strange coincidences that happen from time to time in real life as well as in books, that the first item on the local news should concern the very girl whose picture Gabriel had just been studying. The trial of Maddie Cambay - or Madeleine Wetherby as they called her, Cambay being her stage name - was continuing at Bristol's largest Crown Court. A reporter had attended the trial and now was shown standing outside the Court building, giving the salient points.

Perhaps it wasn't quite such a coincidence after all. The case had been very closely followed by the press and media all along; since it was assumed that public interest in a local murder with the added spice of an actress's involvement would be strong. And as Gabriel had not been able to help hearing about it in the previous days and weeks - in the papers, television, radio, not to mention talk by friends and strangers in pubs and on the street even - it had been consciously or unconsciously present in his mind during that time, which maybe was why he hadn't thrown away the theatre program and why he looked at it from time to time.

Gabriel couldn't draw his eyes from the screen. He watched and listened, as the reporter detailed what had happened that day. An artist's impression of the girl, the prosecuting counsel and the judge flashed up on screen. The reporter asserted that the defendant had seemed tense and nervous during her questioning and cross-examination.

Gabriel turned the television off and went into the kitchen, where he had to rescue the carrots, which were about to boil dry, and the pork chop, which was by now done far too well. As he served out his spoiled dinner on to a plate, he recalled two words the reporter had said - "no witnesses". But of course there had been a witness. One witness. Perhaps the girl's case might be entirely different if he came forward and gave his evidence. But he couldn't now - it was too late. Perhaps - if he attended the Court the next day and watched the proceedings for a while - he'd be able to ascertain for sure whether the girl being tried was the same one he'd seen on the bridge. Perhaps he could just sneak into the courtroom without anybody recognizing him or wondering why he was taking an uncharacteristic interest in a murder trial.

Going up to the chest on the landing outside his bedroom, Gabriel rooted about underneath towels and sheets and photographs of forgotten relatives in wooden frames, until he found a small pile of faded letters tied with a blue silk ribbon.

He brought the packet down to the dining room with him and read through them one by one, something he hadn't done in years. Each letter was addressed to "Helen Blandford, Manor House, York" and had a stamp on the front from the post office saying "return to sender". The letters were written on the same heavy vellum paper and the pages were covered with Gabriel's small, neat writing, so different from Helen's large, round hand. Gabriel stifled his regret and shame and forced himself to read them all, taking an almost masochistic pleasure in the pain they evinced. Gabriel felt his face grow hot and his nose began to prickle with the onset of tears.

"I know I said I wished you'd stay in Bristol, but I didn't mean like this," said Paul with a grin, as he stroked Maddie's hand. The couple was sitting together on the beige sofa in Paul's tiny living room, Andy having already departed for the evening show at the theatre. Although the sky had now darkened to a navy blue as they'd watched it through the window, neither of them had yet moved to draw the curtains.

"I wish it was all over."

"I bet you do."

"More tea?"

"No thanks. It's O.K. I'll have to get back to the theatre soon for the evening show."

"Wish I was coming with you" Maddie said with a sigh.

Paul put his arm around her. "It's so unfair what happened to you. You were...you are such a good actress. Why did this have to come along and spoil things?"

"I won't let it ruin my career. Not unless..." Maddie didn't finish her sentence, not wanting to name her greatest fear, that she might be found guilty and sent to prison. "It's cold in here." She distracted herself by lighting the gas fire with a match from the mantelpiece, glancing at the photograph of Paul and his brother, which hung on the wall, as she straightened up. Her body felt stiff and awkward, the result of two months without dancing, or even classes to keep her in shape.

"How did you feel it went today?" asked Paul.

"Terrible."

"No. You don't mean that, do you? I was watching from the public gallery and I thought you looked fine."

"Nice of you to say so. But I could tell I didn't make a good impression."

"How could you tell?"

"Reginald didn't even want to speak to me afterwards, he just told me to go home and try to forget about things. I know what that meant. He thinks I blew it."

"Oh come on. I think you're being a little paranoid. He probably just thought you'd be tired and wouldn't want to talk."

"He told me not to get angry and I did get angry." Maddie slumped down on to the sofa beside Paul with a moan, grabbed one of the cushions and held it against her chest.

"That prosecution guy was really giving you a hard time."

"It's his job."

"He was really snide. What a bastard. I couldn't stand him."

"It's not personal. He has to try and make me look bad, so he'll win his case."

Maddie was staring straight ahead of her. When Paul put his arm around her and gently lifted the hair from her eyes with his other hand, he could see that she was quietly weeping. "Oh, look, it's not that bad. You got a little cross. That doesn't mean they'll think you're guilty. Because you're not."

Maddie was struggling to control her sobs and her voice trembled. "They'll think I'm emotional. Which I am." She sniffed and her breath came out in choking gasps. "I'm not a killer. But they'll think...because I fly off the handle easily I could have...killed him deliberately. I can't convince them. I'm going to lose this case. I can just feel it. I'm going to lose..."

"Now then, now then." Paul held her slender quivering frame with both arms and rocked her gently back and forth. He didn't know what else to say. What consoling words were there, when nobody could predict events? Only the usual platitudes, and he'd run out of those.

Paul was secretly afraid that Maddie's intuitions about the jury may not be as spurious as he pretended. He couldn't put his finger on what was wrong, and, never having attended a trial before, he found it difficult to foretell the outcome. But he'd watched the faces of the jury almost as closely as Maddie had, and he'd seen little compassion there.

All he could do now was comfort Maddie as best he could and hope - and pray - for a miracle.

CHAPTER NINETEEN

A NYONE OBSERVING THE two men who stepped on to the double decker bus and wound their way up the stairs to seat themselves on the top level at the front, would have thought them an unlikely pair: a man in his early fifties in a smart business suit carrying a briefcase, and a black youth who couldn't have been more than twenty-five, dressed in denim jeans and jacket and with a black leather holster slung cowboy-like over one shoulder. They were not chance acquaintances either, as they conversed at length in animated whispers throughout the entire journey from the outskirts of Bristol into the center of town.

"It's been killing me, not talking about it to my girlfriend, you know. I bet she'd have something to say."

"My wife doesn't seem to mind not knowing. I never discuss my work with her anyway, so I suppose this isn't much different."

"Tilly keeps pestering me, going *Oh Carl, just tell me what it's about at least, how are they ever gonna find out,* but I won't tell her nothing."

The older man bent his head until it was almost touching that of his companion, and remarked softly: "We shouldn't really talk about the case here, even."

The black youth gave a quick glance round before imitating his colleague's action: "No one else sitting up top behind us, so we're O.K."

"For the time being, at least."

"Well, Neville man, you've done a few of these cases before. Is it always this hard? I mean, we don't know nothing for sure yet, do we? I thought it would all be sort of coming clear to me by now."

"I usually find that my gut reactions are fairly accurate. I know we can't make any assumptions yet, but I didn't find her very convincing." The older man had a large and protruding nose and his bushy eyebrows jiggled up and down as he spoke.

"I got my doubts. She don't look like a murderer. She's pretty, ain't she?"

"Don't be fooled by appearances. Just because she's pretty--"

The young man started to guffaw, then covered his mouth with his hand, and added quietly: "I'm always like that, you know."

"The pretty ones are the worst." The business-suited man nodded his head sagely, as if this comment provided evidence of his vast experience with attractive members of the opposite sex.

"Yeah, you're right."

"She's guilty, if you ask me. I mean, what doubt is there?"

"It's early days yet. We ain't heard the other witnesses." The young man had a low-pitched voice, with a gentle Bristolian accent.

"We've only got her story to go on, since no one else saw what happened. I wonder who else they can possibly call for the defense."

"I dunno. They might have something up their sleeve."

"I think it's obvious she killed him deliberately. She practically admitted to it yesterday." The older man muted his normally rather nasal voice and spoke with the conviction of one used to being in authority.

"Why though?"

"She worked herself up into a rage. She's one of these feminist types who hates men. Been rejected by one and wants to take her anger out on the whole sex."

"I don't think so..." the young man offered, dubiously.

"She didn't need to kill him. Even if he was attacking her, she could easily have broken free and run away. I mean, we saw the photographs of him yesterday. Only a little chap, wasn't he?"

"You know that bit with the handbag, I didn't get that. I thought she said it was self-defense. So does that mean, even if she did the murder, we've got to let her off?"

"Listen, I was on a similar case last week - another murder, would you believe, although it was less clear cut than this one, two chaps outside a pub and one knifed the other one in a fight. It all depends what you mean by self-defense. It has to be *reasonable* force. But, if it's unreasonable force, then that's manslaughter."

"So if he had a knife to her throat...?"

"Yes, *if*. Nobody's actually seen this damn knife" the man in business suit hissed. "In my opinion, it doesn't exist."

"Well, I just hope we don't have to give our verdict today. I can't make my mind up." The young man smiled and shrugged his skinny shoulders.

"Don't worry, you'll find after the summing up that you know what you think. I always do."

"If you say so. What's the time?"

The older man glanced at the watch on his wrist, and tutted impatiently, allowing himself to raise his voice slightly: "Five to ten. I think we're only just going to make it. Why do these damn buses have to go so slowly! I would have come in the car, only they don't think to provide you with any parking spaces near the Court, of course."

The black youth sighed and squeezed himself out of his seat: "I hate being late. Normally, I'm late for everything and I don't care. But the judge always makes you feel so guilty, don't he, and everybody looks daggers at you..."

"They're paying a lot of public money for our services, you see, so they want to get good value..." The older man followed his companion, and the two of them descended the staircase and hovered by the bus exit, waiting to alight.

The bus grumbled to a halt at a stop peopled by shoppers anxiously awaiting transport, as the two companions descended in front of an ornate Victorian building bearing a sign which said *Bristol Crown Court*. After waiting a few moments for the queue of commuters to file up the step into the vehicle's interior, the conductor pulled the bell twice in quick succession and the bus began to slide into the stream of traffic.

Gabriel was disconcerted to come across a mass of people standing outside the Court, and he walked hesitantly towards the crowd wondering why the building had become such a popular meeting place. Then, as he looked around him taking in the scene, he understood what was happening. Reporters with cameras and microphones were poised like vultures on the steps of the building, obviously waiting to catch a glimpse of - and maybe a word with - the defendant, who had by this time become quite famous in Bristol, as murder suspects often are, her case being given an extra glamour by the fact that she was an actress.

Gabriel positioned himself a little way from the spectators, on a wooden bench, which was conveniently situated for the benefit of weary shoppers. A woman - who looked to be about the same age as himself - was already seated on the bench. She wore a crisp linen suit in pale lilac, stockings and neat brown shoes, and her maroon leather handbag was carefully placed on the seat beside her. Her face was discreetly made up and her hair - golden blonde with flecks of grey - was secured into a prim bun at the back of her head. She sat with her folded hands on her lap, staring straight ahead with an expression of reserved calm. Everything about the woman suggested poise, refinement and the lack of display for which the English are renowned.

As Gabriel seated himself beside her, he felt a prick of recognition. Some quality about the woman was familiar, but he couldn't remember where or when he might have had dealings with her before. Gabriel was disinclined to turn his head blatantly and stare rudely at the woman. So he stole sidelong glances at her and swung his eyes in her direction, pretending to be noticing a passing bus or someone across the street. The more he observed her, the more it dawned on him who the woman must be, although he hadn't seen her for over twenty years. She was more lined, stouter than he remembered, but there was something unmistakable about her bland expression and her air of assurance. Those qualities had wounded him before.

Still, Gabriel kept silent and made no attempt to introduce himself. Surely - he reasoned - the woman would eventually recognize him and make the first move. It would be impolite of her not to acknowledge him. And she'd always been one for propriety. Maybe she wanted nothing to do with him and was therefore feigning ignorance of his presence.

After about ten minutes, the woman rose from her seat, without a glance at Gabriel, and started to meander towards the crowd, where she hesitated, looking about her as if unsure what to do next. Gabriel - forgetting his earlier discretion in a rare burst of candor - ran up to her.

"Margery! M...Margery" he called from behind her. The woman turned to him, and her expression remained completely blank.

"It's Gabriel, G...Gabriel Thatcher. Don't you remember me?"

Recognition gradually dawned on her face, which registered complete and genuine amazement as she realized who had approached her. "Good heavens. Gabriel Thatcher. Yes of course I remember you. How are you?" She presented him with a stiff little close-mouthed smile and a formal hand to shake.

He obliged, feeling awkward and foolish. "Wh...wh... what are you doing here?" The question was blunt, but Gabriel's curiosity impelled him to ask it.

"Oh. Didn't you know? My daughter's on trial." She said it simply, but it was obviously an effort to retain her composure under the circumstances. She didn't mention the fact that the trial was for murder. "I might ask the same question of you, actually."

"*Your* daughter?" Gabriel replied, too stunned to take in Margery's last comment.

"Yes. Oh I see, you didn't realize. I think Madeleine must have been born after we...lost touch with you."

"It's just that...she looks so much like H...Helen. Don't you think?"

Margery gave a bitter little laugh. "People are always saying that." She replied softly, with a look away from Gabriel. "Strange coincidence. It happens in families sometimes. Of course, they are blood related."

"Yes." Gabriel looked down sadly at the ground.

"I'm sorry," said Margery more kindly. "I suppose you didn't know. Helen died. Two years ago." She slightly extended her arm as if to touch him, give him succor, then thought better of it. "It was a car accident." Margery compressed her lips. "Tragic. She was very young. We were all heartbroken. Especially Madeleine. She was very close to her aunt."

"How did it h...happen?"

"Don't ask me please, Gabriel. I still don't like to speak about it."

"I'm sorry."

"Yes. I know you are." She gave him a smile, which was almost warm. "My husband died too. Did you ever meet him? James Wetherby."

"I d...don't think so."

"Cancer. Nobody knows why with that sort of thing. It just happens. Not a very lucky family, are we?" she commented ironically. "How about you? You're looking well."

"Oh...same as ever."

"Are you married?"

"No."

Suddenly there was a movement from the crowd, and a surge of interest around a vehicle that had just pulled up. It was a police car, and Gabriel craned his neck to see who was getting out.

"Excuse me." Margery slipped away and deftly forged her way through the mass of people to the waiting car.

Gabriel watched as a policeman got out of the driver's seat, opened the back door and led out the girl. It was the girl he'd seen at the theatre - he recognized her now, even without the blonde wig - and she blinked her eyes in the sun as if not used to the bright light. She was trying to avoid looking at the persistent reporters around her, ignoring their demands for a comment. When she saw Margery, her face lit up with relief and surprise. Margery went to her and hugged her and said something softly in her ear that Gabriel couldn't catch.

Gabriel could see the girl mouthing the words, "Thanks mum", then she was led through the throng - flanked by the two policemen - and into the Court.

Terry wasn't keen on accompanying his girlfriend to the Court that day, but he didn't intend to let her face the experience alone. To his mind, Bella's loyalty to her friend was misplaced. Although he had always liked Maddie, her current involvement in a murder trial made her far less attractive a person in his eyes. Bella had made the automatic assumption that Maddie was innocent, but he was more dubious. After all - as he'd pointed out several times to Bella - how much did they really know about Maddie, after an acquaintanceship of only a few weeks? Despite these arguments, the generous-hearted Bella had insisted on being Maddie's sole character witness.

If the truth be told, there was a large dose of compassion mingled with Bella's fondness for Maddie. Bella was conscious of her good fortune in having a large, warm and supportive family. But her friend's situation was obviously very different. Maddie was an only child and adopted: of her adoptive parents she talked little, and then with a certain antipathy. Perhaps that was why the bond between the two girls was so strong, and had been so quickly formed. Bella needed to give to people less fortunate than herself, and Maddie appreciated having an ally to protect and support her.

Bella and Terry sat together outside courtroom number ten, Terry immersed in a book and Bella unwilling to talk about the desperate state of her friend. Madeleine Wetherby's trial had been delayed because the one being heard before hers was dragging on for longer than anticipated. Barristers hurtled past, clutching files or deep in earnest conversation with their colleagues or young reps from solicitors' offices. Bella amused herself by watching a great horde of people who waited outside the adjacent courtroom, number eleven. Most of the crowd seemed to be members of a large extended family of garrulous and articulate Asian people. Eavesdropping on their conversation for want of anything better to occupy her, Bella gleaned that the younger son of the family had been arrested for knifing a white youth at the garage where he worked, but the family believed he had been acting in self defense after his father's shop had been set alight by a local racist gang who were terrorizing the neighborhood.

The only other people waiting alongside Bella and Terry for Madeleine Wetherby's trial to commence, were a prim woman in a lilac suit and a quiet, rather dignified looking man in his sixties, who drank in his surroundings with a somber expression.

———⟡———

The next witness to be called for the defense was Bella Marconi. QC Reginald Flowers confirmed to the judge that this was the only other witness the defense would be calling. Bella was Maddie's only trump card, and everything rested on the impression this lone character witness would make on the jury.

Bella was perhaps aware of the responsibility thus placed on her, as she was so apprehensive when entering the witness stand that she stumbled over her oath and had to repeat it. The incident served to demonstrate that actors, once removed from their character mask and the security of a script, are as vulnerable to nerves as any ordinary person.

Bella, however, did well under her questioning by the counsel for defense. She painted a portrait of her friend as lively, quick-witted, generous and outgoing, sensitive and emotional in a positive way. Some of the jury members were smiling when Bella finished and Flowers resumed his seat, and one or two of them made notes, possibly revising their original opinions of Maddie. So Bella had been lulled into a false sense of security and was therefore unprepared for the onslaught she was due to receive from the prosecution barrister during her cross-examination.

"How long have you know Madeleine Wetherby, or Maddie Cambay as you no doubt know her?" Taylor Coleridge made it sound like a sin to have a stage name, and as if he believed that Maddie travelled about the country killing people under various aliases.

"About three months" Bella answered promptly.

"Three months. That's not very long, is it? Would you say it was possible to really get to know someone in as short a period as three months?"

"It's different in the theatre. You can get very close in a short space of time" replied Bella, sticking to her guns with a fortitude admired by some members of the jury.

The prosecution barrister seemed amused by this example of thespian eccentricity, and allowed himself a discreet smirk. "Do you, for example, know anything about Miss Wetherby's childhood?"

Bella appeared a little thrown by the question and hesitated briefly. "Well, yes I do. I know she was an only child..."

"Do you know anything about her background? Whether she was a good student at school? Whether she's had any operations or accidents or convictions even?"

Bella seemed unable to reply. Reginald Flowers opened his mouth to object to this mass of questions, then decided it wasn't going to harm the defense case unduly, so allowed his colleague to roll on.

"Do you know anything about her previous relationships with men, for instance?"

The judge - having caught the defense barrister's eye - leant down from his perch to intervene: "Could you confine your questions to the witness to one at a time, please, Mr. Coleridge. I, for one, have forgotten what the first question was."

There were a few titters amongst the watching crowd, and a couple of the jury members turned and whispered softly to each other. A brief pause ensued, as Coleridge studied his notes and prepared his next question. Then Bella surprised everyone in the courtroom by asserting tartly: "OK, so I don't know much about Maddie's past, but I do know what she's like now, and that's what's important isn't it?"

"All I'm trying to ascertain, Miss Marconi, is the depth - the level, I should say - of your friendship with the defendant. You see, it's possible to think we know someone very well and then be quite surprised when their true character is revealed."

"I know Maddie very well and I know she doesn't have it in her to kill anybody or want to kill anybody" Bella replied firmly.

"Quite." The smirk on Taylor Coleridge's face was so pronounced now that it must have been visible even to the judge.

Bella felt a strong desire to punch the prosecution barrister and call him a patronizing bastard, but she held her tongue for the sake of her friend. Bella glanced across at Maddie - who sat forlornly in the dock - but Maddie wasn't looking at anyone. She was gazing down, her face obscured so that Bella couldn't tell what her friend might be feeling.

Suddenly, Bella was aware that Maddie's defense barrister was on his feet: "Your Honor, this line of questioning is quite unacceptable, not to say irrelevant. I'm going to have to ask that my learned friend stops harassing the witness."

The judge seemed unsurprised by this outburst. "Very well. Mr. Coleridge, please confine yourself to the facts in this case. I feel that your questioning is becoming somewhat too personal and, as such, has little relevance to the guilt or innocence of the defendant."

"I apologize, Your Honor," replied Mr. Coleridge deferentially but without a trace of humiliation in his demeanor. He turned again to Bella: "When the defendant came to your party on June 2nd, did she come alone?"

"No, she came with her boyfriend Alan, but he left before her."

"I see. Why was that? Had they had an argument?"

"Well - a sort of argument, yes. He left with...some girl."

"I see." The prosecution barrister rolled the words around in his mouth and pondered his next line of attack. "And what was the defendant's reaction to this?"

"She was angry with him of course."

"She was angry with him?" Coleridge echoed.

"Who wouldn't be? I'd have been angry." Bella gave a bark of laughter, then caught Terry's eye and saw him looking at her with his chin cupped in his hands.

"So how did she express this anger?"

"She didn't express it. She just...decided she might as well enjoy herself."

"Didn't she want to take some revenge on her boyfriend, for neglecting her in this way?"

"I suppose so...yes...I don't know...no, she didn't want to take revenge on Alan. She just wanted to forget the whole thing."

"I'm afraid, Miss Marconi, you're being rather ambiguous now. Please tell the jury, did the defendant or did she not wish to take revenge on Alan?"

"No, she didn't, she'd forgotten all about it in five minutes. She's not the sort to harbor grudges."

"So she decided to enjoy herself by...how did she choose to do that? By flirting with other men, perhaps?" suggested Coleridge.

"Well, not just flirting with men. That came into it, I suppose. It was a party. But we were also doing other things, like singing for example."

"According to the statement of Ted Bown - the friend of the young boy who was killed - he says he saw the defendant dancing with and kissing Darren Webster. Would you accept that this was true?"

"She might have been. I don't remember seeing her myself. I was probably in the kitchen. You're trying to get me to say Maddie sleeps around. Well I won't. She's just a normal girl."

"Miss Marconi, I'm simply trying to discover the truth."

"The truth is, maybe she danced with Darren. Maybe she kissed him, I don't know, but she didn't invite him home with her. I know that because I made her a cup of coffee at about 5 o'clock in the morning and she said she was walking home alone."

"Could the defendant have made an assignation with Darren in private, without mentioning it to you?"

"She could, but why should she?"

"I asked you whether she could have done."

"Yes, I suppose so, but--"

"Thank you. Can you tell the Court how long the defendant had known her boyfriend, the young man Alan?"

"About two weeks."

"And do you happen to know where the defendant and this Alan originally met each other?"

"They met through me, funnily enough. Alan came to one of my parties; he's a friend of a friend of mine. I'd met him before, though I didn't know him well."

"So the defendant met Alan at one of your parties, in a similar way - in fact - to the way she met Darren later on. When the defendant met Alan, at that particular party, did she go home alone on that occasion or can you remember if she asked the young man to go home with her?"

"Yes, I remember she did ask him home. But that was different. She was interested in Alan."

"How do you know she wasn't interested in Darren?" Coleridge invested the word *interested* with as much salaciousness as possible.

Bella, nonplused for a moment, took a while before replying: "I don't know what you're suggesting."

"I'm not suggesting anything, Miss Marconi. But by your own admission, the defendant has been known to take a young man home with her, a young man she had just met at one of your gatherings. And the jury must draw their own conclusions from this."

Taylor Coleridge asked Bella a few more questions, but they were inconsequential compared to the coup he had just scored with Bella's disclosure regarding Maddie and Alan. A person with a practiced eye observing this courtroom drama as it unfolded may have come to the conclusion that the case was already a *fait acomplis* for the prosecution. Coleridge had only needed to demonstrate the possibility that Maddie had been accompanied home willingly by Darren, to plant the seed in the jury's mind - a nugget of information that could be true, couldn't be discounted - that her motives in hitting him sprang not merely from self-defense. And this seed would grow into a tree, which would be Maddie's undoing. Because the fact was, nobody knew for sure.

Gabriel - watching from his vantage point at the top of the public gallery - took note of the expressions on the jury members' faces, and he felt his heart sink. Gabriel knew now the truth of the horrible coincidence that not only was this the girl he had accidentally witnessed on the bridge, but it was also the girl he had seen on stage a few weeks before, the girl whose photograph had reminded him so much of Helen that he had been moved to try and find his daughter after all these years. These links to Maddie and her fate were like cords that constricted and imprisoned

277

him. He wished that she were just a stranger for whom he could feel little pity, someone whose guilt or innocence would mean nothing to him. But he couldn't escape the significance of the events that had led up to this moment.

Gabriel could tell that the trial was not going well for Maddie. Although he'd never before been in a courtroom, he sensed the atmosphere of despondency that clung to the place like a fine mist. Gabriel found it hard to comprehend why none of the jury members could see that Maddie was innocent. To him it was as clear as glass. But then, he had witnessed part of the event and knew the full story as no one did but the participants. He pondered why he felt so disturbed by the progression of events: was it simply guilt at not having revealed to anyone his covert information and the oppressive knowledge that he would have to tell, sooner or later, if there was no other way to save Maddie? And why did he care so much whether she were saved?

Gabriel felt his eyes drawn to her again and again. He had thought her beautiful on stage and when he'd seen her publicity photograph in the theatre program. Anyone may have thought that - she was a pretty girl. But she seemed even more beautiful to him now, as she sat so small and vulnerable in a plain frock with her untended hair and no make-up on her young face. It wasn't a romantic or a sexual feeling Gabriel had for Maddie, more a desire to protect her and save her from the injustices of the world. She was so young, so alone and - in his eyes at least - so innocent of wrong.

Gabriel remembered with a pang that Maddie was Margery's daughter, not Helen's. He knew it must be true because he had seen the girl call her *mum*, had seen the look of relief on her face when Margery approached her. And Margery had always been so cold towards him, probably believing him to be beneath her sister in social standing and therefore worthless. Somehow - looking at this young girl now, who still reminded him powerfully of his beloved Helen - he couldn't connect Maddie with the dry conventional woman who had given birth to her. It was a peculiar quirk of Fate that she resembled her aunt so much, both in looks and personality.

In the afternoon of that day, Taylor Coleridge called his first witness for the prosecution - Darren's friend Ted Bown. Gabriel was still in the courtroom, unable to drag himself away from the proceedings, having spent a rather miserable hour in the canteen trying to console himself with a limp ham sandwich and a cup of tea. Bella was now seated beside Terry in the public gallery, to watch the completion of her friend's trial.

When the judge had called everyone to order and the jury members and audience were seated, the prosecution counsel began his questioning.

"Is your name Edward Bown?"

"Well, Ted my friends call me, Ted Bown, yeah."

"And do you normally reside at 12 Larkspur House, Coleraine Mansions, Bristol?"

"Yeah, I do."

"What was your relationship to the late Darren Webster?"

"I didn't have no relationship with him. He was just my friend. School friend, you know."

"Now, you made a statement to the police on June 13th, I believe, shortly after Darren's body was found and identified. If you wouldn't mind, I'd just like to take you and the jury through that statement." Here, there was a brief pause while copies of Ted's statement were circulated to the judge and jury. Taylor Coleridge read out the comments made by Bown and the investigating police officers in a flat voice devoid of feeling, while the jury studied their papers.

"Are you still in agreement with everything you said in your statement to the police?"

"Yeah, I am."

"So, you say you and Darren Webster went to a party in Clifton on the night of June 2nd last, because you had been invited by a friend of the hostess?"

"We did."

"Did either of you know the hostess, Bella Marconi, personally?"

"No, we didn't. But my friend Will knows her - he works as a technician at the theatre."

"And who do you remember seeing there, at this party?"

Ted Bown answered punctually as if he'd been well rehearsed: "I saw her there." He pointed to Maddie, who was staring hard at him.

"The witness has indicated the defendant, Madeleine Wetherby. You remember seeing her at the party at Bella Marconi's?"

"I remember her. Definitely."

"What was she wearing? Do you remember that?"

"She had on a red dress. Kinda low cut at the back. Shimmery material."

"And do you remember seeing the defendant with anyone?"

"Oh yeah, I remember, 'cos they were dancing together."

"Who were?"

"Darren and...the defendant. Madeleine."

"For quite some time?"

"Yeah, it was a long time, yeah."

Maddie again glared at Ted, trying to humiliate him into retracting this blatant lie, but Ted stubbornly refused to return her gaze. Maddie felt so furious and frustrated at her inability to say anything in her own defense, that a red flush started to burn her ears.

"Were they dancing...intimately?"

The young man seemed to ponder this, and then replied with conviction. "Yeah, at one point, yeah they were. And then they started kissing and that."

"And did Darren tell you that he was going to go home with the defendant?"

This time there was no hesitation: "Yes."

"What did he say to you, exactly?"

"He said he'd got off with this girl and she was going to take him home with her."

Maddie motioned furiously to Eva Goldstein to approach her in the dock, and handed the solicitor a slip of paper with some hastily scribbled words. The paper said: *That's a lie!* Eva handed the paper to Flowers at the first opportunity.

"When was the last time you saw Darren?" continued Coleridge.

"It was sometime in the morning, that morning after the party, I don't remember exactly when. Probably about three or four o'clock."

"Did you see Darren or the defendant leave the party?"

"No, I didn't see anything, because I passed out." The young man grinned sheepishly and acknowledged the sniggers from the audience.

"So, was that the last time you saw your friend alive?"

"Yeah, it was."

"No further questions, your honor."

Taylor Coleridge resumed his seat and then it was Reginald Flowers' turn to cross-examine the witness. Flowers tried valiantly to establish that Ted was lying about his friend's presumption to have been invited home with Maddie, or that Ted was simply an unreliable witness. But the young man stuck stubbornly to his story and wouldn't be swayed in his assertion that Maddie had taken Darren home with her deliberately. Since it was simply a case of her word against his with no possibility of proof either way, after about half an hour or so Flowers moved on to another topic.

"How long had you known Darren Webster?"

"All me life, pretty much. We was at school together."

"And to your knowledge, did your friend ever come into contact with the Law?"

"What do you mean?"

"Was he ever charged with a criminal offence?"

"No, I don't think so..." Ted Bown scratched his head.

"Did anyone ever bring a charge against him--?"

"Your Honor" interrupted the prosecution counsel, springing from his seat. "I really don't see what relevance the victim's possible criminal record can have in this case." Coleridge stressed the word *victim*.

"Can you enlighten us, Mr. Flowers, as to the relevance of your questioning?" enquired the judge, leaning forward.

"If you would just allow me a couple more questions, the matter may well become clear, Your Honor" wheedled the defense barrister, swishing his cloak so that the more observant members of the audience caught a glimpse of orange and pink tie.

"Very well" sighed the judge. He waved at Coleridge, who resumed his seat with a weary air.

"As you were at school with Darren Webster and a good friend of his" continued Flowers to the witness, "You surely cannot have been unaware that he was in fact charged with a criminal offence - though the case never actually came to Court - by a certain Winifred Evans?"

"Winnie Evans, that's right" replied Bown.

There was a pause as Flowers waited for the witness to elucidate further. When no more explanation came, the barrister continued: "Do you know the nature of the charge that Winifred Evans brought against Darren Webster?"

Bown replied with a blank look.

"What was it she accused your friend of?"

"Oh. She said that he'd raped her."

"I see."

"But she was lying..."

"That is your belief, is it? That Winifred was deliberately lying?"

"I mean, she was his girlfriend, wasn't she? They'd been going out together two years."

"How old was Darren at the time of this incident?"

"About fourteen, I think."

"And the girl? Winifred Evans? How old was she?"

"Erm..." Bown scratched his head again. "She was two years younger, so she would have been twelve."

"And do you know if the case ever came to trial?"

"No, it didn't. He wasn't charged or nothing. Winnie took it all back."

"She retracted her statement?"

"Yeah. That's how I know she was lying."

"No further questions, Your Honor."

As it was already 3.30 p.m. the judge decided to finish, and no more witnesses were heard that day. Gabriel was disgorged from the Court with the mass of other people who had been sitting in the public gallery. He tried to sneak a last look at Maddie, but she'd already been taken away. He'd hated it in the courtroom - the very atmosphere of so-called justice oppressed him - but he knew he'd have to come again. He was drawn to it like a drug user with a habit.

He'd have to come again tomorrow. And would he act this time? Could he steel himself to act? He didn't know.

CHAPTER TWENTY

IT WAS NOW half-past eleven in court number 10, and the room was getting hot. Quite a few people were already looking forward to the luncheon adjournment. But they had to wait until Taylor Coleridge had finished with his next prosecution witness, who was now occupying the witness box. Her name was Sharon Collier, and she had also been to the fateful party on June 2nd.

"What is your current occupation, Miss Collier?"

"I'm an actress. I'm...not working at the moment."

"What job were you doing at the time of the party in question?"

"I was in *Puttin' on the Ritz* at the Bristol Old Vic. I was playing a small part and understudying one of the leads - the part of Henrietta."

"And who normally played that part?"

"Maddie Cambay, I mean, Madeleine Wetherby."

"The defendant?"

"Yes."

"Did you see the defendant at that party?"

"Oh yes, I saw her. I remember, because she made quite a scene."

"What kind of a scene? Could you describe it to us?"

"Well, she had this terrible argument with her boyfriend, Alan. I know because I was standing near her at the time. She started ranting and raving at him."

"Do you know what they were arguing about?"

"I'm not sure. I think it was something about another woman. But anyway, she shouted at him like anything and everybody just stopped and looked. We were all shocked, you know."

"And what happened to Alan after that?"

"Oh, he left. I didn't see him any more."

"What effect did this argument seem to have on the defendant?"

"I don't know. She was pretty hyped up, I guess."

Gabriel had stopped listening to external voices. All he was hearing now was the voice in his own head, his guilty conscience, telling him that he must act. But even the thought of getting up in the courtroom and telling what he knew - especially now at this late stage when he would be ridiculed for not having come forward earlier - made his heart race with terror. He heard again the voices of his childhood classmates - the cruelest voices in the world - chanting *Gabriel Thatcher, never has an answer, stutterer, stutterer, Gabriel Thatcher* and their vicious, gleeful laughter. He wiped his brow with his handkerchief and realized that he was dripping with sweat.

Now the defense counsel was cross-examining the witness. Reginald Flowers held his robe by the shoulders and poked his head forward as he spoke, his rather beaky nose sticking out like some comical bird. "After the defendant had a slanging match with her erstwhile boyfriend, what happened next?"

"What happened?"

"Well, did Alan just walk away or did he retaliate in any way?

"Oh, he retaliated. He knocked her over."

"Who? The defendant?"

"Yes. He punched her. In the chest I think." There was a gasp of astonishment and disapproval from the public gallery. "Then he walked away."

"I see. And did you feel that the violence of his reaction was justified?"

"Well...she had provoked him but...no, not really."

"And what did the defendant do then?"

"Well, she sat on the floor for a bit and...I think she was crying. Bella was comforting her. I'm not sure what she did then. I went into the other room."

"To your knowledge, the defendant didn't follow Alan or attempt to prolong the argument in any way?"

"No..."

Taylor Coleridge rose to his feet and addressed the judge. "Your Honor, where is this questioning leading? We seem to be digressing somewhat from the facts and going off on some sort of tangent."

"I agree," said the judge. "What is the purpose of your current line of questioning, Mr. Flowers?"

"I'm merely trying to establish" replied the defense counsel, "That the defendant's level of reaction to what must have been a fairly traumatic incident - being knocked to the ground, physically punched by her boyfriend - was not beyond what might be considered normal. I'm endeavoring to show that the defendant is basically an ordinary girl caught up in exceptional circumstances, and does not possess an unusually hostile nature, which might have lead to her attacking the victim with no due provocation. In my opinion, this has clearly been demonstrated by her behavior at the party prior to the events we're considering in this case."

"Very well. But I must ask you to turn your attention now to other matters" said the judge.

"I have no further questions, Your Honor."

———

The next prosecution witness was Alan Leigh, who mumbled so much when giving his oath that he had to be asked to repeat it. He lounged into the witness box and stood with his hands resting on the edge of the box, arms wide and legs apart, as if prepared for a fight. He stared unflinchingly at the prosecution counsel and refused to even glance at his erstwhile girlfriend. But Taylor Coleridge treated him with such gentlemanly courteousness while questioning him that the young man could be seen to visibly relax his hitherto taut body and he replaced the scowl on his face with a self-assured grin. When Reginald Flowers got up to cross-examine, however, Alan resumed his tense and wary expression.

"Mr. Leigh, can you tell the Court how long you had been friendly with the defendant at the time of the party on June 2nd?"

"I dunno. About six weeks."

"You've told my learned friend Mr. Coleridge that the defendant assaulted you verbally. Had there been any other incidents of this kind during your relationship with her?"

"We always argued a lot. But not that bad usually."

"So this was your worst, I mean to say your most violent argument, would you agree?"

"Yeah, I suppose so."

"Mr. Leigh, in your opinion, what kind of person is the defendant?"

"Erm...well, sort of...I dunno...ordinary really."

Maddie glared at her former boyfriend. She felt aggrieved to hear her personality summed up as *ordinary*. But Alan didn't appear to notice her. She glanced at the jury and noticed that one of the members at the front - a youngish black man with a pleasant face - was looking at her, as if trying to size her up. Immediately, she ducked her head and pretended to be very interested in doing up the top button of her shirt.

"So in your opinion the defendant is an average person, not especially prone to losing her temper or overly emotional?"

"Well - she is an actress. And a woman. What can I say?" Alan gave a grunt of laughter and looked at the watchers in the public gallery, courting their approval. "They're all emotional, aren't they?"

"Did the defendant ever lose her temper with you?"

"Oh yeah, she got mad a few times, yes. I got cross with her and all."

"And when she was cross with you, how did she express her feelings?"

"She'd nag me, you know. She'd say stuff like I was no good and she was going to leave me. We always made it up, though."

"But she never expressed her feelings by hitting you or physically assaulting you?"

"No way. Well, I mean, she wouldn't dare. She's smaller than me, isn't she? And I'm a trained boxer."

"When was the last time you saw the defendant that night? The night of the party?"

"Just after...after we had the argument. I left after that."

"What would you say was the defendant's mood when you left her at the party? Was she still angry?"

"I dunno. I don't think she was still angry, no. She was upset. She was in a bit of a state, crying like. But I suppose she must have got over it."

"No further questions, Your Honor."

The soaring notes of the flute washed over Gabriel, filling his soul with tenderness. The music seemed to stir something deep within him, evoking feelings he had almost forgotten. The sight of the man playing distracted him - his long black hair falling over one side of his face as he swayed to the rhythm of the notes he created - and Gabriel wished he could close his eyes and cut off from the outside world, letting only the music speak to him. But he didn't want Kate to think he was sleeping through the concert.

As if she felt him thinking of her, Kate lightly pressed his hand, and he turned to catch sight of her smiling at him contentedly. She gave his hand a gentle squeeze with her own and then withdrew it, turning back again to view the musicians.

All too soon - it seemed to Gabriel - the concert was ending. The music swelled to its final climax and, after a few seconds of awed silence, the audience broke into enthusiastic applause. Gabriel and Kate - from their seats in the front row - clapped even louder than the rest. When the pianist stood up to take his bow accompanied by the young male flautist, they looked flushed and triumphant and at the same time bashfully surprised that this delighted reception was for them. Gabriel liked to be near enough the stage to see the expressions of the musicians; it made them seem like human beings rather than just creators of beautiful music.

"Thank you for bringing me. I've r...really enjoyed it" he said to Kate, and took her arm to lead her out of the hall.

They made their way slowly through the throng, and once out in the street, Kate suggested they walk back together to her son's house in Bristol where she was staying for the evening.

Gabriel was aware of how little Kate had changed, in the thirty years since he'd last seen her. She'd been very pretty as a teenager, in a fresh-faced, English sort of way, and she still had the air of a woman who realizes she's charming. Gabriel remembered how they'd played together as children, he, Kate and her brother. The three of them had been inseparable playmates. He wondered if Kate still recalled the time they'd climbed the apple tree in his family garden and thrown rotten apples at unsuspecting passers by from their vantage point. Now, it seemed impossible to imagine that this rather stout, self-possessed and, yes, elderly woman had ever been that cheeky little girl poking her head between the branches and laughing at strangers.

Kate recognized his reflective mood. "I always wanted to live in that house of yours. Did you know that?" Gabriel shook his head. "But then I married Hamish and moved to Scotland and, well, vets don't have as much money as you might imagine." She laughed a little, a sweet girlish giggle that Gabriel remembered from the old days. "It's been a good life, though, all in all, and the children are a blessing. What would I have done without them just after Hamish died? They really were a comfort."

Their steps echoed a little as they walked down the quiet avenue, lit dimly by street lamps, their arms linked. A feeling of peace suffused the couple, and Gabriel felt as relaxed with Kate as he had always done. Thirty years of distance had done nothing to staunch the depth of their friendship.

"It was the garden, I think, that appealed to me about your house," said Kate, still in her reverie. "So big. We only had a little cabbage patch. But you and that lovely big garden, with all the flowers. Is it still the same?"

"Very much. I t...try to keep it up."

"You always were good with growing things. Get that from your father."

It had seemed only natural, when they became teenagers, that Gabriel and Kate would start courting, even tacitly assumed by both families that they would one day marry. And perhaps they would have done, or should have done. But Gabriel had moved to Bristol to work as a photographer for the local paper there. He wondered, now, how different his life might have been if he had married Kate. He would never have met Helen, never have gone to India or Nepal, never have... But it was useless and pointless to speculate on what might have been.

"Do you see much of Rex's boy - Ian, isn't it? And his children?"

"Oh yes. Every S...Sunday."

"That's good."

Gabriel smiled at her. He knew what she was thinking. It was good that he saw his nieces and nephews, because he had no children of his own. He was conscious of Kate's pity for him, that she felt he had led a rather lonely life as a bachelor. But he had made his own choices. And he had been happy, in his own way. Or, had he?

"Do you still paint?"

"Paint?"

"Yes, don't you remember your watercolors? I used to think they were very impressive."

"Oh, that's right. Of the D...Downs--"

"And the seaside. And, you did one of Cheddar Gorge once, do you remember? I loved that one. Do you still have it?"

"S...somewhere. I suppose."

"I thought you were very talented you know."

"Really?"

"Of course." She seemed surprised that Gabriel should question this. "You were a gifted artist. A natural. I suppose, when you took up photography...?"

"Well, yes, that did rather t...take over. It must be years since I p...painted anything."

"You should do. You shouldn't let these things go. If you've got a talent."

"Yes. M...maybe you're right."

They walked on in silence for a few minutes, each locked in their own thoughts. Now they were crossing the bridge, and Gabriel shivered a little as he looked down at the cold water beneath them and thought of the trial, something he'd been glad to put out of his mind for one evening at least. He felt a great urge to tell Kate all the things that had been on his mind. Perhaps she would understand. She had always been sympathetic and compassionate.

But the words didn't come easily to him. He rehearsed several ways of opening the conversation. He had to begin at the beginning. "D...did I ever tell you, Kate, about my trip to N...Nepal?"

She looked at him in mild surprise. "No, I don't believe you ever did. When was that? Recently?"

"Oh no. A long t...time ago. I went with a f...friend."

"Which friend?"

"My g...girl friend. H...Helen."

"Oh, I remember you mentioning her. That must have been after I moved to Scotland."

"Yes, I think so."

"A long time ago. It must have been very exciting to see the East. Especially in those days. Such a different culture. Did you paint any of the temples?"

"No. I took some pho...photographs."

They were in Kate's street now, only a few doors away from her son's house. Soon, Gabriel knew, he would be at the front door saying goodnight and maybe making an arrangement to meet again. He couldn't possibly get to the heart of what he wanted to talk about in the few seconds remaining to them, the subject was too vast, too painful and too indefinable to be squashed into the tail end of a conversation. And so he closed his mouth and shut the lid on the suitcase marked *secrets*.

They walked to the door and Kate thanked him for a lovely evening and kissed him on the cheek, embracing him momentarily with her fragrant warmth. They promised to meet up again soon and Gabriel knew it wasn't an empty promise, but one they would both be glad to keep. They were both alone now, in their different ways.

That night, Gabriel let himself in to his quiet house, and looked for Liquorice, softly calling her name, but she was nowhere to be seen. It was unusual for the cat to be out on nocturnal jaunts these days, so he looked for her in all her favorite hiding places - under the kitchen table, in the cupboard under the stairs - but she had disappeared. He didn't usually bother to ascertain her whereabouts at night, since he knew she was perfectly capable of looking after herself, but on this occasion he felt in need of her company. Like a typical cat, she was never there when he needed her warm feline body to reassure him.

Gabriel went up to his bedroom and turned out the lights. He'd left the curtains open so that he could look out at the sky, tonight lit up by stars and a low white moon, almost completely full. The silence of the night descended as it does in the country with absolute stillness, and yet Gabriel couldn't sleep. He tossed about in his bed, alternately throwing off the bedclothes in a hot impatience, and clawing them back around him against the chill air. He got up twice to go to the toilet and both times called out for Liquorice, but she was never there. He left the bedroom window open, in the hopes that a long black shadow would jump in and deposit herself on his bed, but she didn't come.

Gabriel felt as though he didn't sleep a wink that night. His mind was full of tangled thoughts and emotions that clamored to be heard and would give him no rest. But he must have dropped off, at least for a little while, because he was aware of waking from a dream to the dawn chorus at about 5 a.m.

The dream was still fresh in his memory, and he held on to it as with slippery fingers clutching a slithery fish. He lay for a few moments and tried to revisualize the dream, to piece together the fragments of the jigsaw into a coherent whole and make sense out of what he'd seen.

Helen had been in the dream. Helen and the daughter Gabriel had never met. It had left him feeling confused, bewildered, although he couldn't work out why. It hadn't been a bad dream or had the frightening impact of a nightmare. Yet it had seemed very real, more real than any other dream he'd ever had, as if it had been an actual waking experience. He wondered if it had been that way because it was unusually significant, or because he had been so close to the threshold of wakefulness. He didn't know. But he felt he must try to remember the dream. He had an impression it might give him some clue what to do.

He and Helen had been in Nepal, as they had been in reality, all those years ago. That part of the dream he'd had many times before. They'd been on holiday, as before, and happy. They were always happy. Gabriel never dreamed about their arguments or the bad days, it was always the good times that stayed with him.

But this time, he'd come back with her to England, and then to her parent's house in York and they'd been together. They'd got married. Gabriel smiled at the blissful recollection of what had never been; basked in the memory the dream had given him. They had married and Helen had had her daughter, the daughter she'd conceived in India. The daughter was born and they called her... Gabriel searched his memory looking for this pearl of information but it wouldn't come, he couldn't remember.

She'd been a happy, fat baby with lots of dark hair, he remembered that. She'd laughed and gurgled and played, just like Rex's children, to whom Gabriel had been a favorite uncle.

And then, all of a sudden, she'd fallen ill. Gabriel couldn't remember why, or what was wrong with her. All he could see was the fat little body wasting gradually away, the baby screaming in pain, and Helen crying and begging him to do something quickly, before it was too late.

Helen was asking him to do something, but what was it she wanted him to do? Gabriel tried to go back into the dream in his mind, to remember more. He heard distant music; as if the dream were a film with an accompanying score and they were all characters in it. He saw Helen's tear-stained face, and the baby's thin wasted body *(what was her name?)* and heard Helen's voice telling him to please save her. But what was it he had to do?

Gabriel tried and tried, but he could remember no more. It was disturbing to have only these pieces of the dream revealed to him. He'd wanted an answer, but the dream solved nothing, just posed more questions.

It was impossible to sleep now, and the day had by now become almost fully light. Gabriel got out of bed, put on his slippers and dressing gown and padded down to the kitchen to make a cup of tea. There - in the middle of the room - was an offering from Liquorice, obviously the fruit of the previous evening's labors. A dead bird, its head bent back, its feathers matted with blood, lay in a clump on the floor.

CHAPTER TWENTY-ONE

IT WAS WELL after 1.45 p.m. by the time Gabriel managed to reach the Court. He'd had to work at the Camera Obscura building that morning and his mind had been far removed from his work, as he showed the groups of tourists into the small dark room and carried out his demonstrations with practiced and automatic precision, his head full of juries and verdicts, arguments and decisions, snatches of courtroom jargon which kept whirling about in his mind.

At one o'clock, Gabriel had ushered the last of the tourists out of the Camera Obscura and quickly locked up the building, hanging a *closed* sign on the door. Then he'd walked swiftly to the bus stop to catch the bus into town. Naturally the bus had taken longer than usual to arrive, and Gabriel had waited impatiently in the queue, cursing the bad luck that had stopped him being free that morning.

As the bus pulled up outside the County Court, Gabriel could see that the area outside the building was deserted, and he guessed with a sinking heart that the trial must already be in progress. He raced up to the large front door and looked at a white sheet pinned to it, to confirm in which courtroom the Madeleine Wetherby trial was being heard that day, then made his way to courtroom number ten as fast as he could, and arrived breathless and panting.

Gabriel saw to his relief that a knot of people were hovering outside the courtroom, murmuring in low voices. He recognized the barrister who was defending Maddie, currently deep in earnest discussion with the prosecution counsel. Margery was also present, attired today in a lemon-colored suit and sitting demurely by herself on a bench by the door. Gabriel was on the point of approaching her, when an incident occurred which brought him to an abrupt halt.

Maddie came out of a back room, as usual accompanied by two policemen, one on either side of her. She looked haggard and drawn, her face made to seem thinner by the stark style of her hair, which was pulled back in a tight ponytail. But Gabriel's attention had been caught by something else about the girl's appearance.

Maddie was wearing something around her neck, whose vivid colors contrasted sharply with her drab wardrobe. It was an article as familiar to Gabriel as the pattern of the wallpaper in his own house. Had he not stared at a fragment of the same material a thousand times?

It was an Indian shawl, faded slightly now after many washings, and still with one frayed edge where a piece had been ripped off. It had been bought in Kathmandu, where Gabriel had been with Helen twenty-five years ago. And now - as if seeing the whole trip flash before the retina of his memory in a split second - Gabriel realized the significance of Maddie's stage name, her chosen name. Cambay. It was the name of the place where Helen had found out she was pregnant with her child, when Gabriel had been too ill with a stomach upset to realize. A little place on the West coast of India.

And suddenly Gabriel knew the truth. He knew it in his bones, without needing confirmation from anybody else.

Maddie had been taken into the courtroom to give her evidence and Margery was standing up now, about to follow her in, along with the rest of the waiting crowd. Gabriel advanced on the woman calling herself Maddie's mother and declared without preamble: "You lied to me!"

She swung around, startled. "What?"

"You said Maddie was your daughter."

"Good heavens, Gabriel. Please lower your voice. What are you talking about?"

"She's not your daughter. How could she b...be? She's H...Helen's. Isn't she? Tell me the truth, M...Margery. P... please!"

Margery sighed. "Oh Gabriel, what does it matter now? Helen's dead. We brought Madeleine up, James and I. She thought of us as her parents."

"D...doesn't she know?"

"We didn't want to disillusion her. It would only have caused her suffering."

"B...but...b...but..." Gabriel's mouth felt as if it would explode with the force of all the words he wanted to say. "She's m...my daughter too. M...mine. And you k...kept her away from me!"

Margery spoke in a quick forceful whisper. "Don't make a scene, for heavens sake. Of course we didn't keep you from her. It was Helen who didn't want to see you again. Can't you understand? It was all her idea."

But now Gabriel wasn't listening to her. He didn't care any more what she felt, didn't care any more about what had happened in the past, only what was happening now. He broke away from Margery and bolted for the doorway of courtroom number ten.

"Gabriel, come back! What are you doing? Gabriel!" Margery's desperate injunctions made no impression on Gabriel's retreating back, as she hurriedly followed him into the courtroom.

CHAPTER TWENTY-TWO

G ABRIEL APPROACHED EVA Goldstein who was sitting
on the left-hand side of the bench, next to the stack
of law books which marked Reginald Flowers' place: "I
have some evidence" he uttered in a forceful whisper.

Eva was startled by this unexpected confession from
a stranger, and wondered vaguely if he were some crank
wishing to draw attention to himself, but she remained
composed as she replied under her breath. "You do realize
that all the evidence has been heard in this case? The
defense is just about to conclude."

"Yes, but I want to speak. I witnessed the k...killing.
I want to give evidence."

Reginald Flowers was at that moment on his feet,
speaking in a clear and vigorous voice to the judge: "Your
honor, I call no more witnesses. That concludes--"

"Excuse me one moment!" To the astonishment of
everyone in the courtroom, the defense barrister was
unceremoniously interrupted in the middle of his speech
by a voice at his rear, and a hastily waved arm. Reginald
Flowers turned to see his client's solicitor beckoning
him frantically, excused himself with as much dignity
as he could muster, and had a hurried counsel with

Eva Goldstein, while the judge and jury looked on in amazement, wondering what on earth could be happening.

Reginald and Eva regarded Gabriel as if he were an angel come from heaven to save them, and they took only a few moments to arrive at their decision. Flowers again addressed the judge: "Your honor, I must apologize for the delay. It seems that the defense do have one more witness to call. However, I would ask leave to consult with my client first. Could I ask for a brief adjournment?"

Gabriel could see the crowd in the public gallery beginning to shift disgruntledly in their seats, and heard their voices grumble in dissatisfaction at the prospect of having their verdict further delayed. He caught a glimpse of Margery's lemon suit right at the front of the spectators. Maddie was in the dock, staring at him with an amazed expression and a glint of recognition in her eyes.

Gabriel's hands were sweating. He prayed to God that he was not too late. He didn't think about what he was going to say to Maddie or her barrister or how to prepare himself for the conversation. He didn't care any more about how he would come across when giving evidence or whether people would laugh at him. That no longer mattered to him at all. He only prayed to be able to take the stand, to have the opportunity of saving the girl he now knew to be his daughter.

The judge announced in sonorous tones to the assembly: "As there is further important evidence to be heard in this case. I am calling a brief adjournment. Members of the jury, you will retire to your room for one hour. We will reconvene at 3.00 p.m."

There was an audible sigh of discontent from the public at being denied their conclusion, and looks of bemusement from the jurors. Gabriel, however, was overjoyed.

———m∾∾⌒⊙⌒∾∾m———

The jurors were grouped around the large wooden table, talking in animated voices. The debate which had been raging about the guilt or innocence of Madeleine Wetherby ever since the commencement of her trial several days ago had become even more heated, now that there was an unexpected pause in the proceedings and the possibility of a surprise defense witness whose evidence nobody could predict. A couple of the male jurors stood in one corner of the room, smoking and carrying on a private conversation which may or may not have concerned the case. The other ten remained seated, some sipping cold coffee from plastic cups, some fingering their already worn notes, some reviewing for a third or fourth time the witnesses statements which had been given to them as exhibits, and hoping that somewhere a gem of information in them would make their decision clearer and the correct verdict more obvious.

"I think we should take another vote" asserted Gloria, pushing back her mass of red hair with one hand.

"What good would that do?" questioned Neville. His business suit had begun to take on a crumpled air, after the hours spent in Court, but he kept on his jacket despite the stifling heat inside the small and windowless room.

"Some people might have changed their minds. I want to know--"

"Good idea. Let's take another vote" interjected Carl, the young black man who had stared at Maddie in the courtroom the day before. He alone among the jurors managed to maintain his enthusiasm, perhaps because this being his first case, he still found the whole process novel and exciting. "Hands up, all those in favor of acquittal." His hand shot up in the air.

"Hang on" bossed Gloria aggrieved at having the initiative whipped out of her hands. "We're not all ready yet. Ben! George! We're taking a vote."

"What, another one?" whined George from the corner, unwillingly stubbing out his third cigarette that hour.

"All those in favor of acquittal" repeated Carl, and this time four other hands joined his in a straggly line. Carl swept his eyes around the room eagerly, to see if any of the others would change their minds.

"That's five" noted Neville, and wrote down the number on his spiral notepad. "Right. All those in favor of conviction." This time, seven hands were raised, counted and noted.

"What do we do now?" sighed Carl.

"You know, this is a bit premature anyway," remarked Ravi, a quietly spoken Indian man who was seated at the end of the table. "We haven't heard all the evidence yet."

"Who is this new witness?" demanded Gloria, now busily buffing her long nails with a file which she'd withdrawn from her pocket at the first sign of boredom with events.

"I saw him going up to Madeleine's solicitor and whispering something in her ear" interposed Maureen from her seat beside Gloria. "An old man with white hair."

"When did he come in?" asked Gloria.

"Just after Judge Collins did the summing up. He walked straight in and went up to the solicitor. I don't think she'd ever seen him before, she looked that surprised." Maureen's large pale eyes were glittering behind her wire-rimmed spectacles.

"Do you really think the defense knew nothing about this new witness?" said Neville skeptically, taking a sip of coffee and wrinkling his nose in disgust at the taste.

"It doesn't matter, though" opined Carl. "What we should do now is just go round the table and ask everybody why they think she's guilty or not, so that we can all come to the same decision."

"Exactly" agreed Gloria. "I mean, this is stupid, seven against five. We've got to all agree on the verdict--"

"Or come to a majority decision" added Neville.

"Well, we're not very near that at the moment, are we?" retorted Gloria.

"God - we've discussed it enough" put in George from the corner. He and his smoking pal sniggered in a superior way, having maintained their air of detachment ever since the start of the trial. "Over and over. People should make their minds up and stick to it."

"Let's go round the table," insisted Carl. "You go first, Gloria. What do you think?"

"Well, as I pointed out before" replied Gloria, glad of a chance to put forward her point of view. "You see I can't really believe that she didn't know he was following her. I mean, I've been followed down the street, at night, by some creep. And as soon as I heard his footsteps I just ran. I think it's ridiculous that she says she didn't hear him - and it was in the early morning for God's sake when it must have been totally quiet. How come she didn't hear him? And how come she didn't just run away?"

"I'm not sure I agree" began Ravi. "If he was wearing soft sneaker type shoes and keeping a long way back, she might not have heard him. And even if she did hear footsteps, she might not have thought they meant she was in danger, being followed or whatever..."

"That's right," agreed Carl. "And even if she did hear him and that, what does it prove?"

"I believe she's lying and that she invited him home with her and now she doesn't want to admit it," said Neville.

"How do we know she invited him home?" said Carl.

"How do we know she didn't?"

"I agree with Neville," said Maureen timidly. "I think she invited the young man home and then regretted it."

"Why?"

"Well, she's that sort of girl, isn't she? I mean, she's an actress, she's young and unmarried--"

"She sleeps around--" added Gloria.

"We heard from her friend that she took that other young man home after meeting him at a party, that Alan. Why didn't she do it again?"

"So it was a date rape?" suggested Carl.

"I don't think date rape exists," asserted Gloria. "I mean, if you really don't want to sleep with a guy you don't get yourself into a sticky situation where he could jump on you."

"I think you're being rather flippant, actually. I mean, if a guy just suddenly leaps on you from behind and sticks a knife to your throat, what are you supposed to do then?" queried Ravi in a reasonable tone.

"That's right. It's not always so easy," agreed Carl.

"Well, it's all very well for her to say that, *He had a knife to my throat*, but we don't know that he did, do we? I mean, the police never found the knife, although they did look for it. Nobody else can back her up."

"The knife might be a convenient bit of drama that she's added to make it look better for her," said Neville, nodding his head and causing his large eyebrows to bob comically up and down. "We can't assume it's true, if we've got no evidence of the knife and no other witnesses."

"We can't assume it's not true, either" Carl pointed out.

"Yes," said Maureen with a sigh. "That's why it's so difficult. How on earth are we supposed to judge this case? We've got the girl telling her side of the story and the rest of the evidence is just other people saying *Oh yes, I think she was feeling angry enough to kill him* or *Oh no, I can't imagine her doing that*. So how do we make a decision? I mean, it's impossible."

"We've got to go on our gut feeling," suggested Gloria. "My gut feeling is it wasn't self-defense. I don't like her. Have you seen her sitting there? She never shows any expression."

"You're not supposed to let that influence you, what you think of the defendant," objected Carl. "Just stick to the facts."

"There aren't enough facts. And we've got to decide something. I think she did it; she deliberately pushed him over the bridge. And I'm not going to change my mind" said Neville.

"Neither am I" declared Gloria.

"Why not? You've only changed it five times already" sneered George.

"Let's wait until we hear this new evidence. That might change everybody's mind" interjected Ravi, hoping to restrain his colleagues from further pointless argument.

"Yes, you're right," groaned Maureen. "I hope they let us back into the courtroom soon. It's getting awfully hot in here."

———

When he came to stand in the witness box later that afternoon, Gabriel found the experience to be different from how he had always imagined. He felt excited, but not at all nervous. Perhaps because all his energies were concentrated on doing the job he had to do, or because for the first time in his life he felt an overwhelming urge to communicate something to a group of people. He was the only one who knew the whole truth and so he had to speak out. Gabriel didn't look at anyone in the crowd, but spoke directly to his questioner, who was at this moment QC Reginald Flowers.

"Mr. Thatcher, could you tell the Court what you saw from the Camera Obscura building on the morning of June 3rd?"

"I saw a c...couple...two people, on the bridge."

"Could you see the people clearly at that distance?"

"They were quite small of course, being a long d... distance away, but I know it was a m...man and a woman and the woman was wearing a red c...coat or a red dress, something like that." There was a murmur from the watching crowd. It had already been established in earlier evidence that Maddie was wearing a red party dress on the fateful day, because Taylor Coleridge had used the point to suggest that she was acting the siren at the party. Maddie herself was looking up now, leaning forward in her chair, her taut gaze intent on Gabriel.

"And what did you see these people do?"

"Well, I saw the girl w...walking along and the man behind her. At first I thought they were s...strangers. Then the girl stopped and looked round. M...maybe the man had called something out to her. They seemed to be t...talking. Then the girl walked on some more and the man f...followed her again. Then..." Gabriel paused, searching his mind, trying to recollect the image he had seen precisely, to give a faithful and accurate rendition of what had happened. "I s...saw the man...he seemed to g...grab the girl from behind and they seemed to be f... fighting. Yes, they s...seemed to be struggling. She had her b...back to me. He had her p...pinned against the wall. And I was thinking m...maybe I should go and h...help or something b...because it looked like he was attacking her."

"So, did you go and help?"

"Yes. I ran down to the b...bridge. It took me a few minutes, because it's ab...bout half a mile away. When I got there, I didn't kn...know what to do, I was f...frightened. I could see that the man had a kn...knife, a big long knife... and he was p...pressing it to the girl's th...throat."

An audible sigh seemed to be expelled from all members of the audience at once, as they heard mention of the knife.

"Was the girl screaming while this was happening?"

"I don't think she was able to. She was sort of ch... choking...gasping..."

"What happened next?"

Gabriel continued: "I think the man h...heard me because he suddenly turned round and s...saw me. And then, the girl seemed to s...swing something at him and she hit him on the h...head and he fell...into the river. It all happened very q...quickly."

"From what you saw, do you think the man could have been attempting to rape the girl?"

"Yes. That's what it l...looked like."

"No further questions, Your Honor."

The bubble of conversation which burst from the crowd at that point was so excited that the judge had to command silence in the courtroom, as the prosecution counsel got to his feet to begin his cross-examination. Gabriel felt punch drunk with elation. He was only now realizing that he'd given his entire evidence with hardly any stuttering.

"Mr. Thatcher, if as you say you witnessed this whole event from the Camera Obscura building, why did you not come forward before?" Gabriel opened his mouth to speak but the prosecution barrister continued in a hectoring manner. "You must have been aware, were you not, of the controversy surrounding this case and the impact your evidence was bound to have on its outcome. So why have you been kept back by the counsel for defense until this moment?"

"One moment!" The defense barrister sprang up. "Defense knew nothing about this witness until today, Your Honor."

"Very well" responded the judge. "Prosecution will please allow the witness to answer the question. Mr. Thatcher?" The judge turned to Gabriel with a not unfriendly expression.

"To tell the honest truth, Your Honor" Gabriel began. "I was aware of the importance of my evidence and I want to apologize to you and the Court for not coming forward till now. The reason is only...that...I'm...very n... nervous of sp...sp...speaking in public and I h...hoped I wouldn't h...have to. I'm s...sorry to put you to all th... th...this inconv...venience." Again, as on that day when he had spoken in defense of his brother, Gabriel's stutter almost overwhelmed him. The words were practically choking him, so desperate was he to release them. But to his surprise, this time the audience seemed to understand what he was trying so hard to communicate.

There was a hushed silence as Gabriel finished speaking. Then - slowly and deliberately - one person started to clap. Gabriel looked up in surprise. The lone clapper was joined by another and another, until the whole courtroom - public and jurors alike - was applauding. Gabriel flushed scarlet, but his heart swelled with a pride he had never known before.

———✦———

The defendant sat apart, in a pretty yellow dress she had been advised by her defense counsel to wear for the occasion, her long sandy brown hair tied back from her face in a ponytail. Maddie felt numbed by the harrowing events of the past few weeks. When she'd heard her name spoken in Court it was as if somebody else were being discussed: at any moment she expected to wake up from this horrible nightmare and walk the streets again, with no more attention paid to her than any other pretty young girl. Maddie's face betrayed no emotion and indeed she felt none, as her life and her character were due to be summed up by two people who hardly knew her. From the back of the public gallery, Gabriel watched and listened and waited.

The prosecution barrister, Taylor Coleridge, was the first to rise. The jury sat expectantly, some with pencils hovering over notebooks ready to jot down words of wisdom, hoping that in the next couple of hours everything would suddenly be made clear to them and their decision would be made easier.

"One human life is never more important than another, and a human life was lost in this case. It is up to us to make sure that this does not go unheeded. Is all human life precious, should it be precious to all of us? I submit that it is and it should be, and if a human life is taken justice asks for a fair punishment to be given.

Darren Webster was twenty-three years old when he fell to his death. He was a young man on the threshold of life. Whatever he may have done in his youth, whatever misdemeanors he may have committed, he did not deserve to die for them.

Madeleine Wetherby is a young woman of strong emotions. We have witnessed these emotions as she gave her evidence in the witness box. I'm not saying emotions are a bad thing. But when they are not sufficiently controlled - as in this case - they can lead to unpredictable and ultimately criminal behavior.

Now I'm well aware that the defendant - as you see her sitting there today - does not look like a criminal. She is a young lady of great charm and personal attractiveness, which she uses to win herself loyal friends like Bella Marconi. That is indisputable. But this charm and personal attractiveness masks a very different inner character and it is this inner character that we are seeking to judge today. Madeleine Wetherby is an actress who is used to appealing to an audience's emotions and exciting sympathy for herself. That is her job. But beneath that calm and serene exterior, what seething cauldron of emotions is lurking, waiting to bubble over and explode?

Miss Wetherby is very good at disguising her true feelings. That is, after all, what she has been trained as an actress to do. And we know that she is very good at her job. But we have evidence, and that is the evidence of Miss Wetherby's past, as it has been related to us by the witnesses we have heard.

The defendant's friend, Bella Marconi, told us that Madeleine had just had a row with her boyfriend on the night of June 2nd. This boyfriend was flirting with other women and possibly even doing far more than that. When Madeleine found out about this she was very angry. In Bella's own words, she wanted to get back at Alan by flirting in her turn with other men. The unfortunate Darren Webster was therefore used by Madeleine in this way, in an unsuccessful attempt to make her boyfriend jealous. When this attempt failed, she became even more angry, seething with rage in fact, at the behavior of her boyfriend and her own inability to stop him. This rage of course was kept hidden throughout the rest of the party that evening, but it was still there beneath the surface.

Now I'm not asking you to believe, members of the jury, that the defendant deliberately placed the ceramic burner in her handbag with the intention of killing anybody with it. That is patently not the case. But she did know that it was there when she swung her handbag at Darren's head and she must have been aware of the likely consequences of her actions. In the event, it proved to be a very useful weapon.

Madeleine tells us that she left the party alone at 5 o'clock in the morning, having forgotten all about Darren, with the intention of walking home and spending the night alone. It was true that she left the house alone, because Bella Marconi saw her go. But Darren followed very shortly after. Could not the two of them have made a secret agreement beforehand, to leave separately but meet up later, on the road? Perhaps Madeleine was still careful enough of her boyfriend's feelings despite their row, to hide from him the fact that she had invited another man back to her flat. Perhaps that was the reason they didn't leave openly together.

At any rate, they were together by the time they got to the bridge. Now, if we are to believe the defendant's assertions that the streets were completely quiet and free of people, as would be expected at that hour, how is it that she did not hear Darren's footsteps long before they reached the bridge? He must have been reasonably close behind her in order to follow her, in which case she must have heard him behind her. I put it to you, ladies and gentlemen, that Madeleine Wetherby was well aware of

Darren Webster's presence, in fact she had invited him to accompany her home.

That being the case, what was it that caused the couple to argue so violently once they reached the bridge? That we may never know. But certainly they *did* argue and certainly there was some kind of a struggle, which culminated in the defendant attacking Darren Webster with her handbag and causing him to fall to his death. The question I suppose is, who had the upper hand in the struggle? Was it a case of rape and self-defense, as the defendant would have us believe? Or did Madeleine Wetherby - in her rage and frustration over her boyfriend's recent betrayal - give vent to the emotions which had suddenly bubbled to the surface and take out her anger on Darren Webster, by lashing out at him with the only weapon she had to hand? I submit to you that the latter scenario is the correct one.

Darren Webster was not a large man. He was 5'6" in height - hardly taller than the defendant - and slight in build. He had also been drinking steadily throughout the evening and must therefore have been somewhat the worse for wear. Could a small young man in this inebriated state really have restrained a woman such as Madeleine Wetherby - who is by the way, also a trained dancer in the peak of condition - to the extent that her only recourse to save herself was to hit him over the head with her weighted handbag? I doubt it. The question for you to decide, members of the jury, is did the defendant use reasonable force to defend herself against an attacker? It is also up to you to decide what constitutes reasonable force in this case. Is it reasonable to hit a young man a fatal blow on the head, even if he is "raping" you? I leave that you for to decide.

Madeleine Wetherby may be many things, ladies and gentlemen, but she is not a fool. Even in the midst of her argument with Darren, she was well aware of the precarious position they were in, standing as they must have been, near the edge of the bridge's guide rail. She was well aware of the heavy ceramic object she had in her handbag, capable of smashing a man's skull if applied with enough force to his head. She was not a desperate girl in fear of her life, but an angry and embittered woman whose emotions got the better of her in one fatal moment. Her move may not have been calculated in cold blood, but it was deliberately executed with the full realization of its consequences.

I therefore submit, ladies and gentlemen of the jury, that if you search your consciences to apply true justice in this case, you will find Madeleine Wetherby guilty of manslaughter."

The prosecution barrister sat down and straightened his cloak, and this time the silence in the courtroom was as tense and full of vibrations as a taut string. Maddie's face was grey and drawn. She felt drained and exhausted, as if she had been physically assaulted. She couldn't summon up the courage even to look at her defense counsel for support.

"Ladies and gentlemen of the jury" began the modulated tones of Reginald Flowers, whose robe was partially open almost exposing a lurid pink tie, "my client Madeleine Wetherby has never denied the facts which we all know. The facts are - and she has admitted to them - that she was alone with Darren Webster on the 3rd of June in the early hours of that morning on the Clifton Suspension Bridge. The facts are that she struck Darren a blow on the head with her handbag - a blow that was forceful enough to knock Darren off balance and cause him to fall into the river to his death. We know that in Madeleine's handbag on that day was a fairly large and heavy ceramic object, which she'd been given for her birthday, referred to as an aromatherapy burner.

This ceramic burner was not an offensive weapon. Madeleine wasn't carrying around in her handbag a... hammer or a brick or anything that was calculated to cause damage to the human skull. It is entirely coincidental that the burner was in her handbag at the time. It was in her handbag because it had been given to her by her friend Bella for her birthday the night before and carrying it in her handbag was the most convenient thing to do. Which one of you ladies - if I may be sexist for a moment--" here he fixed his bright blue eyes on the two female members of the jury - "has not carried in your handbag a book or a bottle of perfume or some other object which would be heavy enough to knock somebody unconscious if you hit them on the head with it? What I'm saying is, the burner was not carried in the handbag deliberately as a weapon. When Madeleine hit Darren on the head with her handbag she had no thought in her mind of killing him, she just wanted to do anything she could to protect herself.

But let's get back to the facts. Madeleine has admitted all along that she did swing her handbag at Darren's head, causing a blow that knocked him into the river. The question you have to resolve, members of the jury, is why she did this. Was it deliberate homicide, calculated and planned beforehand? Or was it the action of a desperate young girl, who was being raped, to try and defend herself? I put it to you that the latter scenario is the true version of events.

I find it very interesting, ladies and gentlemen, that my learned colleague Mr. Coleridge has failed to even mention the evidence of the last defense witness, Gabriel Thatcher. And I would suggest the reason for this is that Mr. Coleridge is well aware of the significance of Mr. Thatcher's evidence. Gabriel Thatcher is an independent witness, with no bias towards the defendant, whom he doesn't even know. He tells us that in his opinion the struggle he saw on the bridge was a rape. And I think we must believe the evidence of his eyes.

Now let's take what we know about Darren Webster first. The prosecution would have us believe that Darren was a blameless victim in this matter. That he was just an ordinary young man who happened to fall foul of a neurotic and vindictive woman's bad temper. But we heard Edward Bown telling us a bit about this 'blameless' young man's rather sordid past, didn't we? At the age of fourteen Darren Webster was accused of the attempted rape of a classmate, a girl two years his junior. The girl subsequently dropped the charges and he was let off. But, ladies and gentlemen, is this the action of a normal young man? I sincerely hope not, no. This is the action of a young thug - if I may put it that way - who resorts to violence to get what he wants out of life. A young man who won't take no for an answer, but would be prepared to force his attentions on a woman where they were undesired and unlooked for. This is no blameless victim.

Madeleine tells us that at the time just prior to his falling into the river, Darren was attempting to rape her. And I think we can safely assume that this was indeed the case.

What then do we know about Madeleine's character? We know she is an actress." Here the barrister paused to let his comment register and a few members of the public smiled, anticipating his next words.

"I know that some people have an image of all actresses as morally lax, that a girl who spends all her time dressing up and parading about on the stage must be some kind of degenerate who deserves all she gets." There were titters from the audience. "But I fervently hope, members of the jury, that you are more enlightened and can appreciate that acting is a profession like any other.

Great play has also been made of the fact that Madeleine and Darren weren't strangers - that Madeleine danced with and even kissed Darren at her friend's party. But I would also ask you to remember, ladies and gentlemen of the jury, that 90% of all rapes are attributed to people known by the victim! I would ask you to bear this important statistic in mind when assessing this case. A rape is a rape, whether it's carried out by a stranger, a lover, a husband, a friend or someone you've just met.

We've heard from Madeleine's friend, Bella Marconi, about the defendant's character. We know that Bella, for one, thinks a lot of Madeleine and for reasons of loyalty and friendship is prepared to speak up for her friend in Court, which is not an easy thing for anyone to volunteer to do. Madeleine has inspired this loyalty and friendship after being known to Bella for just three months. I think that is testament in itself to the virtue of Madeleine's character.

Madeleine has just turned 25. She is a young woman of, we may say, fairly average hopes and feelings. She is not an especially vindictive or aggressive or neurotic young woman. Where is the evidence to suggest that? Nowhere. She is simply a young woman with a promising acting career. Why would she throw all that away with a deliberate act of manslaughter? What for? The prosecution has come up with no convincing motive for Madeleine to have deliberately killed Darren Webster, other than that she was seized by a fit of uncontrollable rage. Where do you see the evidence in her character to suggest that she is the sort of person who is subject to uncontrollable fits of rage that cause her to kill innocent people for no good reason? Nowhere.

The answer is, ladies and gentlemen, that we must believe the defendant when she says she was being raped. We must believe her when she says she swung her handbag at Darren in self-defense and we must believe her when she tells us that Darren fell to his death accidentally. We must believe her, because that is the truth."

The barrister did a little bow to the jury and the judge, before seating himself with something of a flourish. The atmosphere in the courtroom was hushed, as if everyone had been holding their breath until Reginald Flowers was finished. His speech seemed to have stifled all conjecture.

CHAPTER TWENTY-THREE

I̲ T̲ W̲A̲S̲ T̲W̲O̲ days later, as Gabriel was having tea in the living room of his cottage, that he heard a knock on the door. When he opened it, he was surprised to see a young woman whose face was becoming increasingly familiar to him. She was wearing the Indian shawl that had helped him to recognize her.

"I came to thank you," Maddie Cambay said simply, handing Gabriel a gift-wrapped box. "My mother told me where you lived. She says she knows you."

Gabriel was smiling so much he could hardly speak. "I'm g...glad you came" he stammered eventually. "Would you like to come in for some tea?"

"OK." The young woman looked a bit bemused, as if she hadn't expected such a warm welcome.

"What a lovely cottage," she replied, as Gabriel ushered her in.

"Thank you." Gabriel beamed and clutched his gift, as his new friend stood looking about her.

"Have you always lived here?"

"Yes. I was b...born here."

"It reminds me of my parents' house. A bit. I lived there all the time till I was twenty-one. Then I left home to be an actress." She grinned self-deprecatingly. "It's like... the sort of house where nothing ever changes. Secure. D'you know what I mean?"

"Oh yes. You're right. N...nothing changes. Not usually anyway." Gabriel indicated the box he was clutching. "You didn't have to give me anything."

"I wanted to." Gabriel's visitor sat down, uninvited, on his favorite armchair. Liquorice - who had been sitting on the window ledge - immediately leapt on to her lap and started to preen. "Open it - why don't you?" encouraged the young woman, with a winsome smile.

"I w...will. I'll just get you some tea first." Gabriel disappeared into the kitchen and when he returned he found his guest studying the photographs displayed on his mantelpiece, with great interest. She turned to him with an expression of mixed surprise and pleasure.

"Did you know Aunt Helen as well?" she asked.

"Aunt?" The cup he was carrying rattled slightly on its saucer.

"Were you a friend of hers?"

"Yes. More than a friend." Gabriel handed her the tea and proceeded to open his present with trembling fingers. It was a photograph album. A very expensive-looking one, of real leather with his initials embossed on the front in gold.

"I couldn't think what to get you" Maddie explained, "not knowing you or anything. But I thought that was sort of...personal. Mum helped me pick it out."

Gabriel was overcome. "It's p...perfect" he said, fingering it lovingly. "Th...thank you."

"No - thank *you*" Maddie responded earnestly. "You saved me, you know. At least, I think they would have convicted me if it hadn't been for *your* evidence. I was terrified. I'd tried to explain but it came out wrong and... that prosecution lawyer made me look like a murderer, I mean he really did! But then, thank God for you. What you said changed everything."

Gabriel looked down at his hands, embarrassed. "Oh, you would p...probably have been acquitted anyway," he said modestly.

"No. I'm sure that's not so. Things were looking bad for me, my barrister told me that later. But then you came along and...they knew you wouldn't lie. That you had no cause to lie because you didn't even know me."

Gabriel hesitated and realized he was looking at her strangely. He was bursting to tell her his secret – *was she ready to hear it yet?* He wondered.

"I know you put yourself on the line for me" Maddie continued, appearing determined to express her thanks, "And I'm truly grateful. You didn't have to do that. I hope they didn't penalize you for withholding evidence, did they? I've heard they can do that."

"No. The judge was sym...sympathetic. He j...just gave me a telling off. No punishment."

"That's good." Maddie sat back and sipped her tea.

"Maddie?" said Gabriel suddenly.

"Yes?"

"What you said. About my not kn...knowing you..." He hesitated, his lips parted slightly. "Wait there. I want to sh...show you something." Gabriel ran upstairs to his bedroom, pulled an object out of his wooden chest and ran back downstairs with a pounding heart. The time for revelations had come.

He drew Maddie's shawl from her shoulders and spread it out flat on the living room floor, with its one frayed edge towards him. Then he took the piece of material in his hand and carefully placed it alongside the frayed edge of the shawl. It matched perfectly.

Maddie gasped in amazement. "The missing piece! Where did you get that?"

Gabriel said nothing but just smiled. Maddie went down on her hands and knees to examine the cloth more closely. "It's not so faded as mine. You must have kept it out of the light. But how do you come to have it? That was Aunt Helen's shawl."

Gabriel knelt beside her and took her hands in his. "It's a very long story," he said. "Do you want to h...hear it now?"

THE END